DEADLY ADVICE

ROBERTA ISLEIB

WHEELER
CHIVERS

This Large Print edition is published by Wheeler Publishing, Waterville, Maine, USA and by BBC Audiobooks Ltd, Bath, England.

Wheeler Publishing is an imprint of Thomson Gale, a part of The Thomson Corporation.

Wheeler is a trademark and used herein under license.

LIBRARY OF CONGRESS CATALOGING-IN-PUBLICATION DATA

Isleib, Roberta.
    Deadly advice / by Roberta Isleib.
      p. cm.
      "An advice column mystery" — T.p. verso.
      ISBN-13: 978-1-59722-524-3 (softcover : alk. paper)
      ISBN-10: 1-59722-524-X (softcover : alk. paper)
      1. Young women — Fiction. 2. Dating (Social customs) — Fiction.
    3. Large type books. I. Title.
    PS3609.S57D43 2007
    813'.6—dc22   2007009974

BRITISH LIBRARY CATALOGUING-IN-PUBLICATION DATA AVAILABLE

Published in 2007 in the U.S. by arrangement with The Berkley Publishing Group, a member of Penguin Group (USA) Inc.
Published in 2007 in the U.K. by arrangement with the author.

U.K. Hardcover: 978 1 405 64158 6 (Chivers Large Print)
U.K. Softcover: 978 1 405 64159 3 (Camden Large Print)

Printed in the United States of America on permanent paper
10 9 8 7 6 5 4 3 2 1

For my mother

ACKNOWLEDGMENTS

I'm grateful to the people who helped bring this book to life:

Carole Chaski, for her insights on the linguistic analysis of suicide notes; Paula Baird, for putting me in touch with her; Bernd Becker, Angie Niehoff, and Annabelle Lee Hart, for their charitable donations to the Scranton Library, the EWGA Foundation, and the Rally for a Cure, and for the use of their names; Dr. Doug Lyle, for his wisdom about medical forensics questions; and Judy Eckhart of the Portland, Oregon, Police Department; Officer Timothy Bernier from the Guilford Police Department; and Judge Pat Clifford, all for details on police procedure. Any mistakes are definitely mine!

Tracy Groth from 8MinuteDating.com; Amy, Gina, and Yvonne, for firsthand details; Joanie Piccolo, who was left out last time; the Reverend Dwight Juliani, for PEWSAGL; Penny Colby from the Guilford Library; Hallie Ephron, for the roast chicken; Cathy Crook, for the cheese puffs; Barbara Thomason, for the loan of sweet Yoda; a special tip of the hat to the lovely Nancy Cash, former secretary at the First Congregational Church in Madison, who would never, ever have disclosed personal information.

The faithful and supportive Shoreline Writers Group: Chris Falcone, Angelo Pompano, Karen Olson, Cindy Warm, Chris Woodside; Hallie Ephron, for a voice check; Susan Hubbard, for thoughtful comments on several drafts; Susan Cerulean, for steady enthusiasm and encouragement; Deborah Donnelly, for hashing out plot points.

Independent editor Nora Cavin, whose input leads to improvement by leaps and bounds; my thoughtful, cheerful, and responsive editor, Katie Day; Susan McCarty and the rest of the wonderful staff at Berkley Prime Crime who gave Rebecca Butterman a chance; my friend and agent, Paige Wheeler.

Thanks to my dear friends in Sisters in Crime and Mystery Writers of America and all of my family — what a wonderful world . . .

What would I do without John?

Roberta Isleib

May 2006

9

- A Tuttles Point resident reported that she had the sense that someone had been in her home six weeks ago, and she cannot locate her jewelry.
- A prowler was reported on the side of the building under a ramp. Police investigated and found a cat under the deck.
- A dog left his property on Dunk Rock Road and was very aggressive. There were no specifics as to the goals of the animal.
- A Canberra Court resident reported that someone wrote on her window, "I'm always watching."
- Neighbor trouble was reported on Great Hill Road.

From the
SHORE LINE TIMES
Police Log,
August and October 2005 and April 2006

CHAPTER 1

"Single again? Opportunity, not tragedy!"

Dear Dr. Aster:
After twenty-nine years of marriage, I'm single again. I won't bother you with the whole pathetic story of how it came to be. But now I'm ready to dive back in to the dating world. What's the best place to meet potential partners? No singles bars, please. I'm not looking for Mr. Goodbar and I don't drink anyway. Thanks in advance.

Sincerely,
Ready to Rock 'n' Roll

Dear Ms. Rock 'n' Roll:
May I assume you've taken the advice I've given other readers (wink, nudge) and spent enough time alone to sort out

what went wrong in your marriage? If so, get ready for a strange adventure! Believe me, the world has changed since you were last on the dating scene. You have dozens of online dating services at your fingertips, offering many potential new friends. The key here is to use these services wisely and screen the respondents with care.

On the other hand, your question makes a very good, old-fashioned point: Why not meet someone with similar interests rather than a lounge lizard? Are you a tennis player? Sign up for a round robin of mixed doubles. Always wanted to play golf? Take a clinic at your local country club. Bridge, crafts, town politics, writing, church committees . . . the opportunities are as wide open as your interests and imagination. Even if Prince Charming doesn't show up, you'll have spent pleasant and productive time doing the things you love! Good luck and be careful!

I leaned back in my chair and grimaced at the words on the screen, my latest "Late Bloomer" advice column for *Bloom!,* an online magazine. *Good luck and be careful!* Sheesh. As a clinical psychologist taught to believe that unraveling human angst takes time, suffering, and lots of patience, playing the e-zine's expert in life confidences and love doesn't exactly come naturally. And since my new editor, Jillian, started pressing hard to "youthanize" the magazine and take the women's market by storm, I've had to push back, explaining that any woman can feel like a late bloomer, not just senior citizens.

But hassles aside, the column pays handsomely. And the divorce hit my wallet hard, even though it may have been good for my soul. *May have.*

I skimmed the draft one last time. The advice wasn't bad and the tone was chipper, but somehow it fell a little flat. Just desserts for waiting until my drop deadline — I could feel Jillian panting at the other end of the high-speed cable, definitely pissed that she had to stay late on Friday. That kind of pressure doesn't help Dr. Aster much when she's trying for the breezy but personal wisdom readers expect.

Besides, I hate to push golf too hard on lonely housewives — it's D-U-L-L, expensive, and impossible to master if you haven't been fitted for clubs as an infant. On the other hand, you *will* find men on the golf course. They might have plaid pants hitched up over their beer guts, but they have the requisite anatomical features. And interest can be feigned — I did a damn good job of faking it while dating a golf psychologist last spring.

I hit *send,* swearing I'd start next Friday's column this weekend. Then I went out to the waiting area of my office — I'm a clinical psychologist, in my day job — and spent a few minutes straightening magazines and swabbing fingerprints off the coffee table's glass top with Windex. Apparently my colleagues' current caseloads don't include obsessives. All square, I locked the doors and drove to the Hunan Wok.

On the twenty-minute ride home to my Guilford condo, the smell wafting from the backseat filled the car, nearly driving me mad. If it hadn't been raining, I would have pulled over. I've learned the hard way not to transport Chinese takeout within reaching distance after a long week of listening to people's problems. For me, drama and tragedy are great appetite stimulants. Last month, trapped for forty minutes in Friday's rush-hour traffic over the Q-bridge and through the construction zone out of New Haven, I opened the dumpling container at the half-hour mark. And what are dumplings without dipping sauce? Both my upholstery and my brand-new, barely-out-of-the-plastic, three-hundred-dollar Eileen Fisher pantsuit had required professional dry cleaning. Sometimes a physical barrier is the only way to avoid temptation.

I turned off Route 1, drove past the town green, up Whitfield Street, and onto Soundside Drive. Flashes of red and blue bounced off the treetops like a bizarre outdoor disco scene. Police again? I had to lay odds on the Nelson couple at the end of the row. They'd threatened to punch each other's lights out several times over the past six months, screaming loudly enough for the neighbors to move from orange alert to red and call the cops. Mrs. Dunbarton, self-appointed condo captain, pressured me to check in on them two weeks ago.

I tried to weasel out of the assignment. "Even the cops don't like getting involved in domestic disputes. It's dangerous."

"But you are trained in this, aren't you, dear?" Mrs. Dunbarton said. A real professional could handle this no problem, was clearly the implication.

So I buckled and knocked on their door — softly. Maybe they wouldn't hear and I could go home and tell the old biddy I tried. But the Nelsons had answered together, breathing whiskey clouds but admitting nothing, deflecting my tentative expressions of concern. The ranks had closed, at least against the outside world. At least against a nosy neighbor.

I glanced at my watch. Just before eight o'clock. Both Nelsons worked until six. Unlikely that they'd already had enough to drink to launch their cycle and force the complex into high alert. Besides, their end unit was completely dark.

A fire then? I sniffed the air and pressed on the accelerator, my neck muscles stiffening with fear. My sister, Janice, had nagged me for years to make copies of the family photos. And I'd meant to transfer my financial files to the safe-deposit box. And my cookbook collection . . . my mother's signed copy of The Joy of Cooking —

Around the bend, there were no fire trucks in sight, but two patrol cars and a white minivan had parked in front of the condo next to mine, partially blocking my driveway. I sucked in a deep breath, grabbed my purse and an old newspaper, and struggled into a khaki raincoat — the one my ex-husband, Mark, insisted made me look like Sal Spade. Dumb bugger couldn't even get his insults straight. I held the newspaper over my head against the rain and dashed to the plastic-covered policeman lounging beside the nearest cruiser.

"Excuse me, Officer. I'm Dr. Rebecca Butterman. I live next door." I gestured to my own apartment with my purse. "What's going on?"

"Sorry, ma'am," said the uniformed man. He looked babyishly young, with a buzz haircut and a round, pink face. "Can't really tell you anything. But the detective will want to speak with you. Hold on. I'll call him."

He switched his umbrella to his left hand, put his rosebud mouth to his walkie-talkie, and reported that a next-door neighbor was now available to interview. The rain began to pelt us in earnest.

A burly man in rumpled khakis and a tweed jacket emerged from the condo clutching a battered black umbrella. He strode across the lawn in our direction, then peered at me over his rain-spattered reading glasses.

"I'm Detective Jack Meigs," he said in a deep voice. Bass, if he were singing. He extracted a wallet from his back pocket and flashed an ID. "Dr. Butterball?"

"Butterman," I snapped.

"Sorry." He nodded at my unit. "You live here?"

"Yes." I frowned, swallowing another jolt of fear. "Has something happened to my neighbor?"

A third police car wheeled onto my street and cruised to a stop several yards behind Meigs. The boyish face of the young cop bobbed over to greet the arriving uniform.

"What's up?" the new officer asked him.

"Woman ate her gun," the rosebud lips reported, plenty loud enough to overhear.

My mouth went dry.

Meigs nudged a damp, reddish curl off his forehead, turned to the young cop, and pointed to the last cruiser. "Wait there," he said in a grim voice.

He turned back to me. "Sorry about that. It appears to be a simple suicide."

"Suicide?" Questions flooded my mind.

"What happened?" I continued. "When did — ?"

"Do you have a moment?" asked Detective Meigs, already grasping my elbow and propelling me toward the unmarked van.

I hoisted myself into the passenger seat of the detective's minivan, woozy and nauseous with disbelief. There's no such thing as a simple suicide — that much was hammered home to me in graduate school fifteen years ago. "The natural human urge toward preservation of self is so powerful that rage, hopelessness, or despair has to be that much stronger to overcome it," I remembered Dr.

Novick telling my class. "Some of you will face the suicide of one of your own patients during your career."

We'd squirmed in our seats. Which one of us would fail in such a staggering way? And why? Novick went on to lecture us about the emotional toll taken on the people left behind. Let's just say I'm careful — obsessive, Mark the psychiatrist would tell you — when one of my patients hints at suicide. I don't want to feel the terrible weight of having missed a signal they tried to send.

"Were you acquainted with the deceased?" asked the detective.

"We were neighbors. I live next door."

My neighbor — Madeline was her name — had cooked out several nights earlier. She'd filled her small black Weber with charcoal briquettes, then soaked them with lighter fluid. Half an hour later, she'd grilled one hamburger. Hockey puck territory, I'd guessed, from the length of time it sat on the coals. I waved at her from my deck while watering the last of my impatiens and a pot of declining cherry tomatoes.

"I guess fall's on its way," I remembered saying to her. "It always makes me feel a little sad." Damn. Just what a depressed person would not need to hear. Had she been depressed? Angry? Hopeless? Not that

21

any of that would necessarily show itself in a casual chat.

"I didn't know her well," I told the detective, feeling sharp rumblings of guilt. "Enough to say hello." I felt my lips twitch. Better tell the whole truth. "We had coffee once, but you know how things are — everyone's busy. You mean to get together again, but it doesn't happen."

"Notice anything unusual the night of September 7? Visitors? Did she try to get in touch with you? Phone calls? Anything like that?"

I shook my head slowly. "We weren't close."

"Were you at home that evening?"

I rummaged through my purse and extracted my Palm Pilot. It seemed important to be exact. "After nine."

"Did you hear a gunshot?"

I swallowed hard and looked at my calendar again. "Jesus. She's been dead for two days?"

I pictured the woman eating a hamburger and then holding the gun to her head. Two thin layers of Sheetrock separated the length of our condominium units. My neighbor never seemed to sleep: Sometimes I could follow the dialogue in the TV program she was watching — mostly crime dramas and sports. Yet in the case of a fatal gunshot, I hadn't heard anything. How was that possible? *You couldn't hear it if you weren't home, Rebecca.*

My eyes began to tear up and I groped in my bag for a Kleenex. Dammit. I hate to cry in front of other people.

"You okay?" grunted the detective.

"I'll be fine. I'm a psychologist," I said. Which sounded ridiculous. I flipped the visor and checked the mirror — my hair hung in dark clumps and rivulets of mascara ran down my cheeks. Drowned rat territory. I dabbed at the worst of it, patted my nose, and stuffed the tissue back in my purse. "Would you mind telling me where you found her?"

Meigs paused. "You're a psychologist?"

I nodded.

"What kind?"

"Clinical — private practice and adjunct faculty at Yale. Anxiety, depression, marital problems. I handle basic human unhappiness, more or less." It's always hard to summarize the job without sounding glib.

"Then you're familiar with the way this works. Some of them like to leave a big mess behind. This lady was neat — or at least she tried. Bathtub." He handed me a card: *Detective Jack Meigs, Guilford Police Depart-*

ment. "Call if you think of anything that could be useful. But from this side, it looks open and shut."

"Did she suffer?" I asked. *Could I have saved her?*

"It looked as though she intended to die fast," said Meigs.

"Did she leave a note?"

Meigs shrugged. "We'll take care of it from here."

"Have you notified her family?" Who was her family? I couldn't remember seeing anyone visit regularly. Not that I studied the woman's habits. Not that I really knew a damn thing about her.

"We'll take care of it."

I gathered my things and pushed open the car door. An ambulance, silent but lights flashing, rolled up to the curb. Meigs swung open his door, stepped into the rain, and went to confer with the driver. Then he climbed Madeline's steps, wiped his sensible brown oxfords on the mat, and disappeared into her condo.

Stopping to pluck the newspaper off the curb, I slipped back into my Honda and drove around the cruiser into the driveway. I tapped the clicker clipped to my visor, and a wash of light spread over the bushes and the small yard in front of my unit. I parked, entered the apartment through the garage, and punched my code into the burglar alarm, grateful I'd remembered to set it this morning.

All clear.

Dropping my stuff on the kitchen counter, I poured a generous glass of Lindemans Chardonnay. Suddenly ravenous, I tore open the sack of Chinese food and polished off most of the Szechwan chicken standing over the sink.

Through the rain-splashed window, I watched two young cops bump a gurney down the steps next door and roll my neighbor's body to the ambulance. I turned away. It surprised me that Meigs had let slip the comment about the woman being neat. Sometimes, in a profession like that one, you must have a terrible urge to unload the haunting details.

After midnight, with my body still churning under the sheets, my mind kept circling back to Madeline. She had laid twenty feet from me — dead — for two days — and no one had noticed. Including her closest neighbor, me. Wasn't that every single woman's worst nightmare?

Who had finally noticed that Madeline was missing?

CHAPTER 2

Dear Dr. Aster:
My husband admits to having an affair with his secretary. He swears it's over and has begged my forgiveness, but he refuses to fire her. I've always stayed at home with my children and now it's hard to imagine how I can survive on my own. He insists that if only we add a little zing to our sex life, we won't have any more problems. Should I believe him?

Signed,
Chagrined in Cincinnati

Chagrined was headed for heartache. Her husband probably couldn't fire his secretary without risking a whopping sexual harassment suit. But how in good conscience could I counsel her to trust that he'd keep his word and his vows? He'd been a royal flop so far. Legal and moral issues aside, blaming their marital problems on a dull sex life was a gross oversimplification. Relationships don't thrive on sex alone. If their communication was lousy, most likely the sex would be too. Last, but far from least, Chagrined needed to work on her own confidence and self-esteem.

Even for chirpy Dr. Aster, this was not a one-column problem. I moved Chagrin's e-mail to a new folder marked "Last Resorts!"

I shouldn't have started working before coffee: I was officially grumpy. Besides, I'd woken with a nagging headache, courtesy of the white wine, MSG — though the Wok denies they use it — and nightmares about the woman next door. It was raining harder too, cold gray sheets that foreshadowed another harsh New England winter. Really not fair in September.

I filled the coffeemaker with filtered water and sat down with two cookbooks to make a grocery list. Just because I was divorced did not mean I had to eat like a bag lady. Hell, I'd given that advice in any number of forms to my own patients and in the Dr. Aster column.

Plan A: Cook a pot of beef stew to serve my girlfriends tomorrow, and then spend the afternoon finding the right words to help anxious women handle next week's

27

crises. The trick is choosing universal questions and then keeping the answers warm, without sounding cocky or patronizing or, God forbid, slick. This is *Bloom!* magazine after all, not *Cosmopolitan.* My readers want reassurance and practical advice, not smart-aleck, sexy chick-lit sound bytes. Or so I tell Jillian.

Shrugging my trench coat over my gray terry sweats, I sloshed outside to get the *New York Times.* I'd add that to my list for the day — a leisurely reading of the Saturday inserts: the Connecticut section, the Book Review, and the Week in Review. If someone turned up to talk things over, I'd have a handle on the issues.

"Dr. Butterman?"

A small, seventy-ish woman in a yellow slicker approached my mailbox carrying a big cat. The cat was the same soft gray as the woman's hair, with pure white paws.

"I'm Madeline Stanton's mother." Her smile trembled as she nodded toward Madeline's empty condominium.

"I'm so terribly sorry for your loss," I said, pushing back the wave of guilt that surged through me. I touched the woman's arm, then the limp, damp cat. "Is that you, Spencer?"

He meowed and slapped Mrs. Stanton's

raincoat with his tail.

"I have a favor," said the woman. She bit her lip. "I hate to ask . . ."

"Anything I can do for you," I answered firmly. Had the woman begun to cry or was it the rain? "Listen, why don't you come in for a cup of coffee? Bring Spencer with you. Madeline's always kind about letting him visit," I added, and then covered my mouth with my hand. I'd spoken as if the woman's dead daughter were still alive.

Dropping my hand, I placed it gently on the small of the woman's back and directed her up the walkway and into my condo. I hung up the sodden raincoats, blotted the cat dry with a towel, and settled both visitors into oversized beige leather easy chairs. Mark had chosen the recliners — hulking monstrosities out of proportion with the other furniture and just the color of dirt, as I'd told him in the showroom. But at the low point of our mediated settlement, I'd insisted on moving them to my new condo. Time to give those ugly suckers back and buy something pretty. Spencer began to purr.

"How do you take your coffee, Mrs. Stanton?"

"Please call me Isabel."

I nodded, smiling my thanks. "How do

you take your coffee, Isabel?"

"My coffee? Oh. Cream and sugar. Or whatever you have is fine."

"I'm so sorry about your loss," I said again as I emerged from the kitchen. I set the tray of cups and a plate of almond biscotti on the tile table in front of Madeline's mother. "I brought biscuits too. Have you had breakfast? It's the little ways you treat yourself that will get you through the impossible." I passed her a steaming cup. "You said you had something to ask?"

"Madeline mentioned to me once how kind you were to her cat."

I felt myself flush with shame. Madeline hadn't given me permission to take the cat in: I had co-opted him on several occasions, hoping his owner wouldn't notice. Never mind the cat, I should have been nicer to the neighbor. She'd invited me over for coffee shortly after I moved in and I never asked her back.

On the other hand, in my line of work, I had to set boundaries outside the office. Once you let every neighbor with a long face inside the door, you had no time for yourself. Hell, hang up a shingle: The entire condominium population could use a mental tune-up. "You can't treat the world, Rebecca," Dr. Novick used to say.

Besides, I've been busy dealing with the details of the divorce. And it was taking me longer to adjust than I liked to admit. Mark had been contrite and malleable at first, as well he should have been. Eight months ago, I'd come home unexpectedly from the office with the stomach flu and found him boinking a compact, wrinkle-free redhead right in our bed. If I hadn't already been queasy, the sight of that woman's bare ass bouncing on my own husband, on my own six hundred-count Egyptian cotton sheets, had done the job. I bolted right past them but lost my lunch before I reached the bathroom. I hadn't ordered lasagna since. I doubted those two had either.

"Would you be willing to take him in?"

"Excuse me?" I asked, pulling myself away from a gathering cloud of familiar indignation. God, shake it off. Time to move on.

"The cat, Spencer. Would you keep him for me? For Madeline? Just for a couple of days, I mean, until I find him a home. I live in a senior facility and they don't allow animals. Besides, I might be allergic." She extracted a starched handkerchief from the pocket of her tweed pants and honked emphatically.

I was reminded of a social psychology study where salesmen were taught to ask a small favor first. Once their potential customer had agreed to the little request, the following large one was accepted easily. God knows I had a crowd of needy creatures depending on me already.

Half an hour later, Isabel went next door to retrieve Spencer's dishes, a sack of low-ash, low-carb cat food, and the litter box. She'd filled me in on the plans for the funeral (a small service in the common room in her assisted-living facility — no obituary had been filed; just too painful and she couldn't stand the fuss that would follow), and on the strained conversations she'd had with Madeline's two older brothers about the suicide. Well, most of the conversation was with their wives, actually. Though Steven's wife, Pammy, couldn't get off the phone fast enough, Isabel had said.

"My daughters-in-law seem to think I've had my turn bossing the boys around." She laughed, her chin rising defiantly. "They want all channels clear for their own nagging."

She was a spunky woman with a subtle sense of humor, even on this black day. How would she begin to make sense of her daughter's death? And where did her husband, Madeline's father, fit in? Was there a history of mental illness in the family? It was impossible not to be curious.

"Had your daughter been feeling very depressed?" I finally ventured, after a second cup of coffee.

Isabel's face crumpled. She pulled out the handkerchief again and wiped away the tears that spilled from her eyes. "This is what's so hard to understand. She's always been on the moody side, but just lately, she seemed optimistic, almost cheerful."

I'd never say this out loud, but sometimes, suicidal people do become euphoric just before the end. They've made a decision to take their lives and have a plan to follow through. The relief can be intoxicating.

"I'm so sorry," I murmured, helpless and guilty as I watched her start down a long, sad path I couldn't travel with her. And didn't want to, to be completely honest.

Once Isabel left with promises to keep in touch, I made a quick trip to the Guilford Food Market. The prices might be a bit higher and the selection more limited than the supermarket, but I could count on fresh meat, old-fashioned service, and getting in and out in twenty minutes. I filled my handbasket with a pound of organic sirloin tips, carrots and onions, egg noodles, and Whisker Lickins' for Spencer. At the checkout counter, I added a small container of maple sugar candy in the shape of perfect, tiny leaves. *It's the little ways,* I told myself with a guilty grin.

Back home, my visitor watched from his perch on the bookcase, tail switching, as I unloaded the groceries and fried four strips of bacon.

"Listen, buddy," I said to him. "We're not getting involved. You heard what she said — a couple of days." I filled one of Spencer's bowls with dried kibble and the other with fresh water, and rubbed my nose on his head. "Just to tide you over until dinner."

I sliced four onions paper-thin and dropped them into the hot grease. The condo filled with their delicious scent. While the beef cubes browned, I booted up my computer and clicked on the e-mail from the magazine. My editor, Jillian, practically young enough to be my own daughter, had forwarded another page of potential questions from readers for my column, *"Ask Dr. Aster."* Dr. Aster seemed like a goofy pen name to me, but Jillian said the staff adored the flower connection.

"It's perfect! Get it? Late bloomers — just like the aster!"

One did not tilt at the enthusiasms of the *Bloom!* editorial board and expect to have much of an impact.

Dear Dr. Aster:
My daughter, just thirteen, is giving me fits.
Everything sets her off. Something terrible
has happened in her life — she's suddenly
realized that her mother is a bona fide
idiot.

I could imagine the woman chuckling through her gritted teeth.

My sweet little girl has turned into a rude,
defiant adolescent. Honestly, I'm not at all
certain that both of us will survive her teen-
age years. Can you help?
                    Desperately yours,
                    Miranda's Mother

This seemed like a good prospect — a legitimate question from a woman whose humor and resilience could be a healthy role model for the magazine's readers. If I trod lightly, it should be possible to slip in some useful psychological facts without resorting to psychobabble. I opened a new document and typed the title:

"Cavalry on the way: A field guide to your young teen!"

Dear Miranda's mother:

As bad as it might seem, your daughter is going through a perfectly normal stage. Ghastly, oh yes, but normal! Teenagers are hardwired to begin the serious business of separating from their parents, and especially Mom, during puberty. And that means pushing parents away — sometimes in an ugly and awkward fashion. Your job is to hold steady, let her have some space, then allow her to move closer when she needs you again. With babies, developmental psychologists call this "secure attachment." It works the same way for teenagers — your oversized, messy, back-talking babies! You are providing the secure base so Miranda can venture out and explore her world safely. One caveat, though! Make it clear to your daughter that you won't tolerate rudeness or abuse. Neither one of you will end up feeling good about that. Good luck!

I got up to pour a bottle of beer into the stew pot, cocking the lid over the bubbling beef. I'd hashed over this mother-daughter separation issue endlessly in my own psychotherapy. As Mark had joked more than once too often, me and Woody Allen. Believe me, a little self-reflection wouldn't hurt that guy one bit.

A loud banging at the front door jarred me loose from the memory loop of marital disasters. Mrs. Dunbarton stood dripping on the mat, a clear plastic raincoat encasing her barrel-shaped polyester pantsuit, matching booties covering her gray lace-up Stride Rites.

"Good morning, Dr. Butterman. I was out for my constitutional and I brought you your mail." She thrust a packet of soggy envelopes at me.

She had no business using her master key to open my mailbox. I snatched the mail from her hands.

"Rebecca, please." We went through this every time our paths crossed. The formality of the title somehow gave her license to ask outrageous questions.

"I couldn't help noticing that you had a visitor this morning. And she went into Madeline's apartment after. Was that her mother?"

I sighed. "Yes."

The folds of skin behind Mrs. Dunbarton's glasses puckered as she squinted. It was difficult to erase the image of a pig's small eyes from my mind.

"Did she say what happened?"

Spencer rounded the corner from the kitchen to the hallway. He spotted Mrs. Dunbarton, arched his back, and hissed. My laugh bubbled up, but I forced it into a cough.

"No. She asked me to take care of Madeline's cat."

Mrs. Dunbarton clicked her tongue. She had been the ringleader of a small but vigorous anti-pet contingent within the condo complex. Their proposal to eliminate all animals from the premises sank like a stone at the August annual meeting, though she did manage to push through a "no rodent" clause. After the meeting, I'd had to squash the urge to ask her if there was anything about the condominium's operations that she had ever been *for.*

"The police said it was suicide."

I stared Mrs. Dunbarton down. Difficult to believe the police had told her anything.

Her neck reddened. "Well, that's what the paper implied this morning. Peter Morgan read it too. I saw him at the mailbox with Babette."

I spread my hands as if to say, "I wouldn't know." Though neighbors Peter Morgan and Babette Finster were credible witnesses, I refused to get washed along in Mrs. Dunbarton's mean-spirited speculation.

"You must have noticed that Madeline had several gentlemen callers over the last few weeks."

"No, I hadn't been looking. Thanks for the mail."

I closed the door firmly, practically pushing her off the porch, and watched her pick her way down my front walk. Such a contrast to Madeline's gentle mother. A vision of "neat" Madeline in her bathtub flashed unbidden into my mind.

I leafed through the pages of the just-delivered *Shore Line Times* until I found Mrs. Dunbarton's news source on page two in the police blotter: "The body of a woman was discovered in her condominium on Friday night." No name, no other details.

I thought about my neighbor's question. Had I seen any men visiting Madeline over the past few weeks? There had been cars in her driveway. More than two but less than, say, seven. And several times I'd heard the low hum of voices under the steady blare of the television in Madeline's bedroom. Not my business, I'd thought at the time.

The phone rang.

"Just calling to remind you about Brittany's birthday party —"

"Next Saturday, ten a.m. I didn't forget, Janice," I assured my sister. "I'll just stop by with my gift. I know she'll be focused on her friends."

"Is something wrong? You sound a little down."

How did she manage to pick that up when we'd barely said hello? If I didn't tell her something specific, she'd assume I needed intervention, which would come in the form of multiple phone calls, offers of outings with "the girls," worst of all, a blind date with one of my brother-in-law's boring partners. I had to give her something.

"Dr. Goldman's going out of town for a month. It feels odd. After a couple of weeks, I'll get used to the free time and my mental privacy and I'll be sorry when he's back." I laughed sheepishly.

"I can't believe you're still seeing that guy. No one goes for psychotherapy anymore. It's so, well, 1980s. Why not have a few Reiki sessions or a feng shui consultation and be done with it?"

I laughed. "If no one goes for psychotherapy, I'm out of business."

"I mean no one *sane.*"

We've had this conversation more than once. My sister can best be described as "buttoned up." If she keeps busy, pressing her own psychology out of sight and under wraps, she can believe that nothing will go

40

wrong. Which was why I didn't mention how much I was bothered by the suicide next door. She'd tell me it wasn't my problem and I should only worry about the things I can control. But when you examine yourself in the therapist's chair, you realize just how little control you have — how complex the layers of the psyche are, and how much boils under the conscious surface, influencing the direction of your life in ways you had no idea.

"The more you know, the less likely you are to repeat the mistakes of the past," I told Janice.

"What did you write about for this week's column?" she asked, moving quickly off the subject. "I loved the one about talking back to your boss."

"A reader asked how to meet a decent man after her marriage ended. I suggested she get involved in activities she already enjoys or would like to explore."

"You should take a little of your own advice."

I chuckled. "Gotta run now. I'll call you later in the week."

Two can play, I thought as I hung up the phone. I fed Spencer a crispy piece of bacon, his reward for hissing at Dunbarton.

CHAPTER 3

Prayers for the Stanton family were requested in the congregational *Joys and Concerns* Sunday morning, sandwiched between one member's broken ankle and what sounded like an older parishioner's hysterectomy. The Reverend Wesley Sandifer tends to describe every life occurrence as part of the human "journey," whether it involves surgical removal of a body part or loss of a loved one, even by suicide. I'd never seen either Madeline or her mother in attendance on a Sunday, but when the chips are down, everyone leans on the church.

The reverend prayed for peace and healing for all the people on his list. I wondered how long that might take for Isabel Stanton, if it was possible. Then the choir warbled through an anthem, way too strong on reedy sopranos and weak on bass. Which got me thinking about Detective Meigs. Did the small parade of cars I'd remembered outside my neighbor's place constitute "useful" information?

I skipped coffee hour in the fellowship hall and hurried home to finish cooking for my friends.

Just before five, I defrosted a bag of raspberries and whirled them in the blender with a tablespoon of confectioner's sugar and a touch of Framboise. The doorbell rang as I loosened an angel food cake from its pan and pulled a loaf of sunflower honey bread out of the oven. I ushered in Angie Niehoff. She's close to six feet tall, with blond corkscrew curls and big brown eyes — and smart besides. She's made a name for herself consulting as a forensic linguist on high-profile court cases. In other words, the kind of woman you'd love to hate if she wasn't one of your dearest friends.

Annabelle Hart followed right behind, petite and freckled with an unfashionable braid and a button nose. I'd dismissed her as a kook a couple years back when she gave a talk on sand tray therapy at a weekly psychiatry department conference. As did most of the medical-model types in the room, including my psychiatrist husband.

"Choosing and arranging the figures during therapy helps my clients crystallize their internal issues and visualize solutions," Annabelle had explained. "I think of myself as a holding tank — a safe harbor — while they do their psychological work."

Sounded silly, but over time she proved herself kind and smart. So I hired her for a year of supervision and since finishing, we've become good friends. She's a quiet foil to Angie's zip.

"White okay?" After both women nodded, I moved into the kitchen and splashed Pinot Grigio into my green goblets.

The white-wine whiners, Mark used to call us. I wouldn't repeat what they'd named him after the redhead-boinking incident. Hell hath no fury like a spurned woman's best buddies.

Before dinner, we munched on brie and crackers and I told my friends about Madeline's death.

"How dreadful," Annabelle exclaimed. "The poor mother." Her gaze moved to the wall that my neighbor and I had shared. If she wasn't thinking it, I was: This was a very thin barrier between me and that ugly death.

I felt near tears. "I should have known what was going on with her," I said with a deep sigh. "She was my next-door neighbor. If I'd taken a little more time to get to know her, this might never —"

Angie and Annabelle shared a glance. "So why didn't you spend more time?" Angie asked.

"I've been busy — my practice, the column, school starting up. Getting settled in here." I shook my head. "And honestly, the one time we had coffee, there was something odd about her."

"It's important to trust your hunches," said Annabelle, leaning forward to give me a quick pat on the arm. "Was there anything in particular you noticed?"

I set my wineglass on the coffee table. "You know how you meet someone and you think she might turn out to be a friend but something holds you back?" Both women nodded. "She kept suggesting I come for coffee. When I finally went to her place, we had this weird interaction about Dr. Aster. My gut feeling told me it was going to be hard to keep it light. And I needed light."

Both of my friends nodded again.

"But now she's dead. Hard to keep that light." I dropped my head into my hands.

"Was she one of your patients?" Angie asked.

"No, but —"

"I tend to agree with Angie on this one," said Annabelle. This didn't happen too often. I picked up my head and saw her mouth curve into a smile. "She didn't threaten to harm herself or say she was suicidal or ask for help or a referral?"

I shrugged. "Not with me, she didn't."

"It's a tragedy — a terrible waste of life," said Angie. "Your feelings sound normal. Even I would feel bad for a while."

I tilted my wineglass to my lips — it was empty. I sighed.

"I bet you're starving." I got up and waved them to dinner, then served steaming bowls of stew and a mesclun salad with balsamic vinaigrette.

"Have you ever read Salzman's *True Notebooks*?" I asked suddenly. Salzman had chronicled several years of his life teaching writing and sharing the meaning of life with incarcerated teenagers. "Now that's a man worth falling in love with — sensitive, loyal, humble."

"And handsome and married," Annabelle finished. "When the time is right, your Mr. Wonderful will appear."

"Are there any single people in this neighborhood?" Angie asked. "Finding a relationship can be like an auto accident. Sometimes they happen close to home. When you aren't looking."

"Only you can't buy insurance." I laughed and mopped up the gravy in my bowl with

46

a chunk of sunflower bread. "Sure, we have single people. There's Mrs. Dunbarton, who probably nagged her husband to an early grave. And Babette Finster, who's too nervous to live with anyone except her dog." I pulled a tube of ChapStick out of my pocket and rolled some balm onto my lips. "And Peter Morgan. Poor guy got divorced not long before he moved in here. Neighborhood gossip says his ex wiped him clean. Nice enough, and a lawyer, but slightly pompous and a little melancholy — still dealing with the fallout, I suppose."

"You have to act fast these days," Angie warned.

"That's not her style," said Annabelle. "All things come in time."

"And Madeline," I added suddenly. "She was single too." I pulled the empty plates toward me and stood to clear the table. I returned from the kitchen with slices of angel-food cake drizzled with raspberry sauce.

"I need your advice about something. The detective investigating the case told me to call if I thought of anything new. Now I remember that Madeline had nighttime visitors. I saw their cars. Do you think I should phone him?"

"This cake is divine," Angie said, her lips

stained red by the berries. "Could she have been a hooker?"

"Thanks. And no, I didn't get that vibe," I said. "Besides, the way this condo association watches, she would surely have been nailed."

"It can't hurt to mention it to him, right?" Annabelle glanced at her watch. "I need to head out. Early patient tomorrow. It was a wonderful dinner, Rebecca. And always good to see you girls."

With the dishwasher humming and the leftovers stored, I lured Spencer out from under the bed with a can of Friskies. Then I dialed Detective Meigs, expecting to get his voicemail, but getting the real thing instead. He sounded testy and impatient, like maybe I'd woken him. Did he sleep at the station?

"What did the cars look like? Make? Model? Colors?"

"One was blue, I think. A black one, maybe a month ago. I'm not really a car kind of person."

Silence on the line. "And the visitors, can you describe them?"

"I never saw the people. But from time to time I might have heard a man in her bedroom." More silence. He was waiting. "Through the wall I mean. I guess I assumed she had a boyfriend. Boyfriends?"

"Appreciate you calling, Dr. Butterman. Really though, nothing in the case has changed."

I disconnected, wishing I'd never called. This man didn't want to see anything but the most obvious solution. The warm halo of caring left by an evening with friends had evaporated.

CHAPTER 4

Monday afternoon, I checked my messages after a run of three patients. My editor, Jillian, had called twice. Her breathy-with-excitement voice was more animated than usual. The column about Miranda's mother was fine, but she *loved, loved, loved* my dating Q and A. She had an amazing new idea! I should call as soon as *absolutely possible* to discuss.

I dialed the New York City number. Jillian's assistant, a high school student from the sound of it, put me through.

"The column is fabulous," Jillian gushed. "And I had a brilliant brainstorm to follow up." She paused for dramatic effect. "We're going to send you out on the road to test the singles scene. And then you'll write an article describing your experience. You can write it in installments and include sidebars with tips for the readers. I'm thinking you should start with speed dating. Your readers will go wild for this. It's just the kind of youthful feature we've been looking for. We'll pay two dollars a word. Doesn't that sound amazing?"

My turn to be breathless. Literally. Gruesome, humiliating, out of the question: Those were the words that sprang to mind. How to say as much without insulting Jillian and the entire *Bloom!* editorial board by proxy?

"Are you there?"

"Yes, I'm here. It's certainly an interesting concept. But I don't think I'm the right person for the job."

"Oh, but you're perfect! You're single yourself now so you'll know just what these women are going through. Plus you have psychological expertise to share. The readers will adore seeing their own Dr. Aster go through the same things they struggle with. It's perfect! It will be huge. Who knows what might be next? You could be the new Dr. Phil!"

I didn't want to be the new Dr. Phil. Why *do* people yearn to expose their most embarrassing secrets in front of a studio audience, a pushy shrink, and national TV? The man's advice isn't all bad — I agree that the best predictor of future behavior is past behavior and that people often stay in bad relationships because they can't face being alone. But I would never expect anyone to absorb enough self-awareness to make major life changes in one hour. In public. Without follow-up support. In my opinion, if you're going to strip the psychological blinders off someone, you'd better damn well be prepared to ride along with them for the long haul while they face what's underneath.

"I'll fax you the contract this afternoon," said Jillian. "Let's shoot for five hundred words out of the box."

I tried several more times to turn down the assignment, but in the end, agreed to think it over. Twenty-four hours from now, I could write Jillian a regretful e-mail — grateful too — explaining how professional ethics wouldn't allow me to go undercover. Imagine if a computer dating service matched me up with one of my own patients, I'd say. What a rhubarb that would be! The closer truth? I'm not an exhibitionist or a risk-taker. The idea of sampling the singles scene and then reporting on my failures held zero appeal. Even for two *hundred* dollars a word.

I walked across the waiting area to the bathroom, splashed cold water on my face, and patted it dry in front of the mirror. Hazel eyes, an occasional strand of silver hair beginning to show through the honey brown, one-eighth of Annabelle's freckles: Imagine *me* in the singles scene. Of all the small signs of encroaching middle age, I hate the fine lines around my lips the most. Angie says no one else can see them, especially if I'm smiling. But I can picture how my lips will purse up over the next twenty years as the collagen holding their fullness shrinks smaller and smaller, eventually revealing a real-life copy of Edvard Munch's painting *The Scream.*

"Stop!" Dr. Phil would thunder. "Time to replace your perceptual filter!"

The rest of the day buzzed by. While waiting for my four o'clock, I pulled the Yale University Peer Counseling folder from the file cabinet next to my desk to review notes for tonight's guest lecture. Once every fall, I train the college peer counselors how to handle depressed and suicidal students — never an easy task, even with Yale's best and brightest. Tonight would be worse, because every word would remind me of Madeline Stanton.

Twenty minutes passed before I noticed that my patient was late.

A mixed blessing. The spare time to relax was welcome. But I'd pay hell next week. I could imagine how it would go.

"Any thoughts about missing last week's session?" I'd ask.

"I just forgot," would come Lorna's sullen response.

"You seemed upset with me for running late the week before. Do you think the two could be related?"

"That's just bullshit, Dr. Butterman. Sometimes shit just happens."

Lorna would plant her arms across her chest. Her head and neck would sink down into her shoulders until she resembled an enormous, baleful toad. In the past, this was the kind of person who came to mind when I thought about suicidal probabilities — a woman with few friends, fewer social skills, and very few hopeful moments in her life. Therapy with Lorna felt like fording through setting cement.

I drove the six blocks from my office to the campus, parallel parked on Church Street, and zigzagged through clusters of chattering students. In early September, the newness of college has yet to wear thin — taking one's life seems unthinkable. October, on the other hand, is infamous in mental health circles as the month with the highest suicide rate. By then, term papers and reading assignments have begun to stack up in procrastinated piles, promising new friendships wither, and emotional problems brought from home to college shoot up like unwelcome weeds. For the unhappiest kids, suicide can look like the only decent option.

I held up my ID to the card reader outside Trumbull residential college and pulled open the heavy wrought-iron gate. Packed dirt paved the courtyard, broken up by patches of struggling grass. The remnants of a weekend bash — airless balloons, beer bottles, and cigarette butts — were scattered around the roots of an enormous oak. I entered the common room, edged past a student playing chopsticks on a baby grand piano, and hiked up a narrow staircase to the classroom where the counselors meet for weekly training sessions.

The chatter of twenty students wound down as I came into the room. A blond girl with eyebrow rings and two inches of bare midriff settled me into a wing chair upholstered in faded roses. Even riddled with piercings, the girl looked sweet and so damn young.

"This is psychologist Dr. Rebecca Butterman," she said earnestly. "She's here to talk to us about handling depression and suicide." She gazed around the circle, almost whispering now. "Please pay attention. This is the most important subject of the year."

I smiled. "Thanks, Margo. It is awfully important, but you're not in this alone. You can always, always call for backup from the health center staff if you have any questions. And you'll be using the same set of skills that you'd use for any other issue. So let's think this through: When a student contacts you, what's your first step?"

"Define the problem," said Margo, bobbing her head. "Why did this student come in to talk to you today?"

"Exactly," I said. "Depression manifests itself differently in different folks, which is why you have to listen carefully. What's changed in a student's physical or emotional life? Ask about eating, sleeping, attending classes, seeing friends. What then?"

The radiator hissed against the wall. The leaded-glass windows were propped open, but it was still way too hot. The image of my dead neighbor's face popped into my mind. I pressed it back.

A tall, skinny boy with a fine sheen of sweat on his upper lip finally raised his hand. "How are they feeling?"

"Perfect," I said. "If your counselee says she's depressed, don't assume you know what she means. Ask questions. Reflect back what you've heard: 'Sounds like you're feeling kind of hopeless, do I have that right?' "

In spite of reassurance last night from both Angie and Annabelle, the conversation I'd had with Madeline over coffee pushed forward. My neighbor had been fascinated with my advice column.

"Do you write with a pen name?" she asked.

"Dr. Aster," I admitted, "as in late blooming flower."

"Nice," said Madeline. "That's cool. So people ask you questions and you make crap up. And then they listen."

"I don't exactly make crap up. I am a clinical psychologist," I said, sounding officious and annoying even to me. Why was it important to impress her?

A knowing smile. "Let me think up a problem and you say how you'd answer." She took a swig of coffee and slotted the cup back into the saucer. "Got it.

"Dear Dr. Aster:
My family can't seem to understand that I'm no longer a child. I get advice from everyone — on my love life, my career choice, handling finances, even decorating my condo. Now I need some real

advice — how the hell do I get them off my back?"

She crossed her arms and sat back, waiting.

I reached down to ruffle and then smooth the gray fur between her cat's ears.

"Communication is the key," I said, straightening up to look at Madeline. "I'd suggest that this reader talk to her family members directly and let them know how she's feeling. I'd probably add a sentence wondering whether there's anything in the way she's conducting herself that invites their worry and comments. Taking risks, spending too much money, showing up with black eyes, that kind of thing."

"Not bad," Madeline said, too quickly. "It's just common sense, isn't it?"

"Common sense is important," I agreed. "But I'm always scanning for an underlying message — trying to figure out if there's a serious problem, so I can recommend the right outside help. I don't want to miss the boat the one and only time someone reaches out for help." I cleared my throat. "Mix that in with doing my best to sound clever and lighthearted — it's not as easy as it looks."

Madeline leaned forward, her eyes sparkling. "Try this one. Suppose I'm dating a guy and he wants me to try something kinky. Soft porn photographs, maybe, or videotaping us while we're having sex. Not to show anyone else, just for us. But I'm uncomfortable about it. What would you say, Doc?" she finished with a sly grin.

"You probably signed your letter 'Kinky in Kansas City,' right?" I said, hoping that would be the end of it.

"No, go on, for real. I want to hear your advice."

I'd look like a first-class prude if I refused to play. "I'd probably say something like you need to trust your gut on this one. If anything your boyfriend or husband asks you to do feels wrong, you owe it to yourself to decline. On the other hand, it could be that he's encouraging you to expand your horizons in a positive way. As long as you're consenting adults, it's okay to let go and be playful — in the context of a safe and loving relationship."

I sounded like an ass. And Madeline was enjoying my discomfort. I shifted the subject to her cat.

"Spenser, I like that name. You must be a mystery fan."

"It's actually Lord Spencer," Madeline had said. "Like Princess Diana's brother."

A dark-skinned boy with dreadlocks and the knees torn out of his jeans raised his hand, jogging my mind away from Madeline and back to the peer counselors.

"What if we ask about suicide and they haven't thought of it before? Then we're putting something in their heads even worse than what they had to start with."

I peeled off my jacket. The hell with worrying about unprofessional sweat stains. "That's a good question," I said brightly, "but if you're getting the idea your counselee has suicidal thoughts or intentions, she's way ahead of you. If you don't acknowledge them, she may feel that her thoughts are so awful, even a Yale peer counselor doesn't dare say them aloud."

A couple of the kids laughed, but not the boy who'd asked the question.

"Let me put it another way. For most people, having someone listen to them and understand them is a great relief, even if their feelings are frightening."

The boy still stared. Goddammit. Why didn't he get the point?

"Look, eight out of ten people who kill themselves have given definite warnings of their suicidal feelings or intentions before they took their lives. I don't want any of you to be left in the position of not having heard and responded to another student's cry for help."

He nodded. Finally.

And I remembered the last conversation I'd had with my neighbor. She'd definitely seemed gloomier than what I'd seen earlier. Dammit. Any one of these *college students* could have picked this up.

"That burger sure smells good. My ex-husband was the grill man — that may have been his only strong point." I chuckled weakly. "I haven't gotten over the hump of doing it myself."

"Almost always a mistake to depend on a man."

Dead end there. I emptied the watering can into the potted tomato and turned to go back inside.

"I guess fall's on its way," I said, my hand on the glass slider. "It always makes me feel a little sad."

How many times had I given this damn lecture, and still I overlooked obvious depressive signs of the woman right next door? More to the point, our interactions had been too limited to allow me to interpret her signals — if there were any. And I'd been the one to limit them. Needles of guilt stabbed me again.

Stop! I was making myself ill. I forced my attention back to the notes.

"Once you understand the student, you can work on generating options and getting closure. Shall we try a role-play?"

Margo stepped forward to act the part of the depressed subject and two other students took their places as the counselors. Leaning forward, shoulders squared, eyes focused: They looked nervous but brave.

"I'm feeling a little blue," Margo began.

CHAPTER 5

I was bone-tired by the time I pulled into my driveway. A two-toned Oldsmobile was parked along the curb, and Isabel Stanton was huddled on the front stoop. My heart sank. I wanted to be supportive toward this poor woman, but my own battery needed a charge — like a glass of Pinot Grigio, a bowl of leftover carbonnade, and a couple of hours parked in front of the TV, watching shows so dumb you didn't need to reach for the Sominex. I parked the car, collected my purse and briefcase, and stepped back out of my garage.

"Isabel, hello! Have you changed your mind about Spencer?"

Isabel struggled to her feet, a worried smile flitting across her face. "No, no, Spencer's fine." She pulled her camel-hair blazer tightly around her waist. "I'm so sorry to bother you."

I smiled back, and walked around the

hedge and up the sidewalk to unlock the front door. "Would you like to come in for a minute?"

Spencer met us in the vestibule, meowing and serpentining through my legs, then hers. Isabel pulled a plastic bag out of her purse. Her face was pale, dark half-moons of papery skin drooping below her eyes. "I wouldn't bother you, but I just didn't know where else to turn."

I waited, fighting the polite urge to ask her to sit.

"The police brought me a note this afternoon. A suicide note. From Madeline." The baggie quaked in her hand as she offered it to me, then let it fall to the coffee table when I didn't take it. "My daughter didn't write it."

I'd seen this phenomenon before with suicides — the survivors run hard through the stages of grief, resting a long time in the first stage of denial. Understandably so. Who's eager to accept that their beloved sister-mother-father-daughter was so miserable, the only solution was to kill themselves? I felt terrible, and I barely knew the girl. For loved ones, moving on usually means facing some ugly truths about the deceased relative and the meaning of their relationship. And then facing their own rage and sadness.

I couldn't just turn her away.

"Sit down for a minute." I shrugged off my coat, perched on the recliner across from Isabel, and pulled the typewritten note from the baggie.

Dear Mom:

I'm sorry to have caused you this pain. Please don't blame yourself for what's happened. My life simply was not going well, and I saw no reason to continue a lonely existence with little hope for change. As you know, life has been difficult ever since Dad left. Lately, I've dreaded every-thing and felt empty, as though I was already dead inside. But I love you and I know we will meet again in heaven. This may hurt at first, but I'm sure you'll see in the end that my death is the best thing for us all. I've tried to make it and failed — just can't keep it together anymore.

Love, Madeline

When I finished reading, I handed it back to Isabel. "Why don't you think she wrote it?" I asked.

"Dear Mom," she read aloud, and then stopped to look at me. "It starts right there. She hardly ever called me Mom. I was almost always 'Mother.' Even when she was little." She glanced down at the paper. Her shoulders began to shake and tears splashed onto the note. I hurried across the room and returned with a box of Kleenex.

"Look, it's heartbreaking to be faced with her terrible unhappiness. I'm sure —"

"That's not it," said Isabel, withdrawing her arm from beneath my fingers. "I'm just certain she didn't write this."

I sighed. "Where did the police find it?"

"On the laptop in her study. They took the computer with them on Friday night, and then called me to the station to pick up a copy of the letter. They said there weren't any fingerprints on the computer except for Madeline's. Detective Meigs insists there was no foul play."

She shot me a pleading look — the big-eyed, puppy-dog-lost look an owner gets when leaving her pet for the day — and held the note out across the space between us.

I crossed my arms over my chest, feeling slightly sick to my stomach. Then I thought of Angie.

"My best friend specializes in linguistics," I said to Isabel. "I'll give her a buzz and run it by her." I left Isabel stroking the cat and went into the bedroom to call Angie and relay Isabel's story.

Angie didn't think much of my ability to set limits with distressed neighbors. "It's police business, Rebecca. Just like we said last night, there's simply no point in getting involved."

I sighed and lowered my voice. "What about —"

"You can't save the world, Rebecca." She laughed. "Hey, I'm starting to sound like Dr. Aster myself. Maybe I should be writing that column. Seriously, even Annabelle agreed you have to leave space for yourself. You're not obligated to take care of every person you meet. It's not humanly possible."

"So you tell me. And so I've told myself. But it still feels lousy."

Angie blew out a noisy breath. "Did you hear anything in the note that sounded unnatural?"

"Not really," I admitted. "But I'm almost certain the detective told me they hadn't found a suicide note at the scene. Why would he lie to me? Doesn't that sound fishy?"

"It sounds like he didn't want the neighbors messing around in police business. The mother is obviously distraught — who wouldn't be, with her daughter taking her own life? But she needs to move on and in this case" — she chuckled — "see the writing on the wall. Or the computer screen, as the case may be."

"Well, thanks anyway." Easy for her to say.

"I can understand how bad this feels. If you absolutely must do something, take the note back to the detective. He can explain his reasoning and maybe then you can help the mother accept the facts. I'm sorry to sound harsh, but that's probably the best you can do."

I knew she was right. We hung up after making plans to have lunch on Thursday.

I returned to the living room to face Mrs. Stanton. "She suggests you go back to the cops if you really believe it's a fake." I spread my hands helplessly.

"Would you take it? You're a doctor. I'm just the crazy mother. They'll never listen to me." She plucked up the paper from the coffee table and held it out.

Angie's advice faded from my mind when I saw Isabel's eyes.

"Please," she begged, her voice quivering. She thrust the note forward again.

This time I took it.

CHAPTER 6

The Guilford Police Station, a new edifice built recently by taxpayer consensus to handle the dirty business of suburban life, lay just off the highway. The waiting area had brick walls, tile floor, and air-conditioning on full bore, despite the cool September air.

"I wonder if I might catch Detective Meigs in?" I asked the uniformed woman behind the dispatcher's window. "It's about my neighbor, Madeline Stanton."

Several minutes later, Meigs pushed the door open into the waiting area, shook my hand, and ushered me down the hall to his office. He still seemed grumpy. Paperwork — stacks of it — covered the desktop and the chair in front of it. He scooped up the papers from the chair and dropped them on a file cabinet, partially obscuring a photograph of him next to a big-boned brunette and a black Lab. At least the Labrador looked happy. With a jerk of his chin, he gestured for me to sit. I was tempted to remain standing.

"Did you remember makes and models? Or hair and eye color?"

He looked tired and rumpled, wearing a coffee stain on his shirt and a dark plaid blazer that was past due at the dry cleaners, maybe even the Salvation Army. His tie was too wide and too loud for any fashion trend in the last decade. I pushed the note in its protective baggie across the desk and summarized Isabel Stanton's concerns.

"If she's correct, and her daughter didn't write this note, then we have a murder case on our hands, don't we?" I smiled, doing my best to align myself with him, professionals together against the criminal and wacky elements of the world.

But he didn't smile back — the impression of an armored tank lingered.

"What else can you tell me about your neighbor? You said you didn't recognize her friends? You said you didn't know her well?"

"Not well, that's right. She was a little melancholy, maybe even a little bitter. Honestly, Detective? I see now that I kept my distance."

"I guess fall's on its way . . . it always

makes me feel a little sad."

Which one of us was melancholy after all? Or were we too much alike?

I was just about to describe the conversation I'd had with Madeline over coffee when Meigs startled me by spinning the note around so my neighbor's words faced me. He braced his hands on the arms of his chair and tipped forward.

"I understand you're trying to be helpful." His nostrils flared. "In your business" — he paused for emphasis — "you would know better than others how difficult it is for family members to accept a suicide. The first reaction is naturally: not my daughter! Mrs. Stanton is no different. I printed out a copy of the note for her so she could see the truth. You can help with that too — help her acknowledge the facts. There was no evidence of foul play," he finished, enunciating each word slowly and loudly.

Just what Angie had said. But Meigs was beginning to irritate me, with the pompous tone and thin smile. And either he or his wife needed to do some goddamn laundry.

"You told me that Madeline didn't leave a note."

"I don't believe I went on record either way."

A standoff. What were the chances of psychologically muscling my way past a detective with more body mass than two of me and an attitude to match? I returned the note to the plastic bag and slid it into my purse.

"Thanks for your time. And advice." The last was sarcasm, though I doubted he'd recognize it. "I can see myself out."

Back in the car, I switched on the NPR news and pulled onto the highway. I forced myself to concentrate on avoiding fender benders with other irritable work-bound commuters, rather than stew about Madeline's nonexistent case.

I buzzed in my last patient, an art history graduate student with pale lips and flat brown hair that was often greasy. Wendy trudged up the last steep steps leading to the waiting area, huffing slightly. Today her hair was clean. She settled into the green upholstered chair across from my rocker and crossed her legs Indian-style.

"The weirdest thing happened over the weekend." She stared past my shoulder, through wavy panes of glass, out to the rooftops of New Haven and the Gothic spires of Yale.

"Tell me about it."

Wendy hesitated, wringing her hands. She folded forward, elbows to thighs. "You know how my new apartment is on the second floor?"

I nodded. After a painful separation from her husband, Wendy had rented the middle floor of a faded Victorian home in a student section of downtown New Haven. Before signing the lease, she'd spent weeks obsessing about whether anyone could see in — or worse yet, climb in — the windows of a second-floor apartment. I'd walked a fine line, interpreting Wendy's fears about being on her own, while helping her evaluate any real dangers imposed by the new living arrangement. I thought we'd explored every nuance of the conflict — in enough detail that I found myself watching the bushes outside my own condo for perpetrators. And I live in safe and mouse-quiet suburban Guilford.

"I saw a man lurking in the yard last Friday evening. I called the police right away, of course." Wendy giggled.

I shifted slightly. Through months of sessions, I couldn't remember hearing my patient laugh.

"The cops came about ten minutes later. That's warp speed for New Haven." Wendy laughed again. "Turns out it was my third-floor neighbor. He thinks the landlord doesn't take care of the place so he went outside to clip the hedges himself. After the cops left, we ended up ordering pizza." She blushed and spent the remainder of the hour chronicling the positive attributes of her new acquaintance.

"We're out of time," I told Wendy at ten minutes to ten.

Wendy stood and took a deep breath. "Dr. Butterman, I can't thank you enough. These sessions with you have changed my life."

"You're welcome. We're doing some good work here," I added, and smiled. "See you next week." Wendy skipped down the back staircase.

"Abracadabra," I said to myself, locking up the office and heading out to my car. Though this gardening man might be a pleasant respite, I doubted I'd heard the last of Wendy's problems. People did change as a result of therapy. I'd seen it happen — people making adjustments that shifted their balance from misery toward contentment. But it was slow going, no personality transplants available. I was on my way to prove that very point in my own therapy session.

I parked a block away from Buttons and

Bows, the premier children's shop in the revitalized theater section of town. I had half an hour to shop for a gift for my niece Brittany's birthday. Any longer and I'd be late for Dr. Goldman. And he'd pounce on that transgression like a cat on a wounded bird, constructing an unconscious tale of resentment and disappointment that would leave my stomach churning.

Bells jingled as I entered the store, and the clerk called out a cheerful "Let me know if I can help!" I sorted through a rack of sale clothing, feeling a tiny jolt at the sight of a gray cashmere coat with black braid trim — ridiculous elegance and price for a five-year-old girl. But one of the tooled leather buttons was missing, hence the 75-percent markdown. It looked a little big for Brittany. I fingered the soft wool, glanced at my watch, and left the store. So much for that idea.

Shopping under pressure isn't a talent of mine. Hell, I can't make any decisions under the gun. (You can tell that much from the length of my divorce proceedings.) The TV game show *Supermarket Sweepstakes* fascinated me as a child. Contestants had minutes to fill their carts with merchandise. The player who racked up the highest bill at the checkout in the allotted time got to keep her loot. While other shoppers snatched up expensive roasts dripping with blood, or navigated straight for the gourmet aisles to select pricey tins of imported salmon or caviar, I would be vacillating over the right strategy. And what would I do with all that meat anyway?

I rang the bell outside my therapist's red brick building and waited on the stoop until Dr. Goldman buzzed me in. The door to his office swung open just as I stepped into the waiting area. I swished across the room, settled onto the brown tweed couch, and folded my hands over my stomach. Goldman lifted his chin in greeting and sank back into his own chair. Therapy sessions have their own rhythm — mine is usually old-dog slow. My unconscious mind has to be dragged out into the psychotherapeutic chamber, kicking and screaming.

I closed my eyes and started an imaginary "Late Bloomer" column.

Dear Dr. Aster:
You often recommend psychotherapy to your readers. What's the best kind and how long will it take to work?

Sincerely,
Prospective Patient in Parsippany

Dear Prospective Patient:

It depends on the problems you need to tackle and the patience, money, and tools you have to tackle them. Behavior therapy can bring fast results, but talk or psychodynamic therapy can offer deep and long-lasting change. And don't overlook Woody Allen's favorite — the granddaddy of them all — psychoanalysis. People sometimes unfairly compare analysis to prostitution. In both cases, you pay the professional for a certain kind of intimacy, and for his or her time. But psychoanalysis takes a lot longer. Ha, ha.

I could hear Dr. Goldman breathing. Waiting.

"What are you thinking?" he asked.

I opened my eyes. "I almost bought my niece a coat." I described the gray cashmere, horrified to find myself tearing up as I talked.

"What are your thoughts about that?" He tented his fingers and wrinkled his brow.

I pulled a Kleenex from my pocket and blew my nose. So embarrassing to be ambushed by lingering sadness from my marriage. After all, months and months had passed since the first bad shock of Mark's unfaithfulness. And truth to tell, we'd recognized problems for several years before that — we just hadn't figured out how to tackle them. Shouldn't I be over this by now?

I tucked the tissue away and sighed. "It's plain enough, I suppose. My patient, you know, Wendy, went out on a date last weekend." You were permitted to discuss your patients with your therapist — but the buck stopped there. "Who would have thought she'd beat me to the punch? Here I am almost forty years old, and there are *no* prospects on my horizon."

Maybe the lack of progress wasn't my fault. Maybe Goldman wasn't as good as his reputation allowed. I went with the time-honored psychotherapeutic patient's code: When in doubt, lash out. Especially when it feels like your shrink's abandoning you by going on vacation for a month.

"And despite two years of sessions at a hundred dollars a pop here, where am I really?"

I lapsed into silence. In truth, the sweet little coat stood for all I had already lost and what I still stood to lose: I was thirty-eight years old and back on the starting line. Out of shape and out of sorts. Wearing sweatpants and sneakers while the competition was decked out in spandex and space-age-technology track shoes guaranteed to make you fly. How the hell, at my age, was I supposed to meet another decent man, beat the other women off him, develop a healthy relationship, plan another wedding, and then pop out a couple of children?

"I still don't even know if I really want a child," I said to Goldman. "I don't know if I can handle the responsibility. But the biological clock marches on."

"You manage a full caseload of patients and many other activities. That's a lot of responsibility."

"Not the same." I shook my finger. "The patients come already formed. I can help smooth out some edges, but I'm not responsible for defining the trajectory of their lives."

Dr. Goldman was quiet for a moment. "Have you considered that you were drawn to the coat because of your losses as a *girl*? Weren't you approaching three years old when your sister was born?"

I shifted on the couch and checked the clock ticking on his bookshelf. Was he doing this on purpose? Fifteen minutes left in the session before Goldman took his annual month-long pilgrimage to the fall vacation psychotherapist ghetto in Wellfleet, Massachusetts. Was he working out the most painful psychological interpretation he could — taking into account the secrets I had shared with him over two years — and putting all this together into a sentence bearing just enough truth that I couldn't dismiss it?

I wanted to kill the guy. Which made our impending separation feel both easier and infinitely annoying. A month would pass before I could blast him, and by then, the angry charge would have drained down like a dying battery. Transferring feelings of loss and rage to your therapist is a good thing in the end: When your deep, dark secrets are hauled onto the examining table of the psychotherapeutic hour, you have a better chance of identifying them and seeing them through. Still, we weren't going to make much progress in the now thirteen minutes remaining.

"Oh by the way, did I tell you I adopted a cat? Not adopted really. I'm keeping him for my neighbor's mother. The one who committed suicide."

Dr. Goldman made a sucking noise. "Committed suicide?"

"My neighbor. It happened last week but they found her on Friday. I guess I haven't seen you since then." I pressed my fingertips into my forehead. "The mother asked me to talk with the police about the note her daughter left, but the detective says the evidence is clear. I do feel badly that I wasn't there for her."

"I think you must be feeling upset with me for leaving," he said. "That I won't *be there for you* while I'm on vacation."

I heaved a sigh and gazed out the window. Rush-hour traffic was picking up on Trumbull Street — I could see the roofs of the cars through the orange-tinged leaves on the maple outside his building and hear them honking. "Oh, and Jillian wants me to write a piece about the singles scene — after sampling the options, of course. I'm thinking I may go ahead. I've sat around moaning about Mark for about as long as I can stand. I'm beginning to bore myself."

"Well, our time is up," said Dr. Goldman in a somber voice. "We'll continue in October."

I stood up from the couch, smiling a sickly grin. He held out his small hand, a burr of black hair rising below each pale knuckle.

I wrung it briefly and flashed a real smile. "Have a nice vacation."

CHAPTER 7

With traffic flowing slow but steady on the drive home, I focused on the soup I'd left in the Crock-Pot this morning: corn and sweet potato chowder, served with oatmeal biscuits I'd frozen over the weekend. I felt relieved and a little sheepish about the session with Goldman. Astonishing just how far one could regress in a therapeutic hour. He would have plenty to chew over on his month-long sabbatical — if he thought about that sort of thing. Or maybe he'd honed a technique for blocking his patients out when they weren't right in front of him: That was one I had yet to master.

Isabel Stanton's Oldsmobile was parked in Madeline's driveway and the condo blazed with light. I felt a flash of sadness — she was probably sorting through her daughter's belongings. When I opened my door, Spencer snubbed me briefly, but then ran to his monogrammed bowl, complaining that it was empty.

"I'm hungry too, old boy," I said, rubbing the diamond of white fur under his chin.

The phone rang just after I'd finished dinner and started on the dishes.

"Rebecca? It's Isabel Stanton. Next door. Am I interrupting? I wondered if you had any luck with the police this morning?"

"Not really." I had absolutely nothing to gain by beating around the proverbial bush. "There's no evidence to encourage them to consider anything other than suicide." *Smooth, Rebecca.* "I'm so sorry."

"There's something now," said Isabel, her voice vibrating with intensity. "I found what looks like a section of Madeline's diary. These notes absolutely do not sound depressed. Would you mind awfully taking a look at it? When you have a minute?"

I had braced myself when I first heard her voice. Counseling her on a regular basis was a lousy idea, an emotional brain drain for me and not fair to her either, assuming she needed *objective* professional help. But she had piqued my curiosity. And I had to return Madeline's note anyway. Which Isabel didn't think was Madeline's.

"I'll be right over."

I grabbed a sweater and crossed the small area of lawn to the steps and portico that mirrored mine. Isabel answered my knock quickly and ushered me into Madeline's condo.

As I remembered from my one previous visit, the living room was plain, bordering on spare, furnished with a gray leather couch and armchair and a glass coffee table. A wall of bookshelves housed a printer, fax machine, and gear for a wireless Internet connection. But no computer. Cardboard boxes lining the floor along the far wall had been partly packed with books. The only bright spot in the room was a small Oriental carpet woven in jewel-like colors.

"I made some tea." Isabel patted the cushion beside her and held up a mug painted to resemble a grinning cat. "You look worn out. Everything okay?"

I shrugged. "Just the usual long day. Show me what you found."

She reached for a manila file folder that lay on the coffee table.

"I didn't mean to snoop. Madeline would hate that. She was so private." Tears shimmered in her brown eyes. "Anyway, I found this in one of the file cabinets." She extracted a folder labeled "Mad's diary" and held it out.

"You want me to read it?"

Isabel nodded.

I was learning a lot more about my neighbor dead than I ever had alive. I sighed and flipped the folder open. It contained a sheaf of typewritten notes. The top one read:

Dear Diary: Rip-roaring good time. "Fast Connections" — stressful, but seize the moment! A hottie, proud member of the Red Sox Nation, with a cleft chin. Weak in the knees. Yowza, fireworks! But only one side?

I glanced up. Isabel was waiting expectantly.

"I agree — this doesn't sound like a depressed person wrote it."

But people often hide their true feelings behind their words. Otherwise, I'd be out of business. I couldn't make an informed assessment based on these notes. I laid the folder on the coffee table.

"What was Madeline like?" I asked, sinking back into the couch. "I'm embarrassed to tell you that we hadn't gotten to know each other very well."

Isabel stood up, crossed the room to the bookshelves, and selected a photograph from a small cluster of frames. She returned and handed it to me. It was a good likeness, capturing Madeline's imposing eyebrows, long straight nose, and a pretty smile I hadn't seen very often. She had her arm around her more petite mother, who looked younger and happier than she had the last few days.

"As a girl, she was very private. The boys were so much more outgoing, it seemed as though there wasn't a lot of room for her personality in our house. I always imagined that if I had a daughter, we'd be so much alike and I'd understand her through and through." She tucked her face into her hands.

"But you didn't?" I prompted.

Isabel dropped her hands and shook her head. "She had a wonderful imagination. She loved to play with dolls. She wanted Barbie dolls and stuffed animals for birthdays and Christmas, and all the accessories for the dollhouse her grandfather built. She spent hours in her room, making up stories. I always thought she might be a writer, but she had her father's aptitude for math too. So I wasn't surprised she went into computers."

Isabel was crying silently now, her voice muffled by the handkerchief she held up to her mouth. I patted her knee and nodded my encouragement. She would need to talk about all of this, and more, before her pain could begin to heal.

"She never seemed to have much luck finding a good man," she said, her voice growing fierce with anger. "A couple of months ago, she turned up with a black eye."

I leaned forward, thinking of the visitors in Madeline's bedroom. "Someone hit her?"

"She said she'd taken a fall. I didn't know what to believe." Isabel sighed. "I tried to encourage her to move to New York City or Boston, somewhere with more young people around. But she wanted to stay near me. 'Where are you going to find decent, eligible young men on the Connecticut shoreline?' I'd ask her. Guilford is such a small town. It's all families here."

I felt a little queasy listening to her. Those same questions had been bubbling up in my mind since the divorce came through. Could a single person find happiness in the suburbs? A city seemed easier. More options, a faster lifestyle — restaurants that stayed open past nine p.m., for one basic example.

"We all gave her advice — I know it drove her crazy, but she was the baby of the family and we couldn't help it," said Isabel, smiling and moving the folder to the gray leather cushion near me.

"Did you know about Madeline's gun?" The question popped out before I could stop it.

Isabel winced. "She told us she could take care of herself — we didn't need to worry." Her dark eyes glistened as she shook her head. "I don't believe it was hers. Where would she ever find a gun?"

"Go to a gun shop, I suppose —"

"Dear, I'm feeling exhausted. I think I'd better get home."

She did look pale. And old. "Are you all right to drive? Can I call someone?"

"I'm fine." She frowned.

"What is it?"

"I just wondered if you might like to take the files with you and have a look through Madeline's papers. I just know you'd get a better idea of her state of mind."

Her face was hopeful — the pleading pet look again.

"Oh no, I'd hate to be responsible for them. They're your connection to your daughter." I stood up and held out the manila folder.

She dropped it back onto the coffee table, pressed a key into my right palm, and closed my fingers over it.

"Please," she said. "You could even look around a little. Read whatever you like.

Look at anything that catches your eye. I know it's asking a lot, but you're more likely to see things that I wouldn't notice. I'm too close." She pushed my hands away and placed hers on her chest. "Suicide? My baby? It hurts me so much to imagine that."

I walked her to the front steps and watched her pick her way through the shadows along the sidewalk.

She stopped and turned. "Did I tell you the memorial service has been scheduled for Saturday afternoon? Two p.m. in the Reis Room at Evergreen Woods, my assisted-living facility. It would mean so much if you came. Assisted living." She jangled her keys. "Isn't that ridiculous? If you need that much help, shouldn't you just move on?"

I waited until I heard the rumble of the big Olds, then closed the door. What the hell was I doing in this condo? Why had I agreed to stay? What was her agenda? Isabel Stanton was not nearly as fragile and help-less as she wanted me to believe. But, I had to admit that something about the young woman's death rubbed me the wrong way. And Isabel seemed so convinced . . . I figured as long as I was here, I could loop through one time.

I headed down the hall and crossed the

master bedroom to Madeline's bathroom. The idea of her lying twenty feet away from my bedroom — dead — haunted me. A gun held at close range had to do some serious damage. Was the physical evidence still there?

A layer of greasy black dust covered the doorknobs, the sink, and the bathtub. Was I imagining a pink ring around the drain? No, the rusty stain that had soaked into the grout a foot above the tub's rim, below the soap holder, was real. My knees buckled as I grabbed for the door, eased back into the bedroom, and perched on the bed. I can handle psychological carnage, no problem, but blood and guts do me in.

Madeline had installed a huge TV with oversized speakers on the wall opposite her bed. No wonder I'd heard her favorite crime shows more often than I would have liked. And the dull roar of what had to be sporting events. Baseball probably. I was no jock, but I didn't think summer was the right season for football or basketball. And I remembered Madeline mentioning the Red Sox fan in her diary notes.

This room was monochromatic like the living area and pin-neat, except for a water glass on the bedside table and the mess the cops had made last week. Everything on the nightstand — phone, lamp, glass — was coated with greasy black fingerprint dust. If Isabel felt compelled to clean it up herself, I didn't envy her.

A small section of the bookshelves that straddled the TV contained books, photos, and videos. Moving closer, I noticed several titles about the life and death of Lady Diana, the Princess of Wales — biographies, a video of the royal wedding, and a collection of interviews after her death.

I'd had a patient several years ago who'd fixated on Diana's life. She talked endlessly about her fascination with the princess, who was tall, blond, gorgeous, beloved by her country, and blessed with two sons. And very, very tragic, as I kept pointing out.

A therapist has to watch for this kind of shorthand. What's the meaning of clinging psychologically to a woman whose royal life resembled a free-falling plane crashing to a fiery death? In my patient's case, the answer had appeared to be a powerful self-destructive streak that eventually led to her discontinuing treatment when we brushed too near the truth. Underneath the chirpiness of her diary entry, Madeline's interest in Princess Diana might fall in the suicidal evidence column.

Enough. I was exhausted and developing

a case of serious heebie-jeebies from snooping in a dead woman's home. On the way out, I grabbed the file folder from the coffee table, locked the deadbolt, and crossed the small lawn to my condo, which seemed safe, cozy, and warm. Especially with Lord Spencer purring on the bed.

I settled under the covers and leafed through Madeline's papers. Each entry was introduced by "Dear Diary" and contained a sequence of choppy but chipper notes. The few diaries I'd read about or been shown by my patients did not try this hard. Was she writing for an audience? Who? When in doubt, I reminded myself, google.

I opened up my laptop and typed "Madeline Stanton" in the Google toolbar. A link surfaced referencing her graduation from the University of Connecticut. On a hunch, I googled "Madeline's diary." I skimmed through a number of references to *The Diary of Madeline Beck,* the graphic description of a baby's birth, and an equally excruciating description of the likes and dislikes of a tabby cat named Madeline. Fifteen unproductive minutes were eaten up reading the diary of Dr. Charles Balis, a therapist (could this be real?) who detailed his patients' sessions. Finally, I found the link I wanted on the third page and clicked.

A website materialized: "Madeline's Musings — my flight into the dating world and beyond."

My neighbor had been a blogger.

On the far right side of the page, Madeline had listed what appeared to be other blogs including thatfish, bloggydog, morethantwentysomething, and girlmeetsboy. On the left were the dates of recent entries. I clicked on the newest, September 6, and watched a Dear Diary entry pop onto the screen. The title was a quote: "If Barbie is so popular, why do you have to buy her friends?" The contents were an expanded version of the notes Isabel showed me.

Dear Diary: I had a rip-roaring good time on Friday. Okay, I exaggerate. Making "Fast Connections" can be beastly stressful, but I tried to seize the moment! Had a couple of drinks at the break with D — a proud member of the Red Sox Nation, a hottie with a cleft chin that made me weak in the knees. I checked him off as a match but he didn't return the favor. Not yet anyway. So I guess I'm still single, no fireworks to report. Am I (sigh, sigh, violins enter here) looking for love in all the wrong places? Yours truly, Madsingleton

I remembered Mrs. Dunbarton's nosy

comments about Madeline's gentlemen callers over the last couple of weeks. Could the visitors have come from Fast Connections?

I clicked on the previous entry, September 3.

Quote for the day:
The best thing a father can do for his children is to love their mother.

Dear Diary: Apologies in advance for wandering off the dating path, but I had to talk about this. Saw an article online tonight claiming Lady Diana could have been saved without the interference of the paparazzi and with faster medical attention. Some doctor said she died of a rupture of the left pulmonary vein but that most times this can be repaired and the victim saved. Oh my God, could things get any worse for her and for those gorgeous princes??? Sorry to be morbid, but maybe she was too beautiful to live. Charles, how could you have destroyed her? Maybe some people are just destined for a tragic life . . . I'm going out tomorrow to see what I can do about mine. Yours truly, Madsingleton

Twenty-seven comments followed my neighbor's entry — most were variations of

"Cheer up" and "Oh my God, I can't believe she died for no good reason" and "If she loved her sons so much, why wasn't she wearing a freakin' seatbelt?"

Then I noticed a faint red light pulsing from my phone. I'd forgotten to check my answering machine. In the kitchen, I punched the *play* button and poured a half a glass of Pinot Grigio for me and a splash of milk for Spencer. Jillian had left a long message: *Bloom!* was prepared to pay all the expenses for the singles article. She'd done some research on the possibilities and wanted me to choose one and get started.

"There are speed-dating singles mixers this weekend in Branford and Middletown through Fast Connections. Isn't Branford the next town over from yours? And I found a singles golf group in Madison and tennis at the Guilford Racquet Club. Doesn't that sound like fun? How about using the name Rebecca Aster? That should take care of the anonymity issue, right? If you could e-mail a draft of the first column by Monday, we would be oh-so-deeply grateful. And just to be clear, we want your regular advice column every week, as well.

"Oh, and please call before Monday if you meet your prince."

I heard a peal of high-pitched laughter and

then the click of the receiver.

Sheesh. I was being set up left and right. What the hell, maybe it *was* time to ride that horse again. Might as well get paid to do it. I returned to my computer and typed in the web address for Fast Connections. Then it hit me hard — my neighbor had attended this same event just days before she died. Before I could second-guess myself, I registered for Friday's session for thirty- to forty-year-olds at Rudy V's Sports Bar in Branford.

I couldn't help wondering whether "D" with the sexy cleft chin would be there too.

CHAPTER 8

On Thursday, I walked past the row of brownstones lining Trumbull Street to meet Angie for lunch at Clark's Pizza Restaurant. Even with all the nouveau Italian places that have sprung up in New Haven over the last five years, once a month we're still drawn by the comforting siren of worn Naugahyde booths, professional waitresses with no urge to introduce themselves by first name, and slightly greasy food.

We settled into a booth in the window and ordered Greek salads with tyropita on the side. The salads allowed us to feel virtuous; the crispy phyllo pies oozing butter and cheese were pure decadent heaven.

"Want to go to a hot vinyasa yoga demonstration tomorrow night?" Angie asked. "Shobhan Barkan's in town from Florida."

I grimaced. Whoever the heck Shobhan Barkan was — probably some hunk with oiled muscles who could twist himself into a pretzel and balance on one hand all the while chanting ancient Tibetan dirges. My yoga class focuses on stretching, stress reduction, and for challenge, holding the downward dog for an extra thirty seconds. Which is why my pants fit more snugly than is quite comfortable and why Angie looks the way she does — slim and toned, as her singles' ad would say. If she had one. If she needed that kind of crutch. Men seemed to tumble into her path at just the right moment. But she's having too much fun to take one on as a full-time project.

"Nothing I'd like better, but you won't believe what I'm already doing."

Our waitress clattered heavy china plates onto the table and refilled our coffees. Between bites of flaky pastry and salad, I described the new singles article and my appointment with Fast Connections.

Angie dropped her fork and started clapping. "Bravo! You move fast, girl. I didn't think you had this in you!"

"Shut up and take a look at what I've written so far." I popped an olive into my mouth and handed my notes for top tips across the table.

1. Be honest.
2. Be upbeat.

3. Be careful.
4. Didn't find your prince? You can still have fun at the ball!

"Number one is already a bust. I signed up as Rebecca Aster — not Butterman. And no one in her right mind would tell a potential date she's a psychologist. Scares them off faster than leg hair or body odor. Announcing that I was a minister might be worse — maybe not even."

"Right." Angie laughed. "At least a minister would have to go through God to read their dirty minds." She skimmed through my tips. " 'Still have fun at the ball?' You are one chipper gal."

"And what will I have to talk about if I can't complain about Mark?" We both laughed.

"You *will* be careful."

"I will."

"Want company? I can cancel the hot yoga."

"It'll be embarrassing enough, just me. I'll call you Saturday and tell all."

Angie stabbed the last square of feta cheese with her fork and wiped the salad dressing off her plate with a hunk of Italian bread. "How'd you make out with your neighbor's mother?"

"Umm, it's a long story." I signaled to our waitress for the check, waffling over whether to show Angie the suicide note.

"I'm in no hurry," said Angie, grabbing my wrist. "Spill."

I explained how I'd gotten myself appointed to take the note to the police.

"And?"

I shrugged. "Detective Meigs pretty much gave me the same line you did. You know, you can help by introducing her to the facts — her daughter killed herself." I sighed.

"And?"

"And so I told her exactly that. But meanwhile, she'd found a folder of diary entries that she begged me to read. Turns out my mousy neighbor was writing an Internet blog." I held up my hand. "I know what you're going to say: This girl's death is none of my business. But honestly, I had to agree with Isabel Stanton after I read a couple entries. She sounded slightly sad, but I didn't see anything suicidal." I unlatched my briefcase and retrieved the plastic bag that still held Madeline's ostensible suicide note. "Would you look this over? Please?"

Angie skimmed the words, then read the last few sentences aloud.

" 'Lately, I've dreaded everything and felt

empty, as though I was already dead inside. But I love you and I know we will meet again in heaven. This may hurt at first, but I'm sure you'll see in the end that my death is the best thing for us all. I've tried to make it and failed — just can't keep it together anymore. Love, Madeline.' "

"Sounds pretty clear cut to me. What's wrong with this picture?" she asked.

"Plenty," I said. "Starting with the fact that Madeline didn't call her mother 'Mom.' And yes, the father left the family, but that was years ago and this woman was in her thirties and out on her own. I'm not buying her parents' divorce as an explanation for suicide. Besides, no one in the family seems at all religious. They may be members of our church, but I've certainly never seen them at a service."

Angie frowned, but I forged onward.

"Generally, with suicidal people, there's underlying hopelessness, grief, forlornness — a sense that whatever needs to change to make life bearable just isn't possible. I don't see that in Madeline's life. She had a good relationship with her mother —"

"Says her mother," said Angie. "What the hell else is she going to tell a shrink?"

"She had a cat whom she adored," I continued, "and she made no mention of

Spencer in the note — no arrangements for his care at all. Don't you find that odd?"

"Spencer? Is that the gray cat I saw outside your condo? Where is he now?"

I lined up my silverware along the edges of the paper placemat. "I'm keeping him until Isabel can make other arrangements. I would have introduced him to you on Sunday, but he was afraid to come out from under the bed."

"Jesus, Rebecca. You've sunk in this up to your neck. I don't get it. You're usually so good at keeping people at a distance."

"It's hard to take that as a compliment," I said stiffly.

"Sorry." She laughed and patted my hand. "I meant it only in the nicest way. But why her? Why now?"

"I'm sure I told you this the other night. I gave Madeline the brush-off. If I'd spent more time with her, she might be alive today. I would have picked something up, and then I could have steered her toward the right help."

Angie groaned. "You could teach the Catholics something about guilt." She arranged her face into a patient expression. She's known me long enough to realize that we never discuss a subject only once. "Tell me more about the time you had coffee with her."

"We didn't hit it off that well. Right before I was due at Madeline's, Mark dropped in with some papers to sign and we got into a screaming match. It was hard to concentrate on chitchat with a slightly odd neighbor." I rubbed my eyes, careful not to smear my mascara. "We talked about her job in computers. And I told her what I did. She got a little weird when I told her I was a psychologist. Although she was quite interested in my advice column. She made up a couple of questions and insisted that I pretend to answer them."

"That's a little off," said Angie. "What did she do with computers?"

"Programming for a web-marketing company, I think. We spent most of our time discussing the cat. She named him Lord Spencer after Princess Di's brother. She had a kind of shrine to Diana in her bedroom — books, videos, photos — and she talked about her in the blog too. Conspiracy theories, that kind of thing."

"Weren't there a rash of copycat suicides after Diana's death?" Angie asked. "Maybe this is related."

"Diana didn't kill herself," I said. "She died in a car crash. And her death was almost ten years ago. Which is," I admitted, "a possibly significant anniversary. I'm guessing Madeline was around Diana's age when she died."

Angie leaned forward and lowered her voice. "Where was the cat when the girl killed herself? Do you remember the case where the pets tracked the owner's blood through the house and mucked up the whole crime scene?"

I hadn't thought to ask. And it could make a difference. Had Madeline shut Spencer in the basement with food and water? Left him meowing outside the bathroom door? Did she think this through before she shot herself? If she did, could I somehow squeeze the details out of Meigs? Ha. Not a chance.

I shrugged and tapped the paper. "What about the letter? She says here she can't keep it together anymore — you'd never know that from her condo. Her bills were paid, she had groceries in the house, her place was a hell of a lot neater than mine — except for the bathroom, of course, where they found the body. And the mess the cops made dusting for fingerprints."

"Don't even tell me how you became an expert on this woman's apartment," said Angie, shaking her head.

"Her mother insisted that I take the key,"

I admitted. "I just swung through quickly. Even her blog was up-to-date, and you know what a time sink that can be."

Angie sighed and read the note a second time. "Suicide notes are often unemotional in tone," she said. "By the time someone has made this kind of decision, they're past feeling much. Although we do sometimes see ambivalence — love and hate — and blame — usually blaming someone specific. More often than not, I'd say the notes I've seen were short, factual, objective, and banal."

"Not desperate like this one, then," I said.

"Right." Angie removed her reading glasses and perched them on her head. "You say she was writing a blog?"

I nodded.

"I could run a syntactical analysis. That's a program that tests for readability, vocabulary, punctuation, and so on. It would give us a better idea whether the person who wrote the blog also wrote the note. Obviously a lot more reliable than eyeballing the thing and guessing."

We paid the check and walked to the shop next door to run off a copy for Angie. "I'll try to get this done over the weekend. Meanwhile, I'm a little worried about your judgment. Don't do anything dumb with these fast connections."

I gave her a hug, feeling a lot more cheerful than before lunch. "You can count on careful, conservative me."

CHAPTER 9

As I pulled down the driveway and into the garage, I noticed a white paper taped to my front door. A trio of horrible possibilities raced to mind: The condo was being condemned, an unhappy patient was suing the pants off me, or my ex-husband had reneged on the divorce agreement. All of them equally logical, equally likely.

Angie says I have a serious case of negative thinking. I say if she had my history, she'd prepare for the worst too. This way, I'm pleasantly surprised every once in a while. Dropping my purse, briefcase, and bag of takeout from Romeo and Cesar's Deli on the counter, I walked quickly down the hall to unlock my front door.

"EMERGENCY CONDO ASSOCIA-TION MEETING TONIGHT!" the notice screamed in slightly blurred red marker. "Your attendance is required at a meeting of the Soundside Homeowners Association in order to discuss the recent tragedy in our complex and the need for increased vigilance and security. Chairman Peter Morgan will call the meeting to order at 7:30 p.m. in the clubhouse. Respectively yours, Mrs. Edith Dunbarton, Secretary."

I could write a year's worth of advice columns about how to deal with intrusive, bossy neighbors who don't know the difference between "respectfully" and "respectively" — as if any of the readers would care about the curse of Mrs. Dunbarton. I was willing to bet that Peter Morgan hadn't called the emergency meeting (attendance required) — Mrs. Dunbarton had parked her rather substantial rump on his doorstep and refused to remove it until he agreed to the plan.

I toyed with the possibility of ignoring the notice — being bullied about mandatory attendance stoked the urge to skip. By closing the blinds and hunkering in the bedroom, I could lay low and make it look like I'd worked late. On the other hand, any number of absurd regulations might get approved if the reasonable members of the association refused to show.

I sliced a fresh tomato and piled it high with shrimp salad from the deli. Then I poured a half a glass of Pinot Grigio. The mocha-swirl cheesecake I'd purchased and another glass of wine would serve as my reward for surviving the meeting. After eating quickly, I scraped the last shrimp into Spencer's bowl, brushed my teeth, and headed over to the clubhouse.

Inside, chatting condo residents filled several rows of white plastic chairs. Our handyman, Bernd Becker, was standing by at the back of the room to set up more if needed. The board had hired him before I moved in, hoping his phlegmatic Swiss calm and mechanical competence might help repel Mrs. Dunbarton's daily assaults. Dunbarton herself peered at me from her position at the table in front of the room, and then frowned and marked her legal pad. Demerits for arriving late, I supposed.

"Thank you very much for coming on short notice," said Peter, a tall, muscular contrast to Mrs. Dunbarton's jiggling mass. The only thing they had in common was Burberry — Mrs. Dunbarton's scarf accented a voluminous black corduroy jumper and thick elastic stockings, while Peter wore a striking plaid tie.

"I'd like to call the meeting to order. Hopefully we can deal with the issues before us in a timely manner." He glanced at his watch and patted his stomach. "I'm probably not the only one who hasn't had dinner yet. I've asked our condo manager to join us tonight. There may be some information he can add." He smiled and nodded to the back of the room. Bernd straightened quickly.

"Glad to help if I can," he said in his soft accent.

Peter's expression shifted back to serious. "As I'm sure you're all aware, Madeline Stanton died last week in her condo. The police have ruled her death to be a suicide —"

"There is absolutely no way they could be certain about that," said Mrs. Dunbarton. "You can assume the gunshot was self-inflicted if you're so inclined. But with a potential murderer on the loose, I'm here to discuss security measures at our condominium." She struggled to her feet. "Did any of the rest of you happen to notice that Ms. Stanton had a number of male visitors over the past several months?" She glared at me as Peter smacked the table with his wooden gavel. I looked away, not wanting to give her any encouragement. I'd told the cops what I saw and heard, and they weren't interested.

"Madeline's visitors are really not any concern of ours," said Peter. "Let's stay focused on the reason for tonight's meeting."

"If one of them murdered her, I would beg to differ!" Mrs. Dunbarton exclaimed. "It's very much a concern of ours."

Peter took in a big breath and sighed. "The chair recognizes Mrs. Dunbarton to share her thoughts on condominium security. Not to discuss Madeline's social life," he added.

I flashed him an encouraging smile. He seemed to be handling the details of life better than me, given his recent divorce status. He'd even accepted the association's leadership position last month when no one else was willing — except for Edith Dunbarton, of course. She'd already served as president — back in 2001 when she'd proposed a ban on flags after 9/11. It wasn't a matter of politics, she'd insisted, it was strictly aesthetics. Peter is a lawyer, a little bit pompous and a lot too certain, but none of us wanted to take off on another administrative luge run with Dunbarton steering.

"I propose we increase the common fees and hire a security guard to patrol the area," she said.

"Are you crazy? That would cost a bloody fortune," said Mr. Nelson. "No way we're voting for that." He jerked his head to include his wife.

How much had he had to drink before arriving at the clubhouse? He would have had time for multiple cocktails, but his words weren't slurred, and for him, he'd been polite. Usually his dialogue with Mrs. Dunbarton consisted of a string of four-letter words. On the other hand, a functional alcoholic could appear quite normal — right up to the moment he stepped over his internal line.

"Supposing we restrict the guard's hours to the night shift?" piped up Babette Finster, the wraithlike woman with straw-blond hair who occupied the apartment on the other side of Madeline.

Besides her work as file clerk in the middle school principal's office, Babette's only activity seemed to be frequent walks with her tiny dog, Wilson. She'd chatter anxiously to anyone in earshot, or the dog, if the neighbors had evaded her. Watching her constricted social life made me want to push out of my shell and mix it up with the young and restless — even Fast Connections. I felt a little seasick suddenly remembering where I'd be tomorrow night.

"I'd be happy to get some estimates," offered Bernd.

Mr. Nelson barreled on. "Let's suppose

the security company charges twenty bucks an hour — and who will you get for that price — parolees, most likely," he said. "Twenty times eight, that's one hundred sixty. One-sixty times three sixty-five, that's fifty-eight thousand four hundred dollars. And that's assuming they wouldn't gouge us for holidays and weekends. We have what, twenty units in the complex?"

Peter and Bernd both nodded.

"We're chewing on three grand a head."

"Oh my goodness," squeaked Babette. "That's way over my budget. Aren't there less expensive options?"

"The Neighborhood Watch has been successful in other communities," said Peter.

"We already have Mrs. Dunbarton," I muttered under my breath.

"Lighting," she said. "Spotlights should be installed in front and back of each unit."

"Give us a Goddamn break," said Mr. Nelson. "We might as well live in a prison."

Half an hour of squabbling and four defeated motions later, we agreed to split the expense of a new streetlight at the entrance to the complex and to keep a close eye out for unfamiliar vehicles. After the motion to adjourn was seconded and approved, Bernd began to stack the chairs in the corner of the room. Mrs. Dunbarton pointed toward me, freshly enraged by her security plan's defeat.

"If you and Ms. Finster had been paying closer attention, Madeline Stanton might still be alive."

Babette gasped and blanched a frightening white.

"That's unkind and unfair," I said firmly, touching Babette's arm.

She blew her nose into a lace-trimmed hankie and hesitated. "I think I remember a man waiting outside Madeline's door last week." She patted her pageboy into perfect shape. "I noticed him because the hair was magnificent — thick and dark and bushy." Her neck flooded with blotches of pink, highlighting the uneven application of a thick coat of foundation. "Well, to be honest, I also noticed him because she'd had a blond man visit not too long before. Or was the blond man earlier and the dark-haired man next?"

"That same night?" Mrs. Dunbarton demanded.

Peter came forward to join us. "It was probably one of her brothers."

"It's just so awful to have been right next door to her with that" — she shivered — "going on." She turned away from Mrs. Dunbarton. "I'm so upset and scared. Have you seen anyone suspicious?" she asked me.

"No," I admitted. "I've been very busy. School starting and all."

"Do you think it was suicide?" Babette asked, her voice wobbling. "You're the medical doctor."

No point in explaining — again — that psychologists have Ph.D.s. No point in explaining much of anything to this crowd: Once on a scent, they were following one trail only. "I'm not certain —"

"Aha!" cried Mrs. Dunbarton.

I raised my voice a few decibels. "I was starting to say I didn't know her well enough to hazard a reasonable guess."

Peter sighed heavily. "Ladies, I think you should leave this discussion to the police. Babette, did you report Madeline's visitors to the cops?"

She nodded.

"If you don't mind, then, Bernd would like to lock up the clubhouse."

I didn't mind. I hung back while the two women left, Mrs. Dunbarton quizzing Babette on the details of Madeline's gentlemen callers.

"That didn't go too badly," I said to Peter, "considering who you have to manage."

"I'd like to nominate you for this board. A sane voice in the wilderness." Peter smiled and shook his head as he helped Bernd stack the last row of chairs. "Before I forget, we need to get into your unit this week to look at the wiring and the circuit breaker in the basement. Bernd has checked out everyone except you and the Nelsons. He's pulling together an estimate for the board meeting next month."

"Can you let yourselves in?" I asked. "Any time tomorrow is okay with me."

"Very good."

"And by the way," I added, "is there any chance of recalling Mrs. Dunbarton's master key? It really annoys me when she retrieves my mail. There's no good reason for her to keep one, especially now that we have Bernd."

"I'll try," said Peter, looking pained. "You can be certain she won't give it up without a struggle."

"Good night," the handyman said. And to Peter: "I'll get the lighting estimates to you by the end of the week."

"That Dunbarton woman is a menace," Peter continued to me. "Too bad we didn't have a screening committee before she moved in — the two of us." He laughed, then grew suddenly serious. "Really, you don't think Madeline did herself in?"

I paused before I spoke. This was a police

investigation after all, and maybe I should keep my mouth shut. Or was it anymore?

"Confidentially?" I asked.

"Of course," he snapped.

Excuse me. "There was a note on her computer that didn't sound much like her," I said. "And often with suicides, there are indications that the person was despondent. No one noticed that with Madeline."

"I thought you hardly knew her?"

"Right. But I've been spending a little time with her mother. Sweet lady. She's totally devastated, of course." I followed Peter outside and paused by the kidney-shaped pool, now covered with a taut green tarp. Not really long enough to swim decent laps, but good for cooling off in the dog days. "And she just adored her cat — hard to believe she wouldn't have made some kind of arrangement for his care."

"Obviously, I'm not a mental health professional," Peter said, "but if a person is distraught, I imagine they might overlook some of the finer details." He shrugged. "Shooting yourself in the bathtub is a pretty clear statement, in my book. And you didn't hear anything?"

"Nothing." I shivered. "Probably I wasn't home at the time. But it makes me wonder just how deep into my own little world I am."

He patted me on the back. "Even if you were home, the condo files indicate we paid the contractors for double insulation in the bathrooms. I guess they did a pretty good job. I'll see you around. Hopefully we've contained the Dunbarton monster — at least for a while."

I returned to my apartment, locked the door behind me, and scooped Spencer into my arms.

"Are you lonely, Buddy? I wish you could talk. Where were you when . . . when your mommy died?" Which made me feel a little silly, but the cat only purred.

CHAPTER 10

Dear Dr. Aster:
I panic when I have to talk to strangers. PTA meetings, cocktail parties, business events — it makes no difference. My mind goes completely blank, and all I can think is how I'll have nothing to say and end up looking and sounding like an idiot. I've reached the point where I'd rather stay home. Any suggestions?

Tongue-tied in Toronto

Dear Tongue-tied:
Glad you asked, because by staying home, you miss all the fun! Psychologists call this problem social phobia or, in its most extreme form, agoraphobia — literally "fear of the marketplace." There are tons of ways to get past the jitters. You might start with deep breathing and progressive relaxation techniques. Two thoughts to remember: (1)

While you're worrying about what other people think, they're worrying about you! And (2) People love to talk about themselves. So go to your events armed with a set of questions to ask when conversation lags. If your fears don't recede, find a good therapist — talking things over with a professional can really help! Good luck!

I'd written an advice column addressing social phobia last month. But none of these self-righteous tips were helping to calm me down tonight. I hadn't been this nervous since the ninth-grade Snowflake Ball. I'd come across an online article in *Single for Now* magazine about how to mentally prepare for speed dating, but that wasn't much use either.

"Everybody wants to be paired with the most attractive people in the room. Be practical about who you are and who you're looking for," the article suggested.

A kind way of saying, fairy tales notwithstanding, an ugly duckling shouldn't expect to bag a swan.

The bottom line was remaining realistic: In a setting that depends heavily on physical first impressions, the beautiful people will get the most bids. Fair or not, the world works this way. Forget about my advanced degree, well-paying job, loyal friends, and attractive condo. If the other women at the session were prettier, younger, and sexier, I'd tank. I'd be just another aging chicken, passed over by shoppers who didn't like the expiration date.

I parked outside Rudy V's Sports Bar and turned off the car. For twenty minutes I watched a trickle of customers flow into the bar. The girls — even with disbelief suspended, I couldn't call them women — wore cropped tops and short skirts, and teetered in pointy-toed shoes. Maybe I had the wrong night — these kids couldn't be over thirty. I brushed out the creases in my green-striped cotton shirtdress. The outfit had appeared fresh and stylish in *Elle* magazine — not prim, bordering on matronly, as it felt now.

I've come dressed as Donna Reed.

Droplets of sweat slid down my chest, pooled under my breasts, and began to darken select stripes on Donna Reed's dress. I scolded myself that it made no difference whether I personally failed at speed dating — I was here for research purposes only, not to find a man.

Ha. I gritted my teeth and stuffed the photograph of Madeline and her mother into my purse along with a small notebook. I'd picked those items up at the last minute. My neighbor had written about Fast Connections. Maybe, just maybe, Madeline's "D" would show up tonight, looking for her. And maybe we'd have the chance to talk so I could ask a few questions about her state of mind the last time he saw her.

The light was dim inside Rudy V's. The TV blared and my nostrils filled with the faint odor of mildew and beer-splashed carpet. A woman approached with her hand outstretched.

"Hi! I'm Traci! Are you here to participate in Fast Connections?" Traci had glossy auburn hair, tortoiseshell eyeglasses so small I wondered how she could see anything through them, and a wide and equally glossy smile.

My first impulse was to bolt.

I nodded. "Rebecca Bu— Aster," I stuttered.

"Come right on in. We're so glad you're here! You're the last one we're waiting for — if you could write your first name and your number — 204 — on the name tag and this card, then we'll get started." She handed me the paperwork. "So sorry, the others had time to snag a drink and some nibbles, but you can do that at the break."

She smiled brightly again, tossed her hair, and rang a filigreed silver bell — calling the lambs to slaughter.

"Attention please, everyone! A warm welcome to Fast Connections, where a small investment of your time can pay big dividends! You will notice that the tables in our room have numbers on them — these correspond to the gentlemen here tonight. If we could take a minute for the guys to find their seats."

The men shuffled into place, leaving a cluster of giggling women near the door. Why, oh, why had I turned down Angie's offer to come along? A friendly face, someone to roll my eyes at, might have made all the difference.

"Before we get started on your conversations, let me run through the instructions for the evening," said Traci. "Each date lasts for six minutes. You all have the numbers of your dates and the order in which you'll meet them listed on your cards. You should try learning enough about each date so you can decide if you'd like to see this person again. If you'll flip your dating card over, you'll find a list of topics to help jumpstart your conversations in case you get stuck."

The questions on the card were similar to the tips I'd had in mind for my article:

Where did you grow up? What kind of work do you do? What do you do for fun? What's your favorite movie or book or magazine or TV show or restaurant? What's the best trip you've ever taken? If you had unlimited money how would you spend your time?

Surely to God I could fill up six minutes with these topics. With anyone.

"I'll ring the bell at the end of each date." Traci laughed and demonstrated the bell's tinkle again. "Now here comes the only hard part: At that point, you take a moment to fill out your card by checking 'Yes' if you'd like another date with this person. You'll transfer this info to our website later tonight when you get home. Then the ladies will proceed to the next assigned table. Any questions?"

A serious man in the back of the room raised his hand. "Supposing we really hit it off, can't we just get the gal's phone number?"

Traci smiled, a little less brightly. "Glad you asked. To make sure this event is safe and comfortable and low pressure for everyone, we request that no one ask anyone else for his or her phone number, last name, or for a date. I know I don't have to remind you to please be polite and respectful. Even if your date doesn't seem like someone you could be interested in romantically, you'll have more fun if you approach each conversation with an open mind. Everyone has an interesting story to tell if you ask the right questions!"

Traci tinkled her bell and I found my way to date number one. Tim was a heavyset guy with a wispy Fu Manchu mustache, a greasy ponytail, and a faded T-shirt. *Hello?* What could we possibly have in common? Which clever question could I trot out to get things rolling and make the six minutes painless?

He straightened in his chair and I saw the Boston Red Sox logo on his shirt. Bingo. If I could get him talking about baseball, who cared if I knew anything about it myself? But let's face it, a guy like that didn't stand a chance in a setting like this. Unless he had a scintillating personality that burst through his off-putting physical presentation. I felt simultaneously sick and guilty about this line of thinking. Some other guy in the room was probably sizing me up in the same cruel way.

"Rebecca," I said, shaking Tim's sweaty hand. "I'm a little nervous about this, but I suppose we just dive right in, right?"

"Right," he grunted without tendering any assistance.

"I see you're a Red Sox fan."

"Not really." He plucked at his tee. "I picked this up at the Army-Navy. Sixty percent off the lowest marked price — seven bucks. What the hell, I'd have bought a shirt with Domino's Pizza on it for that price, right?"

"Right," I said. "What do you do for a living?"

"Nothing at the moment," he said. "Disability. Back injury."

Guess he hadn't read the articles about women's number-one priority — financial security. I hated to make a harsh snap judgment. On the other hand, a recent research report in the *American Psychological Association Monitor* about intuition stated that the essence of personality is displayed in the first thirty seconds you meet someone. Not that all of us are equally skilled at picking up the cues. And people can be fooled.

I picked up my purse and moved to the next table. The organizers had been right about one thing — the dates happened too fast to allow my anxiety to really blossom. Harry was next — balding, plain, and short. But he wore a clean button-down shirt, and he'd bathed before he came. A prince compared to what was behind door number one.

"I don't think I've seen you before — this your first time?"

"Yes." I nodded. *Last time too,* I added silently.

"Let me give you the smart girl's guide to the action." He winked. "I try to get to these once a week or so. I figure I'll never meet the right woman if I'm not out here plugging."

Once a week? He had to be kidding. This guy had a serious masochistic streak.

"It's a little awkward if you meet someone a second time who you've already turned down the week before," he continued with a shrug. "Oh, and you can tell who's hit it off by who's having drinks together at the break and after the formal dates are finished."

"Were you by any chance at the session two weeks ago?" I asked.

"Yup."

"This is going to seem a little strange, but I'm doing some research and hope you can help." I showed him the photograph of Madeline with her mother and asked if he remembered seeing her.

"What kind of research are you doing? Is she a friend of yours?"

"Neighbor. She's in a little bit of a jam and I'm doing her a favor." I offered up my warmest smile, hoping friendliness would overcome the weak explanation.

"I met her. In fact, I marked her online as a match." He frowned and clucked his tongue. "I guess her heart didn't flutter for me. But she seemed to like one of the other guys who was here that night."

"Dark hair and a dimple in his chin?" I asked.

He patted a few strands of thin blond hair into place over a bald spot. "Sounds like him. Like I was saying, you can tell if there's chemistry by checking out the bar. They pounded down the drinks and got into some heavy conversation by the time the joint closed."

"Is he here tonight?" I smiled brightly.

Harry looked around the room. "I don't see him." He squinted his eyes and then smiled back. "He had a preppy name. Derek, maybe? Anyway, enough about them. What do you do for a living?"

"I write an advice column."

"Cool."

Traci rang her bell and I shook hands with Harry, then checked the box to remind myself I'd be interested in seeing him again. I wasn't really, but maybe he'd remember something more about Madeline and her mysterious heartthrob, Derek. Besides, I was no Princess Diana. Who did I think I was to dismiss every guy in the room?

The rest of the night passed quickly. I declined to check the boxes of a handsome, well-dressed dandy with a high probability of narcissistic personality disorder, a man whose doctor had told him he couldn't hang out in bars anymore, and a fellow whose job — cemetery attendant — precluded much opportunity to socialize.

Traci flashed a toothy smile as I staggered to the door after the last round. "Did you have a good time?" she asked.

"Very interesting."

"Please do stick around and have a drink. You may meet one of the guys you didn't get matched up with and really hit it off."

"The babysitter's waiting up," I lied, and slunk from the back room into the outer bar. Then I spotted a dark-haired man with a sexy cleft chin at the far end of the counter, nursing a draft beer and watching the ballgame on a wide-screen TV. I started to push through the crowd, then felt a massive hand clamp onto my wrist.

"Dr. Butterman. I didn't know you were a sports fan." Detective Meigs raised his eyebrows, sipped his beer, and wiped his mouth on his sleeve. Then he dropped my hand.

"I'm not," I answered. Too quickly. Because if I didn't like sports, why the hell was I here? We both looked at the sign posted over the dining room: *Rudy V's Welcomes Fast Connections!*

"I wouldn't imagine that an attractive, intelligent lady like yourself would need a dating service," Meigs drawled.

I flushed. When he wasn't grumpy, he was kind of cute. Especially considering the "dates" I'd just run through. Then my gaze slid down to the ring on his left hand, a gold band worn smooth by some longish number of years of marital bliss.

"When you assume, you make an ass out of you and me," I said primly.

"Can I buy you a beer?" he asked. "Or a glass of white wine? I guess that's what you ladies like."

I looked down to the end of the bar. The dark-haired man was gone. But maybe Meigs had relaxed enough to talk to me about Madeline's case. And damn if I couldn't use a drink after those awkward conversations.

"A glass of wine would be fine," I said.

Meigs flagged the bartender, then turned back and glanced at my purse, which gaped open. Madeline's smiling face gazed up at him. Meigs glowered as I snapped it shut and tucked it under my thigh.

"I was really hoping you weren't going to mess around with this case. Wasn't I clear about staying out of police business?"

"I'm not in any way trying to contaminate your official investigation," I said stiffly. "From what I can see, there isn't much of one going on. For your information, I'm doing research."

"*Re*-search?" His bushy eyebrows peaked in disbelief, a rather startling contrast to the close-cropped ginger curls. He'd had a haircut since the first time we'd met. "On what subject?"

"The singles scene," I snapped, "obviously. I write an advice column. And they've asked me to do an article about speed dating. Why else would I be caught dead at Fast Connections?"

"Something to do with Madeline Stanton? Just a wild guess," he said, pointing to my handbag.

"Listen. This lady killed herself approximately twenty feet from me. It bothers me, okay?" I didn't want to show him just how near I was to tears — exhausted from two hours of smiling chitchat with strangers. "And I'm a psychologist, remember? We pledge to keep people alive, not let them die."

The bartender delivered my drink and

quickly backed away.

"You don't believe in suicide?" he asked.

"Not in my patients," I said.

"Was she one of your patients?" he asked.

"You know I couldn't tell you even if she had been. But I don't like letting friends and neighbors down either."

"You didn't really answer my question," said Meigs. "Do you believe people have the right to kill themselves?"

Why was he asking me this? It felt like a trap — how often does the right to die come up in casual bar conversation? Not that there was anything casual about the way he was questioning me. More like a grilling.

"I see people all the time who are desperate for a little hope — and who might just find it with some therapy or even medication. If you spent most of your waking hours with people like that, you wouldn't be so damn flip about it."

"I'm not being flip," he said, pulling a basket of popcorn across the bar and tossing several kernels into his mouth. "In my opinion — and I understand you don't think much of that — if someone's ready to end her life, who are we to force her to carry on? Who's to say when she's had enough?"

"When a person has a major depression, the pointlessness of life may feel entirely convincing," I said, "but it's crucial not to take that at face value."

Meigs pointed one beefy finger at my chest. "Who are you to say those feelings aren't real?"

"What about the people they leave behind?" I asked, my voice rising high and tight. "What about the children who spend the rest of their lives thinking their parents didn't care enough about them to stay alive? What about the parent who spends the rest of his life carrying the weight of his dead kid's misery? It's not nearly as simple as you make it sound." I slid off the barstool, pushed the wine away, and slapped a ten-dollar bill on the counter. "That should cover mine."

I stalked out of the bar, sucking in the fresh air once I got past the smokers lounging outside the front door. Not until I'd left the parking lot and started home did it occur to me to wonder why we'd gotten into such an intense argument. And why Meigs was hanging out at Rudy V's at all. Years in my business have taught me that very little happens by coincidence.

CHAPTER 11

It made no sense for a grown woman to dread a five-year-old girl's birthday party. But I found myself taking traffic-clogged Route 1 to my sister's fancy Madison neighborhood rather than a reliably trouble-free hop on the highway. All the while rehearsing what I'd told Janice several times earlier in the week: This was a drive-by appearance.

Why the sinking feeling? My niece is a lovely girl — marginally spoiled, but nothing unexpected given the attention Janice lavishes on her only child. For this occasion, my sister had hired two beauticians to provide manicures and hairstyling for Brittany and her five dearest friends. Over the top, but my niece was delirious with excitement. And who could argue with that? My mother died a couple months before I turned five. I didn't have a party that year. *Which explains a lot,* I sighed. At least I had a good excuse for leaving early — attending Madeline's funeral. Funerals trump birthday parties, even with close relations involved.

I coasted to a stop by the curb on Randy Drive and walked up the brick path to Janice's three-story, five-bedroom, four-bath, three-car-garage home. The heavy brass pineapple-shaped doorknocker echoed back from the foyer. My brother-in-law, Jim, opened the door, wearing pressed jeans and a white Oxford shirt that looked to be fresh out of the package. And a desperate expression.

"Janice tells me you're escaping this bedlam," he said. "Can I go with you?"

I mussed his perfect hair and stepped inside. "Sorry, Jimmy, it's a funeral." He faded back toward the den. Brittany burst into the hallway holding out her hands — ten stubby blue nails painted with perfect little silver stars and moons.

"Aunt Rebecca, look!"

"You look gorgeous, honey. Happy birthday!" I kissed her glittering cornrows and followed her to the family room, adding my present to the stack on the coffee table. I'd finally decided on classic books — not the kind of gift that would send a kid into cartwheels on first opening, but she might appreciate first editions of *The Wind in the Willows* and the original *Winnie-the-Pooh* — no Disney illustrations, *please* — in the years to come.

Pink streamers and a large foil Barbie balloon hung from the ceiling. The table near the kitchen was laden with food. An enormous cake rippling with chocolate icing held the place of honor, with *Happy Birthday Dear Brittany!* written in pink.

My sister worked her way across the room, dressed to kill suburbia in a twin cashmere sweater set, pearls, and a polka-dotted bow clasping her chestnut hair. I tested one of Janice's finger sandwiches — three layers, two kinds of filling, and two colors of bread.

"Didn't you get my messages?" Janice hissed, grabbing my arm as I swiped a finger full of chocolate icing from the back of the cake plate.

I had skipped over her three voicemails, assuming they were party-related rants. "I'm sorry. Life's been insane and I knew I'd see you today."

"Two cops came by late yesterday afternoon asking about your relationship with your neighbor," Janice said in a whisper. "What could I possibly tell them? You never even told me she died!"

My stomach tightened. I took a deep

breath, not wanting to scare Janice. Not wanting to scare me. "What did they want?"

Janet's eyes widened. "They wanted to know if you were over here Wednesday night. The detective said they had to check up on all the neighbors. He said it was strictly routine." Her voice crept up toward shrill. "Is something wrong? Are you in trouble?" Two of Brittany's friends' mothers stopped talking to watch.

I gave her a quick hug. "They have to cover all their bases. Was the detective a big guy with messy hair?"

She nodded, her chin still quivering. "Reddish, but not like Bozo. Detective Meigs."

I produced a reassuring tongue cluck. "He's a control freak, that guy. He warned me he'd have to speak with you — they're obligated to cover their butts in case of a lawsuit later." Her worry lines started to let go. "I'll call you tomorrow and fill you in on everything, okay? You need to get back to the party. And I promised my neighbor's mother I'd come to the memorial service."

"Why should you go?" Janice asked, frowning. "You hardly knew the girl. Brittany will be disappointed." She touched her cheek. "You have glitter on your face."

My niece twirled past, trailed by a conga line of little girls flinging handfuls of confetti at the dog. "Brittany won't even know I'm missing," I said firmly. "I'll spend some one-on-one time with her soon. Madeline was my next-door neighbor."

No point in describing the real story — as much as I understood of it: the guilt, the fear, the identification, the missing father, the possibly phony note. And the sense of yearning and pain that Isabel radiated. When you added all that up, I couldn't *not* go.

"By the way, the sandwiches are fabulous." I dabbed my lips with a California Barbie napkin. "I am sorry to miss that cake."

"Yellow sponge with chocolate frosting — your favorite." Janice smiled fondly. "Brittany wouldn't hear of anything else. Speaking of mystery men, what happened with the fast dates? Did you really go?"

I wrinkled my nose but she just laughed. "Angie told me. I saw her at the Stop and Shop."

I'd have to kill Angie later. Janice worries too much, so I tend to keep dicey developments to myself until they're history. "No princes, no kings, no dukes. Not even any earls," I said. "But plenty of frogs. Enjoy the party and give me a buzz tomorrow." I blew her a kiss and fled out the door.

■ ■ ■ ■

As I drove to the memorial service, I wondered why the hell Meigs was checking me out. Didn't he believe Madeline killed herself? Quite possibly he was doing just what I'd explained to Janice — crossing his t's, dotting his i's, and the hell with who he scared to death in the process.

I pulled into the parking lot of Evergreen Woods, a high-end, expansive assisted-living facility set back in the woods off Route 1, about ten miles from Madison. The buildings were sided with pale yellow and green aluminum slats — an attempt to remind residents of home? Madeline's service was scheduled for one of the common rooms. High ceilings tapered up to a skylight, with pickled wainscoting, a brick fireplace, and pink walls warming the space. Isabel's haggard face lit up as I crossed the room to greet her.

"Thank you for coming. It means so much to have you here. I don't think you've met my sons." She grasped the elbow of the man standing beside her. "This is Steven, my oldest —"

"And her favorite, of course," said the handsome bald man in a navy striped suit and a pale blue tie identical to the one the president always wore to televised press conferences. "We're very grateful for your kindness to my mother in this difficult time."

Isabel smiled tenderly. "And this is Tom," she finished, pulling another middle-aged man toward me. "Rebecca was Madeline's next-door neighbor. She's keeping Spencer." Her eyes filled with tears.

"Good to meet you," said Tom, squeezing my hand briefly. "Thank you for coming."

He had dark, bushy hair and more sculpted features than his older brother. Maybe Peter Morgan had been right — the man Babette Finster had seen outside Madeline's apartment could very well have been Tom Stanton. Not that Madeline seemed especially close to her brothers. Hadn't she pretty much come out and said the whole family drove her nuts? Not that I'd bothered to get to know her well enough to learn the truth.

Isabel turned me over to Steven, who introduced me to several older women and then his and his brother's wives. They weren't quite Stepford wives, but close: limp handshakes, expensive-looking jewelry, carefully coiffed hair, and flashy dresses that showed a little too much skin for a funeral, in my humble opinion. They wouldn't be an easy match for Isabel, with her unassuming but strong persona and classic clothes. It looked like someone in the family must have money. From what? I wondered.

A black-robed man escorted Isabel to a chair in the first row and then stepped up to the podium. I recognized the Reverend Wesley Sandifer, the minister from my church. I gave him a small wave. What was he doing here? He widened his eyes in acknowledgment and waited for the rustling to die down.

"Good afternoon and thank you all for coming. Our hearts are heavy today as we congregate to celebrate the life of Madeline Stanton." His lashes fluttered closed, and then open. "Our temptation at a time like this is to focus on the why? Why have we lost a lovely and bright woman in the prime of her life? But Jesus would say to us, 'Come to me, all you who labor and are heavy laden and I will give you rest. Take my yoke upon you and learn from me, for I am gentle and lowly in heart, and you will find rest for your souls. For my yoke is easy and my burden is light.' "

Reverend Wesley took off his glasses and rubbed the tiny indentations on his patrician nose. "With our burdens lifted up to

God, we free ourselves to focus on celebrating the joy Madeline gave us during her short life."

Did he really believe it was all that easy?

He went on to deliver a homily to the effect that Madeline was creative and smart. And a gentle spirit had shone through her brothers' rambunctious presence. Pretty much what Isabel had told me several nights earlier. But Reverend Wesley's rendition somehow felt distant and stiff. Maybe it was the "I didn't have the pleasure of knowing her well but her family told me . . ." that he inserted before every other sentence. At last he wound down and invited Madeline's older brother, Steven, to come forward.

Steven straightened the knot on his tie. "I never realized we were that loud," he said, drawing a polite laugh from the mourners. He arranged several note cards on the podium. "Madeline should have been born into a royal family. She adored Princess Diana. Remember, Mother" — he smiled at Isabel — "when she made the entire family get up to watch that blasted wedding?"

Isabel nodded, her cheeks shiny with tears.

"Five in the morning, and she had us all lined up in front of the television to see Lady Diana and Prince Charles get hitched. For weeks after, she insisted we play wedding. Tom was usually the usher and I, of course, was the prince."

The crowd laughed softly. I glanced quickly at Madeline's second brother. He nodded with a pained smile as Steven continued.

"Our mother cut up a bedsheet and sewed it onto a nightgown so Madeline could have a wedding dress with a train. And didn't you let her borrow your veil?"

Isabel bobbed her head again and blotted her nose with a hankie.

"Even without the royal blood she admired, our sister *was* a princess, beautiful inside and out. And a whiz at math besides. She outscored both of her knuckleheaded brothers on the SAT test — always showing us up was our Madeline." He flashed a crooked grin. "I'm sad I won't have the opportunity to be at her wedding, to walk her down the aisle to present her to her prince, so she could live happily ever after."

His voice was trembling now, and the two older women nearest to me had begun to cry. He looked up at the vaulted ceiling.

"Bless you, Madeline, and forgive us for a lifetime of teasing. Thank you all for being with us today." He tucked the cards into the inside pocket of his suit coat and walked away from the podium.

"Thank you, Steven," said the minister. "I'd like to invite Madeline's brother Tom to come forward."

"As usual, Steve stole my thunder," Tom said, pulling a crumpled paper from his shirt pocket. "The common lot of the second child. I will be brief. Madeline had a soft spot for animals. She kept after Mother until we had them all — dogs, cats, guinea pigs, birds — practically Noah's Ark at our house." His chuckle died away. "She had a kind spirit evident in her love for all the creatures."

He opened his mouth, closed it, and then, working his jaw furiously, strode off the platform and sat down.

Reverend Wesley hustled forward to retake the podium. "Please join me in reading the prayer of the patron saint of the animals, St. Francis of Assisi, which you will find printed in your bulletin."

I glanced down and began to read: "Lord, make me an instrument of Your peace . . ."

It wasn't really fair to make assessments about which brother had been closer to Madeline, based on these brief remembrances. On the surface, Steven would be the obvious choice. But some people have an easier time expressing their grief in public than others. Some people's pain feels so powerful they're afraid they'll never be able to stop it once it begins to trickle out. Hard to guess what else Tom might have said about his sister if he'd been able to finish.

While we waited for a teenage girl in a long black skirt to saw through "You'll Never Walk Alone" on her violin, I flipped over the program. A photograph of Madeline had been printed on the back. It was definitely not recent; her hair was almost waist-length and her eyes unworried. But still brimming with secrets. Or was that my imagination? Even considering the comments made by the minister and Madeline's brothers, I'd learned very little more about her recent life than I'd known before the service started.

With a wave of subdued rustling and murmuring, the small audience got to its feet. It struck me that Madeline's father had not been mentioned. Why wouldn't he have been the one to walk her down the aisle at her hypothetical wedding? I made my way over to a table covered with plates of presliced cheese, crackers, and grapes, as well as a tray of homemade cookies and a cut-glass bowl filled with pink liquid. A small woman in a flowered dress with a prominent dowager's hump served me a drink and introduced herself as Isabel's neighbor.

"We were neighbors for years in downtown Guilford. When Isabel's sons heard I was moving out here to Evergreen Woods, they convinced Isabel she should come too. Why should you lose your closest and oldest neighbor just because you're getting older? Life is hard enough, don't you think?" Her eyes searched for Isabel in the crowd.

"Losing a daughter so young must be terribly painful," I agreed. "The service was a lovely tribute to Madeline — her brothers did such a nice job describing her. The wedding story was so sweet. I haven't had the chance to meet Madeline's dad yet — can you point him out to me?"

"Oh, Isabel divorced him years ago," she said, patting the sweating punch bowl with a napkin. "May I offer you a glass of punch?" she asked the next person in line. It was one of the Stepford wives — Steven's wife, if I had them straight.

I thrust my hand out. "Rebecca Butterman," I said. "We met briefly just before the service."

She shook her head — I guess I hadn't made much of an impression. "I'm Pammy, Steven's wife. Is there alcohol in here?" she asked the punch bowl lady.

"Oh no, dear. It's ginger ale, fruit juice, and lime sherbet."

Pammy scowled and teetered off. "How else are you supposed to get through these things?"

"She was devastated," the punch bowl lady whispered.

I smiled and glanced around the room, hoping to talk with a girlfriend or other nonrelative. A young man in khaki pants, blue blazer, and a thin tie was edging toward the door. I charged over, my hand extended.

"I'm Rebecca Butterman. Let me guess, you knew Madeline from school."

"Work," said the man, straightening his wire-rimmed glasses. "I have a start-up web-design company." He pulled a card from his wallet and passed it over: *Webflight Enterprises*. "We hired Madeline last year."

"Was work going well for her?" I asked.

"She was very creative," said the fellow. "We're going to miss her a lot. Hope you'll excuse me — I have an appointment." He backed out the door and bolted down the hall.

Not much new there. By now, the crowd was thinning, leaving mostly blue-hairs from the assisted-living facility to enjoy the snacks. Sadly enough, this kind of event was probably not unusual in this place, except for the age of the deceased.

I spotted Tom, the less intimidating brother, and decided to try the dumb brunette approach. "Lovely service. I wish I'd had the opportunity to get to know her better."

"She was a private person," he said. "Don't feel bad that you weren't close to her. Not many people made the inner circle."

"I haven't had the chance to express my condolences to your father," I tried, looking around the room hopefully.

"He's not here," Tom said, a pained look on his face. "He and mother are not friendly. It's always awkward with both of them in the same room. Will you excuse me?" He walked away before I could respond.

Had Isabel asked him not to come or did he choose to pass on the occasion? What kind of man skipped his daughter's funeral because his relationship with his ex was tense? Suddenly hit by a wave of fatigue, I wandered the room until I found Isabel surrounded by a cluster of elderly women.

"I'm on my way. Let me know if you need something," I said, squeezing her hand.

She squeezed back. "Thank you."

I walked briskly to the parking lot and collapsed in the Honda, leaning my throbbing head sideways against the window's cool glass. It's important to mark a person's death, but funerals still feel like the devil's own. I started up the car and headed home.

As I turned into my driveway, a small gray shape darted across the lawn. I pulled into the garage and hurried out of the car, pausing at the kitchen entrance: I had not remembered to set my alarm.

I went through the apartment calling for the cat. "Kitty, kitty, kitty? Spencer? Are you hungry?"

Nothing.

I flung open the front door. Spencer waited on the steps, meowing forcefully. What was he doing here? I definitely hadn't let him out. Last weekend I'd decided to keep him in the house until he seemed settled. It would be too damn sad to watch him mooning on Madeline's front porch. And if something happened to him — I could just imagine explaining that to Isabel.

I felt a cold chill. Someone had been in my condo. Should I call the cops? I pictured describing the problem to Detective Meigs.

"So let me get this straight, Doctor, you called to report a cat outdoors?"

Although, honestly, would that be any different from the usual fare in the police blotter?

I stalked through the apartment, feeling crazy and weak, switching all the lights on and talking out loud, pretending someone large, strong, and mean had accompanied me home.

There were no signs of an intruder.

After throwing the deadbolt, I started to drag one of Mark's recliners across the room and wedge it under the doorknob. Then I chuckled. The wiring. Peter said that he and Bernd needed to check the wiring. They must have let the cat escape on their way in or out of the condo. I abandoned the Barcalounger in the hall and crawled in bed with the truant kitty.

CHAPTER 12

One shaft of watery sunlight angled through the Revolutionary-era glass and glinted directly into my eyes. I tore a check out of my checkbook and shifted slightly in the pew, brushing away shreds of foam that had burst through the pale red velvet covering the cushion. During the period earmarked for announcements from the congregation, a constituent from the Women's League had strong-armed us for new pew cushion donations by drawing our attention to their faded and tattered condition. A no-brainer, but then so were the leaks in the Meetinghouse ceiling, the rotted window in the parsonage, and the dangerously low stockpile of canned goods at the soup kitchen. Sometimes the sheer weight of needs provokes an urge to convert to atheism. Or morph into the kind of member who shows up on intermittent Sunday mornings, drops a couple of bucks in the offering plate, and leaves feeling smug: God is on my side.

Two homilies in two days from Reverend Wesley felt a little punitive. He was holding forth on one of his favorite topics — he called it PEWSAGL: pride, envy, wrath, sloth, avarice, gluttony, and lust. Today the focus was lust. The message sounded very similar to a sermon he'd delivered last spring. He was just back from a month's vacation and apparently the Lord hadn't moved him to write new material while he was away.

Besides low-level boredom, the prospect of seeing Mark later this afternoon had completely ruined my concentration. I'd thought I was acting mature two days ago, suggesting he swing by and pick up those ugly chairs. This morning it just seemed like a bad idea.

I found myself thinking more about Madeline's funeral. There had been no mention of how she died: murder, suicide, or even natural causes. If there was gossip about the real story, I'd missed it. Then I remembered the condo meeting Thursday night and Mrs. Dunbarton's bulldog belief that Madeline Stanton had been murdered. Why was it so clear in her mind that a crime, rather than suicide, had occurred? I wished I'd tried harder with Madeline's coworker yesterday.

"Please join us for lemonade on the lawn after the service," said Reverend Wesley. "Now receive the benediction. May the Lord . . ."

I hung back at the tail end of the line of parishioners waiting to shake the minister's hand. He might have information about the Stanton family and their missing father. The trick was how to wrangle possibly confidential data out of him.

"Good morning," I said when my turn came. "Nice service yesterday for Madeline Stanton. That was so sad."

He adjusted his stole over the black robe, smoothed his gray-flecked dark hair, and clucked his tongue. "One of the hardest jobs in the ministry is saying good-bye to someone so young."

"Do you happen to have a record of Mr. Stanton's address? I want to send him a condolence note." I might go to Hell for bald-faced lying to the minister, but I didn't know how else to track Madeline's father down.

"I believe he lives somewhere in the Rockies — Colorado or Wyoming? Or was it New York? Call the church office in the morning and the secretary will pull it up on the computer."

"Thank you. I enjoyed your sermon by

the way. Lots to think about there," I said, smiling through my second lie in as many minutes.

At three-thirty p.m., Mark's blue Toyota truck pulled up along the curb outside my condo. He waited in the cab for five minutes, then walked slowly up the path to ring the front bell. I opened the door.

"You look terrific," he said, bending forward to peck my cheek.

I sidestepped, leaving him kissing air. "The chairs are in the living room. Did you bring someone to help carry them out?"

He stared. "Sure. Al's out in the car." He beckoned to the man in the truck.

"Don't let the cat out," I said, retreating to the kitchen.

"Since when do you have a cat? I thought you didn't like animals."

"Just men who act like animals. Al, for example," I added quickly after seeing the expression on Mark's face.

Al has been Mark's best friend since grade school. We never exactly hit it off — although I briefly entertained the fantasy of setting him up with Angie. Mark's best friend married to my best friend — vacations together, holidays, exchange of godparent duties — but the fantasy worked much better than reality. In real life, Al still hasn't matured past high school or, giving him the benefit of the doubt, fraternity days. And according to Al (as disclosed by Mark during a shouting match just before I moved out), I'm a tight-lipped, humorless bitch with no sense of adventure and probably lousy in the sack to boot. Later Mark apologized profusely for letting that nastiness slip, but the damage was done between me and Al.

I yanked a free-range chicken and four sweet potatoes out of the fridge and banged them onto the counter. Angie was coming over for an early supper — what we didn't finish, I would enjoy tomorrow night when I was too tired to bother cooking. I washed the chicken, patted it dry, and stuffed the interior with a quartered onion and sprigs of rosemary clipped from the pot on my back porch. Mark likes his chicken plain — no flavoring, no vegetables. I added garlic and celery to the cavity, dotted the skin with small chunks of butter, sprinkled herb salt, a grind of pepper, and more rosemary over the top, and slid it into the oven. Dumping the giblets and another onion into a small pan of chicken broth, I turned the heat on low. With any luck, the smells would waft out to the living room to tantalize the men before they were finished.

"We're all set here, Bec," Mark hollered fifteen minutes later. No one else has ever called me Bec, either before Mark or after.

From my post at the kitchen window, I watched Al climb back into the passenger seat of the pickup and pop the top on a Budweiser tall boy. Wiping my hands on a dishtowel, I returned to the living room, working to smooth any traces of tight-lipped, humorless bitch from my face.

"Well, thanks," he said. "I appreciate the offer. I missed those chairs."

"You're welcome."

"It smells good in here. I sure do miss your cooking."

I attempted a real smile, not the pinched spinster look, then started for the door. But when I glanced back, he was just standing there.

"Rebecca, I'm really sorry I hurt you. Sometimes I can't believe things turned out the way they did between us."

"Water over the dam, Mark."

He sighed. "You seemed so closed off. I didn't know how to reach you."

"The naked girl in our bedroom certainly got my attention."

He hung his head. "I said I'm sorry. And I was going to say I miss you."

"Not just the meals and the Bar-caloungers, then?" I didn't like sounding sour, but he'd winged me with the "closed-off" comment. And I was still steaming over the memory of Al's cruel remarks. If in fact they'd come from Al.

"Good luck with what's-her-name." Another pained smile.

"She's out of the picture." His face flooded pink.

I held the door open. "Sorry to hear it. Take care." He strode past without looking at me. I snapped the door closed behind him and went to collapse on the couch. Spencer hopped up and butted me with his head until I rubbed his jowls. Living with an animal seems so easy compared with a man — the connection between us uncluttered and clear. Fill my bowl and rub my head and I'll love you faithfully.

I'd spent more time than I wanted over the past year wondering how I'd contributed to our failed marriage. Starting in my early twenties, I'd been a devotee of the column "Can this marriage be saved?" in the *Ladies' Home Journal.* Well before my formal psychology training began, I understood that the idea of stepping out on your mate was supposed to be related to the quality of the communication between the two spouses.

In each month's *LHJ* column, a featured therapist heard out both sides of the story of another troubled marriage. Then he, or more often she, informed the couple that because they hadn't learned to talk about their innermost feelings with each other, one or both had looked outside the twosome to fill the void.

Not that I'd ever cheated on Mark. The closest I'd come was when Ethan, our next-door neighbor in New Haven, drank too much bourbon at the neighborhood Christmas cocktail party and groped me in the pantry. Full of Yuletide cheer myself, I had felt a small buzz of excitement, even though in the light of day Ethan had all the sex appeal of a graham cracker.

I deposited Spencer on the floor and hauled myself off the couch. Back in the kitchen, I chopped two zucchinis into rounds and then crushed a clove of garlic, scrubbed the sweet potatoes, and popped them in the microwave. The giblets simmered in their broth. Spencer would enjoy part of that treat and the rest I'd make into gravy. Angie was always amazed at the trouble I took cooking for myself.

"At the risk of sounding like the know-it-all Dr. Aster, if you can't bother cooking for yourself, what's the message you're sending?" I answered.

Which reminded me that a "Late Bloomer" column was due tomorrow — not to mention the Fast Connections article. I basted the chicken and moved the sweet potatoes into the oven, and then powered up my laptop and began to type, remembering those wise words from "Can this marriage be saved?"

Dear Dr. Aster:
I work with a wonderful man who has all the qualities I've been searching for in a life partner. The good news? I've found my soul mate and we've fallen in love. The bad? I'm already married. I'm seriously considering having an affair. Before you scold me, please understand that I've never been tempted before! Is there something so wrong with wanting to be with the man I love?

Cheating Heart in Hyannis

Dear Cheating Heart:
It's possible that you truly may have found your soul mate. It's also possible that your feelings for your coworker are more closely connected to your marriage than you might guess. Review your interactions with your husband over the

past year: Can you trace a subtle sea change in your relationship — even before things heated up with the new man? So often couples have never learned to talk about their innermost feelings with each other, and when the going gets rough, they look outside to fill the void. Think carefully before you make a move that could seriously damage your relationship with your husband. At the least, take time to sort out your marital issues thoroughly before embarking on a new relationship. Otherwise, the old baggage travels with you! Bon Voyage!

Next up, part two of the Fast Connections piece. Concentrating on the positive, I described the buzz generated by rapid-fire conversations with five men I'd never met. There was no time to get nervous, I told my readers, and the night had the feel of a challenging crossword puzzle or maybe a mystery. Who knew if it would lead to something more, but the experience definitely took the edge off any worries about meeting someone new. Behavioral psychologists call this flooding, I didn't tell them, and if it works for laboratory rats, why not for you? I ended with a quote from Fast Connections hostess

Traci Smith: "It's so rewarding to see people come out of their shells. Two of my couples from the past year are now engaged. How cool is that?"

I certainly hadn't seen marriage material during my session, but as they say, you can't win if you don't play.

Angie rapped on the front door just as I finished straining the broth for gravy.

"God, it smells good in here," she said as she stepped inside. She drew her eyebrows together and looked around the room. "Something's . . . different."

"Mark stopped by to get the recliners. Your boyfriend came with him."

"Creepy Al?" she said. "I can't believe you ever thought I'd go for that lump. Which reminds me, how did your speed dates go? You never called me Friday."

"No, but you talked to Janice," I said accusingly.

"Sorry, sorry," said Angie, raising her hands like a captured prisoner. "I assumed she already knew. I was dying to hear how it went."

"I didn't get home until late and I was bushed, and then busy all day yesterday. I'm just writing the notes up for the magazine — in fact, I'm about to check for love matches." I laughed sheepishly. "Want to watch?"

"I can't believe you waited this long!"

My heart raced waiting for the Fast Connections page to load — ridiculous. I had no desire for a repeat session with any of the guys I'd met Friday night. Still, one always prefers to be the rejecter than the rejectee. Especially with Angie looking over my shoulder. She watched me type in my e-mail address and then password: *DrAster.*

The first names and identification numbers of my "dates" came up on the screen: The heavy-set, non–Red Sox fan; the cemetery worker; the sociopath; the banned drinker; and Harry the short, balding Fast Connections veteran.

"What now?" Angie asked.

"I click on any guys I'd be willing to see again and if they also chose me, it's a match." I moved the cursor to Harry's box, checked his name, and hit *return.* His Fast Connections e-mail address came up — he liked me too.

"Prince Charming?" Angie asked, rubbing her palms together.

"He was nice enough." I cleared my throat. "The truth? He met Madeline Stanton a couple of weeks ago at one of these sessions. And saw her having a drink with the guy she mentioned in her blog. That guy was at the bar Friday night too, but Detective Meigs distracted me and he left before I got the chance to talk with him."

"Wait a minute," said Angie. "Meigs was speed-dating?"

"Actually, I have the feeling he was following me. Or at least following the same trail I am. He showed up at Janice's Friday night too."

"What the hell did he want from Janice? Didn't he say it was suicide, case closed?"

"I don't know what he really thinks. But he was bugging Janice about whether I'd really been at her house last Wednesday." Angie looked worried so I shrugged and waved my hands. "He can't think I'm involved."

"This doesn't sound like dating," she said. "It sounds like private investigation."

The oven timer began to chime. "Dinner's ready," I said.

Angie followed me to the kitchen where I settled the chicken and yams onto a platter. I coached her on sautéing the zucchini while I whisked a tablespoon of flour and some broth into the chicken drippings.

As we ate, Angie described the results of the syntactical analysis. "You were right about this — whoever wrote the suicide note is not writing in the same style as the blog. It's always possible that a suicidal frame of mind affected her output, but my hunch is Madeline didn't write the note."

We stared at each other.

"I'm thinking," Angie said. She scraped the remaining zucchini slices onto her plate and doused them in a pool of gravy. "No calories in gravy if green vegetables are involved, right?"

She finished eating and angled her fork and knife across the dish. "If she didn't kill herself, who did it?"

"Exactly what I've been wondering." I told her how Babette Finster thought she might have seen two different men visiting Madeline over the last few weeks. "I'm not sure she's a credible witness, but Mrs. Dunbarton said pretty much the same thing. And I did see those cars. And hear the voices through the wall."

"What else?"

"At Madeline's memorial service yesterday, I got the chance to meet her older brothers and their wives. Ugh. Not the kind of women you'd be thrilled to see your sons bring home."

"Vipers in the bosom?" Angie asked.

"Maybe not poisonous, but not my cup of tea. And I don't know what's up with the father. Isabel won't say. But her son implied they're estranged — seriously enough that he didn't come to his own daughter's funeral."

"He's mentioned in the note. If Madeline didn't write it, whoever did had to know something about the guy, right?"

I nodded. "I'm going to get Mr. Stanton's new address from the church office tomorrow and try to reach him."

"Odd that Isabel pushed you into being the detective. Why give *you* the notes and the key to her place? I'm thinking, if it was my daughter, would I want to know all the dirt? Would I want a stranger involved?"

"She's heartbroken, Angie. She's trying to understand. And she knows I'm a shrink. Madeline knew it too. Remember, she wanted me — aka Dr. Aster — to give her 'pretend' answers to questions she made up."

"Remind me," said Angie. "What exactly did she ask?"

"How to tell her family to get off her back — which rings true to life. Madeline was the baby: Everyone in the family gave her advice."

"Families always give more tips than a person wants. We all may want to murder our relatives, but I don't imagine most people take it that far." Angie laughed. "Anything else?" she asked.

"She wanted to know what Dr. Aster would advise if a girl's boyfriend was into kinky sex — and said girl wasn't quite comfortable with it."

"And you replied —"

"It all depends: consenting adults, loving relationship, blah, blah, blah. But it felt more like she was goading me than really wanting answers. If that was a cry for help, I missed it."

"Let's not go there again," said Angie. "You're the most sensitive person I've ever met. But even you aren't perfect."

We stacked the dirty dishes in the sink and returned to the living room.

"I don't think this girl confided much to anyone," I said. "Or at least everyone in her life got a different angle."

"I don't like it," said Angie. "If we're right about this, you've gotten mixed up with a murder case. You need to go talk to Meigs again and give him what you've got."

"The guy's an ass."

"An ass like Al?"

"Hmm. Maybe not that bad." I laughed. "You have a knack for putting things in perspective. But he makes me feel like an idiot." I pushed my hands through my hair and pulled it back into a knot. "That's why I hesitated about calling him last night when I found the cat outside." I snickered. "Good thing I waited because I remembered the handyman was coming to look at my fuse box. Hysterical report in the police blotter averted!"

"Whoa, wait just a minute. Explain."

So I told her about finding Spencer on the front stoop and how I'd panicked, and then calmed myself down with the Bernd Becker wiring hypothesis.

"A repairman on a Saturday?"

"You don't know Bernd," I told her. "He works until the job is finished."

"But how can you be sure it was him? For God's sake, Rebecca, you live alone. You should have called the cops."

After Angie finished a round of horrified scolding, I promised to stop by the police station the next day to report both the unlikely (in my mind) break-in and the results of Angie's analysis.

At the door she turned and kissed me on the cheek.

"Hey," I said, "how did it go with the hot yoga dude?"

Her eyes twinkled. "Awesome. He was dead serious about giving personal atten-

tion. And his pretzel twist is not overrated."
She grinned and swished out to her car.

CHAPTER 13

Monday afternoon came and the bloom was already off Wendy the graduate student's rose. She was furious with the new boyfriend, but unwilling to describe exactly what transgression had occurred. He had tried to e-mail and call his way back into favor but she was freezing him out. I gave up attempting to squeeze out the details of the infraction, although the tease was annoying.

"Sounds like you might want to consider having a talk with him, lay it on the line," I said mildly.

I made a mental note to write another column on the subject. Keeping silent in a relationship — including therapy — only makes for emotional distance and an avalanche of misunderstandings. Hard to think of one example where hashing a problem out wouldn't help. Either you end up feeling closer to the person in question, or you find out maybe you're better off alone.

"Who are you, Ann Landers?" Wendy growled. "Since when do you dole out advice instead of listening?"

"Sorry," I said with a guilty start. "How did you feel when he called to apologize?"

Obviously, my mind had wandered. Some patients barely notice when my attention wavers, but Wendy isn't one of them. With her antennae sharpened by the fluctuating moods of an alcoholic mother, she tracks every slight breach in my focus. I hate to think the advice column has affected my therapy style, but it's certainly possible.

"Jesus, my mother used to do that to me," she said, beginning to cry.

"Do what?"

"Whenever anything went wrong, she got mad at me."

"It feels like I'm blaming you for something," I said, genuinely perplexed. "Can you tell me more about that?"

"You're sticking up for that jerk just like she did with Dad. It wasn't my fault, it wasn't." Now she was crying so hard that her shoulders shook.

And I was on high alert. Some kind of inappropriate sexual contact came first to mind. Had the boyfriend tried something that reminded her of her father? But Wendy had never mentioned incest, nor had I suspected it from her symptoms. And a patient's history often distorts the present — coloring the current-day facts in a way that doesn't match reality, for example, or grooving a pattern of bad choices and unhappiness that can be hard to snap. I had to proceed cautiously, treading the fine line between supporting her exploration of the past and recognizing when her feelings were too overwhelming to continue. With the spate of false memories in the news these days, a therapist has to be exquisitely careful not to plant suggestions in her patients' minds.

"Would you feel comfortable saying a little more? It might help us sort this out."

But Wendy wasn't going any further. She burst into more racking sobs — and was done for the day.

After ushering her through the waiting room and down the stairs, I checked my answering machine. My final Monday patient, Lorna, who had skipped last week's appointment, also called to cancel her session for today. She'd contact me later in the week to reschedule. Which most likely meant she didn't plan to call at all. I made a note in my Palm Pilot to phone her by Friday. Even if she declined to come in, by following up to suggest the option of talking difficult feelings over, I might set the stage for a better outcome next time she tried therapy. Hopefully with another shrink, I couldn't help thinking.

The next message was from Jillian: She'd received my article about Fast Connections. Her response was a little subdued.

"It's very well written, of course. Love the concept. For the follow-up, try to be a little more personal. Your readers want to hear details, darling, personal details. How about report on a date with one of the guys you met speed-dating? And if possible, could you get me your advice column by Friday? I'm going away for the weekend and I want to put this issue to bed before I head out to the Hamptons. Give me a buzz this afternoon and let's discuss."

That made three calls I didn't want to make: Lorna, Detective Meigs, and Jillian. I'd start with one less noxious: Nancy Griswold, church secretary. Saddled with the terrible conflict of overhearing too much insider information while being sworn to confidentiality, Nancy might be an easy nut. Spilling your guts to a psychologist might not count as gossip.

"Nancy, it's Rebecca Butterman." I pressed on, hoping to duck a detailed report on her teenage nephew. She'd asked me for a professional referral a couple of months ago when he'd been on the brink of sinking into the wrong crowd. Her gratitude propelled her to report every nuance of his progress each time our paths crossed. Sweet, but time-consuming.

"Look, someone's knocking on my door, but I have a quick question. Could you kindly find an address for Madeline Stanton's father? I want to drop him a note."

"Wasn't that the saddest thing?" she countered. "I'll pull his info up for you right now."

While on hold, I listened to a gospel rendition of "Amazing Grace" — much more aesthetically satisfying than the amateur violin at Madeline's memorial service.

"He lives in New York City." She read off the address and phone number. "It was such a tragedy, him leaving town and all. That was before your time, right?"

"Um-hmm." I wouldn't push her, but neither would I discourage her if she felt like spilling beans.

Nancy sighed. "Didn't Sigmund Freud say it all comes down to money and love?"

"Sex and work, I think was how he put it."

"That sounds better," she said, giggling.

"Uh-oh, the reverend's here. See you in church!"

Money and love: That could mean anything. My cell phone rang. I checked the incoming number — Jillian. Might as well get this over with.

"Rebecca, you got my message? The story was a good start. But think 'dishing the dirt,' darling. We're counting on you to boost our website hits and advertising with this series."

"Got it," I said glumly. "You're saying it's dull."

"Never dull, but I know you can make things sparkle."

"I really have no interest in dating any of the men I met," I said firmly.

"Then we can send you somewhere else for the next installment." She went on without drawing a breath. "I'm thinking the singles golf group might be a nice contrast to Fast Connections. There's even a website called Dateagolfer.com."

I felt a pit open in my stomach. During the brief time I'd dated the golf psychologist, we'd stopped into the driving range twice. He was polite and encouraging but neither of us could ignore the glaring truth: I had no aptitude for the game. Besides, I hadn't connected with his friends from the golf world at all — attend a social event with his crowd and they nattered about their latest round, newest equipment, or even more obscure topics like the covering on their golf balls. If I was painfully honest, I would also admit that having been dropped by this guy for a neurotic LPGA player had pretty much turned me off the sport for good.

"No golf," I said firmly.

"Fine," said Jillian. "How about an online dating service? Match.com, Yahoo! Personals, Great Expectations — you choose. Your sidebar could focus on how to construct a profile that attracts attention, and then follow up by describing a couple of the guys who are immediately panting on your doorstep. Sound good?"

"Let me think it over," I said, without enthusiasm. "Maybe I could e-mail one guy from Fast Connections and see where it goes." She was on the kind of brainstorming roll that didn't call for discussion or disagreement. At least with an e-mail correspondence, I could stay at home in my pajamas to do the research.

"Let me know what you decide. And don't forget I need Dr. Aster by Friday. Roger that?"

"Roger."

I hung up. Meigs had left a voicemail

while I was talking to Jillian. He'd meet me at the station after five. I glanced at the clock. No point in getting there ahead of time only to have to cool my jets in the waiting room with the suburban criminal element. Might as well start on the new column.

I opened the file of letters that Jillian had forwarded over the past month. Sometimes it's easy to choose the questions. Other times, the problems seem tedious, and my answers, even more tired. In the early days of this gig, I worried a lot about finding the right voice for Dr. Aster and poured over other advice columns in search of the right role model. I didn't want to be a drip or a scold — I wanted to give real advice for real problems, keep an ear out for deeper issues, and cover lots of topics, all while sounding clever and funny. In a gentle way. Piece of cake.

Dear Dr. Aster:
My daughter-in-law needs help. I'm worried about how tightly she controls my granddaughter. God forbid this child gets her outfit dirty or even drops Cheerios on the kitchen floor. When my son's family comes to visit, my granddaughter spends most of her time strapped in her high chair.

I love this child dearly and hate to see her spirit crushed by her mother's restrictions. What's the best way to talk with my daughter-in-law about this problem?

Sincerely,
Fretting in Frisco

Dear Fretting:
Remember the years when your son was a toddler and into absolutely everything? Isn't it oh-so-much easier to see the path someone else should be following than to be in the trenches yourself? Your job these days —

The loud rasp of my outside-door buzzer startled me. Had Lorna decided to catch a few minutes of her session after all? I saved the column I'd started, crossed the room to the intercom, and pressed *talk*.

"This is Dr. Butterman. Can I help you?"

"Dr. Butterman? Rebecca? Steven Stanton here. Madeline's brother? Could I come up for a minute?"

"Uh, sure." I hit the buzzer and stood in the waiting room while he climbed the three flights of stairs. Why hadn't he just called? Or at least called ahead? He finally materialized, striding toward me with his hand outstretched, a big smile on his face.

"Sorry for the inconvenience." He wrung my hand. "I'm assuming you remember me from my sister's funeral? Thanks for letting me have a moment of your time. I'm sure you're busy. May I?"

He gestured to the open double door of my office and started in before I could answer either question. I closed the doors behind us. He settled into my chair, closest to the desk and draped with a rose-colored afghan. Clearly my turf. A supervisor once reminded me never to put myself between a patient and the door and I've always kept to that. In the rare event of a paranoid episode, the patient needs an easy way out. So much for that.

Madeline's brother looked around my office, taking in the bookcase, my honeymoon photographs of Paris in the rain, and the row of African violets on the windowsill. Two needed serious pruning — the third I should probably toss. Healthy plants lend an air of confidence and optimism to the office. Sick ones, obviously not. Steven's eyes drifted to the draft of the new column on my laptop. He'd need X-ray vision to read it, but suddenly self-conscious and slightly claustrophobic, I marched across the room. The scent of a pleasant cologne wafted toward me as I leaned over to put the computer to sleep.

"So this is what it's like to see a shrink," Steven said.

He was wearing another expensive suit — light gray with darker pinstripes, and a gold-and-blue club tie this time. The crease in his slacks was still sharp — he had none of the wilted look I earned by the end of a long Monday.

"My only experience with you guys is watching Tony Soprano on HBO. At least now I know better than to try to kiss the psychiatrist and send her gifts. Tony's therapist wouldn't accept anything from him." He laughed.

"Of course she wouldn't," I said with a smile. What was this all about? "Even if he were Prince Charles — and still single — the idea is to create a safe space that falls outside the patient's life, not to become part of it. It's the only way you can really help your patient observe his issues clearly enough to lay a foundation for change."

"*Observe his issues.* I love the way you guys talk." He leaned back in my chair, resting his elbows on the arms of the chair and tenting his fingers. "Supposing I made an appointment because I had a problem with my wife. How would you handle that?"

I flashed on Madeline teasing me about

Dr. Aster during our first and only coffee date. What was with this family? I decided to play it straight.

"We shrinks always start by exploring the issues" — I made air quotes and grinned — "the patient brings in. So I'd ask you to define those issues in more detail. You say you have a problem with your wife — well, that could mean any number of things, right? Sex? Communication? Money? An affair? I wouldn't want to assume anything, you see." I gave a short laugh. "But you didn't come in for a lecture on my therapeutic technique. Or as a patient," I added quickly. "So what can I do for you today?"

He angled one leg across the other and tapped his expensive leather shoe. "It's my mother. May I be blunt?"

I nodded, quite certain he'd say whatever he wanted whether or not I gave permission.

"I'm aware that she's asked you to look into Madeline's suicide. I'm asking that you stop."

CHAPTER 14

"You don't want me to look into your sister's suicide," I repeated. "Why?"

He heaved a sigh through pursed lips. "My mother is not the most stable person in the world right now. She's in a lot of pain." Steven leaned forward, balancing his elbows on his knees, looking intently at me. "Not that I'm blaming her or anything. But she's suffered a lot of losses. I don't think she's able to face her current reality. She needs to process her feelings about her daughter's death, rather than deny them. You would agree with that, wouldn't you? Doctor?" He flashed another engaging smile.

"It is important to come to terms with a personal tragedy," I said slowly, "but it takes time. Especially with a suicide." I grimaced. Maybe he just didn't understand the possibilities here. "Honestly? There *are* some loose ends in your sister's case that make me wonder whether she killed herself."

He frowned. "Such as?"

"The cat. She made no arrangements for the cat. And the note. Your mother didn't feel it sounded like her." Something about this man made me uncomfortable. And unwilling to back down. "She doesn't believe that Madeline's death could reasonably be connected to grief over your father."

"Christ. Mother has no perspective when it comes to my father." Steven's cell phone rang and he pulled it out of his pocket, rolling his eyes. "Stanton."

I overheard the tinny yammering of a female voice.

"Goddammit, Pammy. Can't you handle this until I get back to the office?" He barked a few phrases about spreadsheets and monthly quotas, then snapped the cover of the phone closed. "Sorry. I hate when people do that. What were we saying?"

"Your father."

He smoothed the angry furrows from his forehead. "My mother can't see anything clearly about the subject of my father. I know she doesn't want to believe that Madeline still has — I mean, had — strong feelings for him. It was a messy divorce. Everyone suffered."

"What went wrong between them?"

He blinked and flicked his hand. "The

usual. Another woman." He stood up abruptly and started to the door. "I do hope you'll honor my wishes and not encourage my mother on another painful wild goose chase."

A tight smile and he was gone.

Behind the glass window inside the police department, the young cop with the rosebud lips told me to have a seat — the detective would be with me shortly. Instead I paced the small waiting area, studying posters that had been colored by grateful schoolchildren after September 11. Not that our Guilford PD had been intimately involved with handling that tragedy, but they were ready then and ready now. A teenager with a pierced lip and a bandanna holding back his straggly hair waited with me.

"Dr. Butterman, come this way." Meigs held the door open but didn't offer a handshake or a smile. And this time he led me to a bare interview room rather than his messy but more human office cubicle.

I lifted my chin in the direction of the one-way mirror. "Somebody think this could be important enough to listen in?" I smiled politely to let him know the comment was semi-friendly fire.

"Nope." He grinned. "Any action yet from

your Fast Connection?"

I flashed my best gimlet-eyed glare. "Really none of your damn business. I came to tell you that my friend, who's a forensic linguist, compared Madeline Stanton's blog entries to the alleged suicide note. She does not believe the two samples were written by the same person."

"And she's basing that on — ?"

"Syntactical analysis. It's a way of analyzing language using content, grammar, vocabulary —"

"I know the definition of syntactical analysis. I did manage to pass my GED exam. And the police department entrance exam too. But I fail to see how I got so lucky as to have two ladies *ass*-isting in my casework." He ran a hand over his hair and grinned again. "Was your friend with you at Rudy V's the other night?"

This guy was a jerk — the worst TV cop come to life — an insensitive, inappropriate bully with poor listening skills and a closed mind. I wished someone on the other side of the mirror would step in and tell him to knock it the hell off. I considered leaving without mentioning my hypothetical condo security problem.

Angie would kill me.

"I'd also like to report a possible break-in

at my condominium Saturday night. Not a break-in, really, more like an incident. Not even an incident really, but I promised my friend —"

"A break-in? Saturday night? And you're reporting it now?" The sleazy smile was gone.

"Nothing was missing or broken or anything. It's just that the cat was outside when I got home. I'm certain I left him indoors earlier in the day. On the other hand, I'm pretty sure the condo manager —"

"Forced entry?" asked Meigs, extracting a small notebook from his shirt pocket. "That means, were the locks on the doors or windows broken?"

"I know what it means." I stood up. "Everything seemed fine. I'm quite sure the handyman came in to do some repairs. The cat probably slipped out then."

Meigs waved me back to my chair. "Was anything missing? Jewelry? Money? Electronic equipment?"

"Nothing was taken, as far as I could tell."

I don't like getting too attached to *things* so I don't keep much valuable stuff around. I do own a few pieces of my mother's jewelry, probably worthless to anyone outside the family. Worst of all would have been losing my computer. Or my photographs.

And cookbooks. Funny how priorities come into focus with a gun to your head. Ouch. Bad metaphor.

"Who has a key to your place?"

"Nobody except the handyman would have gone in without talking to me first," I said. "Or telling me later."

Meigs leaned forward and tapped his fingers on the desk. "Who has a key?"

"My sister, Janice. My friend Angie. They water the plants if I go away. I don't travel that often. Bernd, the handyman at the condo, he has the master. And the neighbor who was our last condo president." I frowned, furious again at the idea of Mrs. Dunbarton with access to everything. I tightened the back on my pearl earring and thought of Mark. "My ex might have one."

"Your ex has a key? What's your relationship like now? Still having problems?"

"Not anymore. Not lately." I flushed. *So* not his business. "I'm planning to get the key back. He's not a bad guy really." I felt the hot blush seep down my neck. "He needed to go through some books and papers that I packed up by accident and I didn't want to see him." I was babbling. Why did I have to explain myself to this moron? Mark wouldn't break into my apartment. He wouldn't set one foot in without an engraved invitation.

"The cat slipped out when the handyman came," I repeated. "Or maybe I didn't notice when I left earlier in the day." I stood up again.

Meigs got up too, looking amused. "I can have an officer follow you home and check things over."

I pictured pulling up to the condo with a police escort. The worried spinsters would come out in full force and I'd be left to calm them down.

"You're right, it's too late now." I leaned slightly forward. "Is Madeline's case closed? My sister said you were at her house on Friday asking about my alibi."

He waved his hand. "Routine police procedure, checking out the neighbors."

He did think I was an idiot. "You might be interested to know that I had a visit from Madeline's brother this afternoon. He told me to knock off looking into the suicide." I raised my eyebrows meaningfully.

"And so?" Meigs asked. "It's good advice. And here's some more good advice, Nancy Drew." He'd been grinning like a monkey, but now his face grew serious. "Next time you suspect there's an intruder in your place, don't go in. Call the cops."

■ ■ ■ ■

Once home, I dumped the mail and my computer on the counter. I turned most of the lights on, toured all the rooms including closets, and checked the locks on doors and windows. Then I filled Spencer's dish with kibble and hit *play* on the answering machine.

The first call was from Mark, suggesting coffee. "Or something." I felt a jolt almost like the first time I spotted him at a psychiatry department brown-bag lunch. I hate to admit he still makes my stomach lurch — that tall, dark, Jewish, Ivy League look — and he's brilliant when he isn't being dense. But what would be the point? It's taken eight months to regain my sea legs after the marriage withered, and damned if I can explain exactly what went wrong. Angie theorizes that two mental health professionals — always analyzing, diagnosing, living in the past instead of the present — are doomed from the start.

On down days, I hash over the low points obsessively: the shock of finding Mark with that girl; the sinking sensation as I confronted the truth of his affair; the wash of guilt, sadness, anger, and terror that followed. Five years ago, we'd constructed a little circle of safety and intimacy with our marriage vows. Then Mark had breached that circle, inviting the enemy in the back way and blowing the hell out of our haven. That's my interpretation on bad days.

Days with more distance, I recognize that earlier losses make this one loom larger. And that if I'd looked hard enough, I would have seen this coming. And that Mark made a big mistake, but he isn't a mean person. He couldn't find a decent way of saying he was lonely and scared. And he couldn't rescue me from my own issues any more than Prince Charles had been able to save Diana. Assuming either one of them had even tried.

Face facts, Rebecca: The marriage hadn't worked the first time. Why go back now? I deleted the message. Next time he phoned, I'd tell him to return my key and not to call again.

Next, Peter Morgan's voice projected from the answering machine, filling the kitchen, reminding me about the all-condo, summer's-over cocktail party around the pool tomorrow night.

"And Mrs. Dunbarton wants you to bring an hors d'oeuvre. I'll just be happy to see another sane face," he finished with a laugh.

189

Hmm. Was this really just condo business? Truth is, until I wash Mark completely out of my system, no one else stands a chance. Though Peter strikes me as handsome and apparently successful. And a little full of himself. Anyway, I'd hate for something to go sour and end up having awkward encounters at the mailbox several times a week.

I pulled the telephone book from a cabinet under the counter, paged forward to attorneys, and found his listing: *Morgan, Schaefer, and Krickstein, Attorneys-at-Law, established in 1973, specializing in second opinions on criminal cases.* Not an ambulance chaser anyway. Enough. I flicked on the TV and started surfing through the channels. Sliding past the Golf channel, I caught the flash of a familiar face and quickly backed up.

An attractive female announcer stood next to a petite golfer in a blue cap. "The Solheim Cup, the semiannual competition between European and American golfers, returns to Sweden next week," she said. "Cassie Burdette was a surprise captain's pick on the American team. How do you feel about the upcoming tournament?" The announcer pushed the mike in front of the golfer's face.

This was the girl my golf psychologist friend had chosen over me while we were dating. It was all for the best really; we weren't a good match. But still: Who doesn't prefer the role of dumper rather than dumpee? Tonight Cassie was dressed stylishly in curve-hugging plaid knee-length shorts and a pink polo. And she didn't have the mousy, worried look I remembered — in fact she was beaming. Practically glowing.

"I'm thrilled to have been selected and look forward to representing our country in this prestigious competition," she said.

"We'll be rooting for you. And congratulations on your engagement," the announcer trilled.

I watched in amazement as Cassie blushed and stammered her thanks. Was she marrying *Joe?*

Life was barreling on around me. Unless I wanted to be left in the exhaust, it was time to start my own engine. I snapped off the TV and checked my Fast Connections e-mail address one last time. Harry, the friendly bald guy, invited me for a drink the next night at Su Casa in Branford. Serendipity.

"I thought you'd blown me off," his e-mail read, "but I guess you were just busy. Look forward to spending more time together!"

In the space of one margarita, I should be able decide whether I wanted to bother seeing him again. And glean enough juicy tidbits to satisfy Jillian's thirst for details. And maybe pump Harry about Madeline's friend Derek.

"See you at eight," I wrote and sent the message off. Then I redialed Angie. "What would you say about me dating Mark again? It would be so much simpler than all this."

"Certifiable," she said, and hung up the phone.

CHAPTER 15

The alarm clock shrilled at six a.m. I pushed Spencer off my legs and rolled out of bed. With a full schedule at the office and two social engagements on the docket for this evening, I had to whip up my contribution to the condo party's hors d'oeuvres before work. That would leave time for me to prepare mentally for the night by sandwiching in a yoga class on the way home. The teacher would hate that concept — squeezing yoga into a frenetic day — but it had to be better than nothing. I'd need all the help I could get to face the condo patrol followed by my Fast Connection. My ideas never sparkle quite so brightly in the morning light.

While coffee dripped through the filter, I pulled up my recipe for cheese puffs on the computer. I dropped a bar of frozen butter into the microwave and grated a mound of sharp cheddar. These rich and slightly greasy wafers, cut by the tang of globs of hot pepper jelly, are always popular. The only question is how many make it through my taste testing to the party. Before leaving the house, I stuck strips of Scotch tape across the front and back doors, set the alarm, and exited through the garage. Angie and Detective Meigs had made me nervous. If someone outsmarted the alarm and broke in, I'd clear out and call the police. I'd demand someone — anyone — other than Meigs.

The day passed quickly. I worked my way through five of my regular patients and then ushered in a psychology graduate student recently assigned to me for therapy supervision. Luke Sawyer was older and more confident than the average grad student, with ten years of experience as a rehabilitation counselor under his belt before he'd returned to school. Early impressions — not always reliable, I reminded myself — suggested that he lacked insight and empathy.

The clinical director had given him a new patient, an attractive woman with psychotic and suicidal tendencies. Luke spent the first fifteen minutes of our session pitching hypnosis as a way to break through his patient's defenses and reveal her extra personalities. Which definitely sounded more dramatic than the long slow route of talk therapy, but also dangerous and dumb.

"Most of your patients have probably never had the experience of having someone really listen to them for an hour a week," I said gently. "You can't imagine how valuable that feels. This lady is no exception."

"She thinks she experienced satanic rituals in her early childhood, but she doesn't remember the details," said Luke. "We've got a very good rapport already. I met with her for an extra hour when I conducted her intake interview."

I groaned inside. A firm time limit allows patients to feel emotionally safe, to believe the therapist understands how to set and keep boundaries. Luke had already breached that fragile levee — which this lady desperately needed if her background was really what he'd described.

"The two of you must work together to sort this out — imagine she's brought you a very complicated jigsaw puzzle. It's slow going for a while, but then the themes in her history will start to emerge. There's no magic. Not that I know of."

"But —" he began.

I held my hand up. "You don't have the experience to do what you're proposing. With the threat of suicide already on the table, you have to tread carefully."

His face reddened. "The literature suggests that multiple personalities respond very well to hypnosis."

"First of all, you haven't told me enough to confirm that diagnosis. And frankly, I'm not a fan of hypnosis, nor am I trained to conduct it. If you'd like to request another supervisor, I'll be happy to call the department and explain my position." I wouldn't mind dumping this guy but I felt obligated to give him my best shot. "What brought her into the clinic in the first place?"

"A date rape," he said in a surly voice. "Though a normal person could have spotted this guy's intentions a mile away. In two sessions of hypnosis, I feel quite certain she'd see what she missed in the guy's signals . . ."

I held my hand up again, really ready to throttle him. "If you choose to work with me, we'll have to do it the old-fashioned way: like peeling an onion, pulling back the layers and shedding tears as you go. Your choice." I glanced conspicuously at the clock. "Our time is up for today."

When the sound of Luke's indignant exit had faded down the stairwell to the bottom floor, I changed into my yoga gear and headed to the car for the drive home to

Guilford. I would allow myself twenty minutes to rant internally about how a "normal person" would have seen a date rape coming.

Chattering ladies of all sizes wearing bright spandex were streaming into the Total Health Center for the five p.m. class. I unrolled my sticky mat on the carpet, stretched out full length, and closed my eyes.

"Okay, ladies." The instructor, a seventy-something woman in white tights and a "Life Is Good" T-shirt, clapped her hands. She attributes her amazing condition to yoga and we're willing to believe. "Let's settle down. Lie back and let the day's problems drop off like heavy winter clothing in spring. This time is for you."

As she guided us through a series of stretches, my thoughts drifted to Madeline. What might I have seen if we'd gotten to know each other, peeled the superficial layers away? I'd learned very little from the stories at the funeral. Why had Steven Stanton come by the office yesterday to warn me off? Possibly, he was telling the truth — he only wanted peace for his mother. Possibly, he didn't want a stranger going through his sister's things. Possibly . . . I made a mental list: Call Madeline's father in New York City, search the local paper's archives for articles about the Stanton family business, and pump my Fast Connections date, Harry, for details he might have forgotten to tell me.

If none of those avenues bore fruit, it was time to let the questions die. Poor choice of words, but sometimes a person on an obsessive quest is just avoiding her own problems.

Back home, feeling calm and relaxed, I checked my Scotch tape intruder early-warning system. All clear. Spencer ran to meet me, his heart-shaped ID tag jingling on his collar. I fed him and changed into a pair of black jeans and a black sweater. Sophisticated without being stodgy, I hoped.

Babette Finster met me at the door of the clubhouse and accepted the plate of cheese puffs.

"These look wonderful." Her voice dropped to a trembly whisper. "Edith Dunbarton is still on the security jag. Do you really think we need a guard? I can take out an equity loan, if I have to."

"We made a good decision last week," I said. "Don't let Edith make you crazy."

I patted her bony back and smiled, wishing the complex were full of interesting young professionals, not nervous old maids.

But most people my age either couldn't afford the price of a Long Island Sound view, or needed more latitude — physical and psychological — for kids and pets. Or both. Across the room, Peter raised a bottle of white wine and an empty glass.

"Can I get you a drink, Dr. Butterman?" he called. "If you're like me, you've had a long day."

"Would love one, Counselor." I smiled, feeling a tiny surge of warmth in my midsection. "It's a gorgeous night, isn't it? Thanks for reminding me about the party."

We were deep into a comparison of the new Spanish and Cuban restaurants in New Haven, when I saw Mrs. Dunbarton waving frantically.

"Excuse me a minute?" I asked. "I'll be back."

Peter clinked my glass with his. "Looking forward to it."

Mrs. Dunbarton slowed to graze the snack table, then barreled toward me. "I need your support on increased security," she announced. "Certain people are holding back."

"I really appreciate you organizing this party," I said.

"I don't think you understand how serious this matter is," she said. "We live here because it's quiet and safe. I, for one, am not willing to allow hooligans to spoil our space. We have to take more steps."

I leaned my head toward Madeline's condo. "But why don't you think our neighbor killed herself? The cops seem quite definite it was suicide."

She puckered her lips and narrowed her eyes.

"I knew another case just like this one," she said, squinting hard.

I raised my eyebrows.

"It was my cousin's daughter, if you really want to know. She had bad baby blues. I told Luellen she should take that baby girl away from her until she was in shape to handle it —"

"So something went wrong, just like you predicted?" I asked.

"I'll say," said Mrs. Dunbarton, straightening her shoulders and shaking her head. "She swallowed two sleeping pills and went to take a bath. Then she fell asleep and drowned right there in the tub. We blamed the husband, naturally, for leaving her alone. He insisted she killed herself and the police said the same. At first."

I swallowed. "But it wasn't suicide?"

"Of course not," Mrs. Dunbarton snapped. "She'd left a bottle of formula warming. The poor girl hadn't slept in two months. By the time the paramedics came, the water boiled down to nothing and scorched the plastic bottle. You tell me what new mother is in the middle of feeding her baby but takes her own life instead? I don't care how depressed you are. You feed that child first." She crossed her arms over her chest and glared. "It had to have been an accident. Or murder."

"And was there something about Madeline's story that reminded you of your niece's situation?" I asked. Holding a gun to your head could no way be construed as an accident.

Mrs. Dunbarton clicked her tongue fiercely. "I'm only saying that my cousin's daughter didn't kill herself. You can't run around assuming things are suicide. Now maybe her husband did it. The police never did look very carefully at that possibility as far as I can see." She rattled on about the dead girl's unfortunate marriage and how the baby's father had subsequently let his daughter grow up wild. "She has a baby now herself." She leaned in so close I could see the pimento cheese spread lodged in her molars. "Out of wedlock," she hissed.

I tried several other times to establish the connection between her cousin's niece and

Madeline Stanton. Had she seen or heard something specific about Madeline that cast doubt on the suicide? She remained obtuse — mired in the tragedy from her own family's history and transposing her suspicions to the present.

Still, that didn't mean her theory was wrong.

Peter approached carrying a fresh bottle of wine. "Mrs. Dunbarton, the Nelsons are talking about getting a pet bunny. I wonder —"

"A rabbit? Not on my watch!" she sputtered and hurried across the room.

"I thought that would get her attention," he said laughing. "You looked like you needed rescuing. Can I freshen your drink?"

I covered my glass with my hand and smiled. "You're an angel, but I'm meeting someone in twenty minutes." Did Peter look disappointed? "A friend," I added, just in case. "I can go weeks without setting foot out of the house and then two invitations the same night. It never rains but it pours."

"So you didn't need rescuing from the Dunbarton monster?" he teased.

"Not this time," I said. "She seems so stuck on believing Madeline didn't kill herself and how we need to take more measures to make the property secure. I was trying to figure out why."

"Always the shrink," he said, "the busman's holiday. Any solutions?"

"She had a tragedy in her family — the death looked like suicide at first but she's certain that wasn't the truth. I couldn't get her to connect the dots with this incident."

"Probably best for the neighborhood if we try to move on," said Peter. "Babette's a nervous wreck. Not that she wasn't a Nervous Nellie before this happened. Makes you wish you lived at a singles' complex, doesn't it?"

"Bingo," I said, pointing at him with an imaginary gun. "I was thinking exactly the same thing."

"We reasonable folks should stick together." He smiled, the skin around his eyes crinkling into attractive lines. "Like dinner at the Cuban place. Would you like to try it some night?"

"I'd like that."

"I'll call you." He raised his wineglass in salute and turned away. I popped the only remaining cheese puff into my mouth — too late to worry that eating the last item on a plate might predict life as an old maid — and walked out of the clubhouse and down the block to drop off my empty plate at the condo. At the last minute, I called

Angie's cell phone and left a message.

"I'm meeting Harry at the Mexican place in Branford. If I don't show up tomorrow morning, send out the dogs." I laughed, not wanting to scare the hell out of her. But I couldn't help thinking of Madeline — dead two days and nobody noticed.

A Guilford police car passed me on the way out of the complex. Had one of our "inmates" convinced the cops to provide extra sweeps? I wished I was staying home tonight in my own safe space. I swore to myself, big-bucks paycheck from *Bloom!* or not, this would be my last date with a stranger.

Chapter 16

Su Casa was to the Soundside cocktail party as an African safari was to a pet store. I parked in the recesses of the back lot and followed the extended happy-hour noise in through the shadows. I felt a little sick to my stomach and wished I'd worn something less clingy. A burlap sack maybe. Or better yet, had just said no.

Harry's face bobbed up at the end of the long bar crammed with twenty-something patrons. He looked shorter and balder than he had last week. I willed myself to relax — it would be hard to get into trouble here. One drink, a quick chat, and on my way.

"Great to see you again, Becky," he said, leaning over to offer a wet kiss. On the mouth.

"Rebecca," I said and patted my lips dry with the napkin the bartender pushed across the bar. "Margarita on the rocks, no salt, please."

"Make that two," Harry added. "Could we get some chips and salsa?" He turned back to me and grinned. "So how was your day?"

"The usual," I said, remembering at the last minute that I hadn't told him I was a psychologist. "Sorted through questions from unhappy readers and then answered them. I'm sorry, I never even asked what you do for a living. Six minutes isn't much time to gather facts, is it?"

"Enough to decide if you like someone." He winked. "I'm in sales. Squash courts, tennis courts, swimming pools — we have a lot of customers in southwestern Connecticut. Martha Stewart sets a high bar down there."

"Sounds interesting." Which it didn't, but what else could I say — I wouldn't be caught dead in sales and I've certainly never dated someone in that field? *Don't be a bitch, Rebecca.* But the past five minutes had confirmed that Harry was not my type. Stay focused and be pleasant, I told myself. Then you can escape, go home, and relax.

"You remember I was asking about my friend Madeline the other night?"

He slurped the last of his margarita and signaled for the bartender. "Ready for another?"

"Not just yet, thanks." I took a dainty sip. "I know this is going to sound silly." I grimaced. "I haven't heard from Madeline in a few days, and I'm worried. She really fell for that man she met at Fast Connections." I tapped my fingers on the bar. "I'm wondering if she could have gone off with him somewhere and simply failed to mention it. On the other hand, she's a reserved woman and that doesn't really fit at all." I shrugged and sipped my drink again. "Silly, right? But she's my friend. Do you have any suggestions about how I could track this guy down?"

Harry squinted at me. This sounded weak. I'd put my psychiatric interview skills up against anyone's, but as a detective, I was sledgehammer subtle.

He glanced at his watch. "When I met her almost two weeks ago — she was anything but shy." His eyes narrowed. "What's really going on?"

"She's missing. I'm worried. I thought he might know something about it." I looked directly at him.

"She's probably on a cruise somewhere — and we're stuck in a dingy bar in Connecticut." He snorted with laughter.

"I don't think she's on vacation," I said. "The newspapers have been stacking up and no one's been by to water her plants."

"So what, you think this dude kidnapped her or something?"

I shrugged. "I'm concerned, that's all."

"The name was definitely Derek," Harry said. "Seems like I overheard he lives east of here — Westbrook, maybe? Old Saybrook? I wasn't that interested in the guys in the room, if you get my drift." He started on the fresh margarita. "Maybe the lady from Fast Connections would help."

"I thought of that. She probably gets all kind of kooks trying to wheedle names out of her." I laughed lightly — I wasn't one of them, I wanted him to know. "They'd be out of business in no time if they didn't keep their data confidential."

The layers of an onion, I thought suddenly. I should be asking about Madeline, not the man.

"I'm curious," I said. "You're a good-looking fellow with a decent job and social skills to match." I smiled. "What's appealing to you in a woman? What made you check off Madeline's name, for example?"

"First of all, she wasn't a blonde." He reached over and twirled a length of my hair between his fingers. "My ex-wife ruined blondes for me — like getting food poisoning after you eat shrimp. You never want shellfish again."

"I know what you mean," I said, shifting farther back on my barstool. "So the dark hair was a plus. What else turned you on?"

"She was edgy."

"Nervous?"

"No, edgy. Like, cutting edge. Like, teasing and wired. I kinda got the idea I'd have to hang on for the ride." He winked again — not an attractive tic for a man with narrow eyes and a chubby face. "I had the same feeling about you."

Oh Lord. I couldn't help myself. "Harry, you have to be kidding me."

His leer evaporated. "I'm trying too hard, aren't I?"

I nodded, feeling bad for him. But it wouldn't do him any kindness to lie. "But it's not only you. This fast dating is a lot of pressure — trying to guess your date's dreams. And then be that man." I smiled. "Somewhere the right girl is looking for *you.*"

"Maybe you're her?" he said wistfully. "I did mean what I said — hanging on for the ride and all."

"It's hard to tell much in a grand total of six minutes," I said. "I'm actually pretty dull. Will you excuse me while I dash to the ladies' room?"

After a quick visit to the bathroom, I said good-bye to Harry, hustled to my car, and started home. I hoped he wouldn't contact me again — he wasn't a bad guy but definitely no sparks on my side. By his report, Harry had been grinding through the dating mill long enough to know the drill.

"I need to get home — long day tomorrow" should translate to "nothing's happening for me so save us both some embarrassment and please don't call." Most guys would get the message just from the fact that the "date" lasted thirty-nine minutes.

The condos around mine were already dark, including Madeline's, of course. I was glad I'd left the porch, kitchen, living room, and garage lights on. There would be no surprises in my pin-neat garage bay. Another advantage of divorce — Mark never did understand the point of storage space if it wasn't crammed with junk. I let myself in, breathing a sigh of relief: My Rube Goldberg Scotch tape security system was still intact.

I washed and moisturized my face, put on a plaid flannel nightgown, and got into bed with my laptop. Spencer hopped up and began to knead my thigh and purr loudly. I was wound up supertight — not a chance I'd fall asleep. Might as well start the next segment of this hideous dating assignment while the images were fresh in my mind. I decided to write some sidebar tips first, before tackling the reality of Harry.

Top Tips for Meeting Up with Your "Fast Connection"

1. Keep your spirits high but your expectations reasonable. Remember this: Every man you meet in a speed-dating session comes prepared to sparkle. It's not so easy to keep up that level of liveliness over the longer haul. So let the buyer beware!

2. Honesty is still the best policy! If you proclaim you love kids but develop an allergic reaction when your new date's offspring come around, you'll have wasted his time and yours.

3. Safety first! This guy may have felt like a soul mate after a few e-mail exchanges — but don't believe it! Don't offer to make dinner for your first date — choose a public, busy meeting place and keep your par-

ticulars private until your antennae tell you he's a go. And let someone you trust know where you went and when to expect you home.

Avoiding my personal essay a little longer, I surfed through other dating sites: Great Expectations, Yahoo! Personal Premier for Deeper Connections, and eHarmony. They all boasted success stories — married three months after first meeting at the dating service, engaged to the love of their life after six months online — hard to believe these relationships really worked. It's an occupational hazard — all the worst possibilities of any given situation come rushing to mind.

Writing this article was going to be painful. I wondered if Jillian would accept a piece on deconstructing online dating profiles instead. I could "break the code" for which guy just wants to hook up, who wants a marriage prospect without doing any of the hard lifting in a relationship, and which hunk of fool's gold might be a find. But no: Jillian wanted personal angst — displayed publicly. And she wanted it to be mine.

Then I had a brainstorm — why not pretend I'd really fallen for Harry and we were e-mailing like crazy? The facts would be distorted, but who'd be checking? No one else knows my password — except for Angie. And Jillian only cared that I was funny and personal. I swallowed my guilt and started to write.

Speed dating is a numbers game, so put on your tough leather skin and get ready. This kind of mate-surfing is tailor-made for the outgoing woman who can view a series of encounters with unfamiliar men as an adventure, not torture. I had a great adventure and a terrific outcome — you can too!

STEP ONE:

Women, polish your five-minute pitch!

Suddenly I thought again of Madeline's disappointment that her Fast Connections date — Derek the dark-haired Romeo — hadn't chosen her. She'd mentioned the guy both in her jotted diary notes and in the blog. Yet Harry insisted there were sparks on both sides. Maybe Derek just hadn't gotten around to contacting Madeline by the time she posted that blog entry — Lord knows I'd waited a full forty-eight hours to list Harry as a possible match. And then needed a sharp nudge from Angie to finish the job. What if Derek had written Madeline, but not right away? What if he'd tried to contact her after she died?

I logged back onto the Fast Connections website and typed in madsingleton@fast connections.biz. What about her password? First I tried *Diana.* Login attempt failed. How many chances would I get before the site locked me out? I typed *Madeline.* Failed again. The cat uncurled from a furry knot and rolled onto his back, purring loudly. I tapped S-P-E-N-C-E-R into the empty box. The familiar match page loaded onto my screen — another collage of happy couples in various stages of infatuated bliss — clinking glasses, smiling and laughing, a couple of chaste kisses in front of Manhattan landmarks.

Two men had written Madeline after the speed dating: Miles and Derek. The messages were dated the night that she died. A chill spilled across my shoulders as I clicked on the icon for e-mail from Derek. He'd invited her to meet him at the Guilford Tavern for a drink the following Sunday. "I'll sit on that barstool night and day until you show," he'd finished.

Of course she hadn't shown — she was dead. And then he'd made an appearance at the bar outside my Fast Connections session at Rudy V's. Hoping to make contact with her again?

What if I wrote him a note now, pretending to be Madeline? Hopefully, I could imitate her breezy style well enough that he wouldn't rush out for a syntactical analysis. I grinned.

> *Howdy partner! So sorry to be slow and miss the drink at the Guilford Tavern. You wouldn't believe the crazy shit that's been going down here! Anyway, enough of the mea culpa — I had a ball meeting you and talking after. Never would have guessed I'd hit it off so easily with a handsome dude from Fast Connections!*

I skimmed back over the paragraph and replaced "I had a ball" with "it was awesome" — my first draft sounded like it came from Madeline's maiden aunt. Handsome dude didn't make the cut either. I deleted that and typed in "a cool guy." Better not to trip myself up with odd language. As far as I knew, Derek could be a regular reader of Madeline's blog, and tuned in to every nuance of her ramblings. I read it one more time and then deleted the whole thing.

It didn't feel right, impersonating a dead woman. Yes, I'd like to know the truth about

Madeline. And I'd given my word to Isabel. What if I wrote to Derek pretending to be Madeline and he'd already heard about her death? He'd know I was trying to pull something. And where were my professional ethics? With a heavy sigh, I logged out of the website and shut down the computer.

I'd sleep on it tonight.

As creepy as the idea of a suicide next door felt, murder was beginning to seem even worse.

CHAPTER 17

Dear Dr. Aster:
My last child started college this fall, leaving me alone with my husband for the first time in twenty-something years. Seems like I've been looking forward to this moment forever! But instead of feeling closer to my husband, I'm thinking about murder! I can't take his carping about my cooking, my housekeeping, my body. Did the kids' ruckus disguise a lousy relationship? Is it time to move on?

Sincerely,
Nagged to the Nubbin in Norwalk

Dear Nagged:
Let's take first things first. No matter how much you've been looking forward to the day, it's a huge emotional and physical change when your last chick flaps out of the coop. And change outside means a psychological shift inside.

And shifting in a healthy way takes time. This is a great moment to take stock of where your life is going — with your career, your husband, yourself. But please don't rush to make decisions about your marriage! Try sitting down with your man and talking about the state of your relationship — he's probably suffering growing pains too. Good luck and enjoy the peace!

I put my computer to sleep and pulled on yoga pants and a sweatshirt. People mock medical doctors who dog it on Wednesdays — but I do the same when I can swing it. Not to play golf, God help me, just time off to do errands, walk with Angie, catch up with Dr. Aster, and clear my mind. When you spend your working hours soaking up other people's pain, you'd darn well better figure out a way to fill your own emotional coffers.

The day was a stunner, the morning chill steamed off by the sun and just a hint of color dabbed on the tips of the trees. I passed a group of young children fitting their palms into handprints that had been pressed into the cement of the sidewalk years earlier. Suddenly it seemed hard to believe I was living in the town where I was born. Dr. Goldman had spent plenty of my high-priced therapy hours nudging me to look at the meaning of moving back to Guilford. He was not happy when I put a deposit down on Soundside Drive.

"As a psychologist, you know how important it is to talk about this kind of decision before you act it out."

"Even a psychologist," I wanted to mimic in a simpering voice, "can't set up a cot in her therapist's office."

But that would open up a whole other can of worms. So instead I explained again how every damn person in the Yale mental-health community knew what happened with Mark and the redhead last winter. Bad enough to tolerate embarrassed and sympathetic faces each time I attended a symposium. I'd be damned if I'd live with half the gossiping department on my block too. I didn't have years to discuss it — I had to get out, immediately.

The condo market had dried up, my Realtor told me. Then the Soundside property popped up on multiple listings, with a manageable commute and the right price — plus close enough to the water that frustrated gulls sometimes dropped uncooperative mollusks on my front walk. Besides all that, the town would be a seller's dream when the time came — good schools and an abundance of stiff-upper-lip New England charm.

Just then I saw Angie, jogging in place on the Gettysburg Memorial side of the statue of the Civil War soldier in the center of the green. Her legs are half a foot longer than mine, which makes for a quick pace: Her fast walk is my trot. But after half a plate of cheese puffs, two drinks, and more chips than I'd intended or wanted last night, I didn't mind.

"I had two desserts yesterday," she puffed and leaned over to hug me. "Mind if we go at no-yakking speed?" We took off at a fast clip. Forty-five minutes later, over coffee at the bagel shop, I filled her in on the visit from Madeline's brother, the date with Harry, and my decision not to post to Madeline's Fast Connections friend.

"It was tempting," I said, "but it didn't feel quite right."

Angie frowned and tapped my forearm with a plastic spoon. "This really isn't like you. I thought you agreed to take the information you collected to the cops."

"I did take it to the cops," I said. "I specifically told Meigs about Steven Stanton."

"And?"

"He essentially told me to butt out."

Angie laughed. "A smart man."

"I'm just looking around a little. If nothing turns up, I'm going to call Isabel Stanton and tell her she needs to move on."

"What if she begs?" Angie asked. "You're a soft touch."

I made a slashing movement across my neck. "Done. If she won't let it go, I'll propose attending a suicide support group. Yale offers them a couple of times a year."

Angie stood and pulled on her jacket. "I'm checking in with you tomorrow. If you haven't turned your leads over to the cops by then, I'll call Meigs myself."

"Fine." We left the shop and I watched while she cut across the street and disappeared into Page Hardware, former bank and now purveyor of housewares, appliances, and mousetraps. Then I perched on an empty bench on the green and pulled out my cell and the slip of paper on which I'd written Madeline's father's New York City phone number. I wasn't finished looking around quite yet.

"You've reached the home of William and Lorena Stanton," a recorded male voice answered smoothly. "We're unable to take your call but leave a message after the beep." Sounded just as self-assured as his

221

son, Steven.

"Uh, Mr. Stanton, this is Dr. Rebecca Butterman, from Guilford, Connecticut?" As if I wasn't sure where I lived. "I'm calling in reference to your daughter, Madeline. First let me say how very sorry I am for your loss. I'm her neighbor. Was her neighbor.

"I was wondering . . . could you call me?" I left my number and thanked him for his time.

Why should he answer a message like that? But I couldn't very well leave the questions I wanted to ask on an answering machine. Did he have any reason to suspect she had been suicidal? Why had he been run out of town? Why had he gotten divorced? And why had he lost contact with his only daughter? And missed her funeral?

I walked to the library in the far northeast corner of the green. One of the local papers, the *Source,* was too new to dish the dirt I needed. Besides, their police blotter took the high road — refusing to name names. I'd already checked the online archives for the other paper, the *Shore Line Times.* They only went back to 2002, and I'd found no recent scandals in the Stanton family history.

A pleasant gray-haired librarian showed me how to use the public computer to search for headlines in earlier editions of the *Times,* and how to load rolls of microfiche into the clanking dinosaur of a machine that would reveal the details.

My eyes started to blur after an hour skimming through screens of text. The Stanton family had shown significant civic commitment over the years, documented by photos and articles about participation in town fund-raisers, Rotary Club appearances, and a large donation thirty years ago to the Shoreline Congregational Church building fund. The patchy photograph of a ribbon-cutting for the new education wing showed a much-younger Isabel Stanton beaming beside her husband, William. Madeline and her brothers — round-faced, dark-haired children — were clustered around a giant pair of cardboard scissors in front of the refurbished church house.

"Wilcox Metal Works has always been proud to contribute to our town, starting with canons in the Civil War," said Isabel Stanton. "My husband and I are pleased to follow in the path carved by my father and grandfather." So Isabel had the money.

But no scandals. Not fit for print in the local paper anyway. Buried deep in the Out and About section from ten years ago, I found a small column announcing Mr.

Stanton's upcoming marriage. In the accompanying photo, the bride-to-be looked no older than thirty — big boobs marginally contained by a plunging neckline, big blond hair, big eyes mooning up at her fiancé. A trophy wife. No wonder Isabel wanted to run him out of town.

I pushed back my chair and rubbed my eyes, thinking about my last conversation with Detective Meigs. It bothered me that he'd visited Janice and then mysteriously appeared in the bar at Rudy V's. Why track me if he was certain Madeline killed herself?

Angie was right — anything I came up with had to go to the police. On the other hand, if I had to face Meigs's sarcasm again, I wanted to be prepared. My gut told me he was the kind of small town cop who did things his own way — off the books. If he was under investigation by his police board or one grievance away from being fired, maybe there'd be some hints in the local news. I returned to the public computer and typed *Jack Meigs* into the search bar.

Meigs's name surfaced in a round dozen headlines — none of them controversial or negative. "Meigs Honored for Fifteen Years of Service to Guilford," "Meigs Keynote Speaker for Connecticut Youth Conference," "Jack and Alice Meigs to Serve as

Honorary Chairs for Youth Center Fund-raiser," "Meigs Leads Charge to Crush Rash of Burglaries." Nothing confirming my unofficial diagnoses: bully, ambitious bureaucrat, or even pain in the ass.

I scrolled down to the last headline:

MEIGS LEAVES ACCIDENT SCENE

I found the corresponding microfiche and slotted it into the machine.

Alice Meigs, 45, 282 Long Hill Road, was charged with driving while under the influence of alcohol, drugs, or both, and reckless driving, following a motor vehicle accident on Route 1 in Guilford near Route 77. She was processed and released on a Promise to Appear in court.

This kind of public humiliation would certainly make a policeman cranky. Very curious now, I returned to the computer and searched on Alice Meigs. I would lay odds on her being an alcoholic. According to the paper, the accident had occurred in the morning. Nonproblem drinkers were not likely to tank up and roar down Route 1 before noon.

I found no further mention of Alice Meigs or her accident.

I filed the microfiche away and left the library. Standing in the parking lot, I decided to try William Stanton one more time. The clumsy message I'd left gave him no good reason to return my call.

"Hello?" That smooth voice again, this time in person.

"I'm Dr. Rebecca Butterman. I'm a psychologist. I was Madeline's neighbor? I'm terribly sorry for your loss."

At first he said nothing, then a quiet "thanks."

"Uh, let me be frank," I said, "your wife — I mean ex-wife — asked me to look into Madeline's death. The police told her it was definitely suicide and Mrs. Stanton was convinced otherwise. I can't say I've found anything new, but I didn't want to quit without talking to you — without getting your side. I wondered whether you'd heard anything from her before she died? You were important to her, I could tell from her diary."

"Isabel hired a psychologist to do police work?" Mr. Stanton asked. "Is she out of her mind?"

"I'm not really —"

"How is this your business?" he steamed. "I don't even know who you are."

"I was her neighbor," I said gently, choos-

226

ing to respond to the sadness rather than the anger. "What do *you* think happened to Madeline?"

"I have no idea."

"You were important to her," I repeated.

Mr. Stanton sniffed. "*Was* important. We hadn't been close in years. Isabel saw to that."

"Would you be willing to say why?"

The phone disconnected. I hadn't reached the guy at all. Hard to imagine how bad he felt having lost his daughter twice, this time for good.

I felt gloomy, and then, as always, hungry. I stopped at the Guilford Food Market to pick up Caesar salad fixings, an acorn squash, and ingredients for meatloaf. My mouth watered: I'd bake the squash and drizzle it with butter and maple syrup in honor of fall.

Once back home with the groceries unloaded, I booted up the computer to proofread the Dr. Aster column I'd dashed off that morning. Ugh. Second time in a row I sounded obsessed with badgering unhappy housewives to give their relationships a chance. What was the deal? Had to be related to seeing Mark on Sunday. But even if I had second, third, and fourth thoughts about my own marriage, it was not fair to make my loyal readers take it in their cotton briefs.

To hell with Mark, I scolded myself. Mistakes were made, decisions followed. Time to grow up and move on. I deleted the column exhorting Nagged to the Nubbin to talk to her man and chose a letter I could answer with more zip.

Dear Dr. Aster:

My youngest son is getting married next spring. As mother of the groom, let me assure you I know not to interfere! Which is precisely why my husband and I offered our prospective in-laws a generous sum toward the cost of the wedding — to use as they please. But the bride's mother is beginning to drive me mad. She wants to control everything: the number of friends we're allowed to invite, who gives a toast and for how many minutes, whether grandchildren may attend. Yesterday, she delivered that last straw: I'm to wear a pastel gown, absolutely no black. Keep in mind that this is a formal affair and that I'm a middle-aged woman with a substantial rear end. And my skin looks hideous in pastel. I've had it down to my pink keister! Can you help?

Ready to Kill in Kansas

Dear Ready:

Watching your children get married brings out all kinds of intense feelings. Your last baby is grown and soon gone. How can you be sure his bride will take care of him the way you have? How can you trust her family won't become more important to him than yours? No wonder weddings have a reputation for bringing out the very worst!

Congratulations on this important milestone and on your generosity. Before you make a fuss about the dress, step away while breathing deeply and remember the skills you honed when you had argumentative teenagers in the house. If ever there was a time to pick your battles, this is it. Good luck and try to enjoy the moment!

P.S. Would navy blue solve the problem? Just kidding . . .

I e-mailed the column to Jillian, poured a glass of iced tea, and sprawled on the chaise longue on the back deck. Madeline's mini Weber grill was still standing sentinel outside her slider. Her potted geranium looked brown and dry.

Who had she been and why had she died? The information I'd gathered over the past several days didn't hang together. Was it possible that Madeline's father's second marriage caused the family to splinter? Seemed unlikely that a mid-thirties woman would kill herself over that — it was ancient history. Why didn't Madeline's brother want me to pursue her death, while Isabel seemed desperate to disprove the suicide? What had Harry from Fast Connections picked up in their short time together?

I could deal with a live person sitting in front of me with mysterious symptoms and bumpy moods — that I knew how to handle. But the secrets of a dead girl were something else. It bothered me not to be able to ask the questions that mattered. I was ready to call it quits. On the other hand, I didn't like being told to butt out of Madeline's business. That didn't sit well at all.

I glanced over at the grill and decided to use the key Isabel had pressed on me to visit Madeline's apartment one final time. My neighbor couldn't tell me what her family was really like. But I might find some answers in her photo albums, her diary, her home. If nothing obvious turned up, *my* case would be closed.

CHAPTER 18

Madeline's place was dim and smelled like Clorox and Pledge. Someone — maybe Isabel — had been by to clean and close the windows and blinds. The film of black dust had been wiped from the bathroom and bedroom surfaces and more of Madeline's books were stowed in cardboard boxes lining the baseboards. An unsigned real-estate contract lay on the coffee table. Life was about to move on. Would the Realtors tell prospective buyers about Madeline? Probably not. Nothing would queer a sale faster than a depressed dead girl haunting the home. I wondered how long it would take Mrs. Dunbarton to put the new neighbors wise.

I perused the row of boxes, bending over to untuck the flaps. Framed photos had been piled haphazardly in the last box. I knelt and lifted them out. Most were family photos — the ones I'd seen displayed on the bookshelves when Isabel first asked me over. I recognized her brothers, younger then, and Steven with more hair. Underneath the family pictures, I discovered a photo of Madeline and another teenage girl on skis, framed in red plaid fabric and titled with the caption "best friends." The girl looked familiar, though with goggles obscuring most of her face, it was hard to say how.

At the bottom of the box was a picture of Madeline as a girl with a handsome gentleman: A crack in the glass spidered between the two of them. Her dad? Madeline clung to the man's hand, smiling up with a look of pure adoration. He stared at the photographer, lips pursed in a frown. I stood up, knees popping, and balanced the photo on the empty bookcase.

Why had they fallen out of touch?

In the master bedroom, I pawed through a boxed collection of photographs of the Princess of Wales: Diana in her puffy wedding gown, Diana gazing into the face of her infant son, Diana with a shy smile wearing a stunning pale blue evening gown and a diamond tiara. On the floor outside the box was another picture of the princess, this time wearing trousers and a military vest — Diana had taken up a cause.

Why weren't more of Madeline's friends

at the memorial service? Or coworkers? It struck me that none of the Soundside neighbors, even those who'd lived here forever, seemed to know her well. I wished I'd had more time to talk with the second brother, Tom, about what really happened between their parents, and where Madeline's loyalty had fallen.

I rustled through the boxes again, looking for the notes from Madeline's online diary. Isabel must have taken them home.

I locked the door and returned to my own condo, hoping the neighbors hadn't noticed the lights on in Madeline's apartment. And the absence of Isabel's car. If one of them called me on it, I'd flat out lie: I needed extra cat food, Spencer's rabies certificate, even his winter collar.

Feeling restless and discouraged, I checked my e-mail — nothing very interesting. Mostly spam and an invitation to attend a continuing-education session on the new patient-confidentiality laws. Important, but deadly. Damn it, why had Madeline died?

Think like a psychologist, Rebecca. I forced myself to sketch out a psychiatric intake interview. Not much data, but I tried.

IDENTIFYING INFORMATION: Madeline Stanton was a 34-year-old single white female, living alone in a condominium in Guilford, Connecticut.

CHIEF COMPLAINT: Dead.

Not funny, Rebecca.

HISTORY OF THE PRESENT PROBLEM: Madeline was reported missing by her mother, Isabel, two days after being shot and killed. Annoying local detective informed Isabel that the death was a suicide, confirmed by regretful note left on the victim's laptop. Forensic linguist believes someone else wrote the note.

PAST MEDICAL HISTORY: Unknown.

PAST PSYCHIATRIC HISTORY: Although the patient was apparently somewhat of a loner, based on historical report and sparse attendance at her memorial service, no history of formal psychiatric treatment is known.

FAMILY HISTORY: Madeline was the youngest of three children; she had two older brothers, Steven and Tom. She was born and raised in the small shoreline town of Guilford. Her family owns a local business, Wilcox Metal Works, and has been active in town affairs. Some years ago, Madeline's parents had a serious falling out, perhaps over another woman. Mr. Stanton has since moved away and remarried. None of the family is currently in regular touch with him, and he denies recent contact with his daughter.

MENTAL STATUS EXAM: Madeline was an attractive, dark-haired woman who appeared younger than her stated age. She made aggressive eye contact during her meetings with the interviewer and gave the impression of wanting to appear both mysterious and clever. Speech was logical and coherent. Mood appeared slightly depressed, overlaid with a forced cheeriness. Based on TV programs heard through the walls, Madeline either was unable to sleep, had difficulty falling asleep, or needed the company of the television in order to sleep. Appetite seemed normal. (Like everything else in my fake report, this was based on a shred of data — Madeline's one grilled hamburger and the junk food stored in her refrigerator.) There was no express suicidal ideation.

IMPRESSION AND RECOMMENDATION: Madeline Stanton was a 34-year-old single woman who defended against her loneliness and the conflict in her family with an active online life.

This was often the way the psychological model of a patient came alive: As I steeped myself in the interview notes and test results, conclusions would begin to take shape. If Madeline's online activities were an important clue to her life — and death — I needed to go back to her blog. I typed the web address into the search bar and waited for her site to load. I hadn't taken the time the other night to read much past the most recent entry. If my neighbor had been as flirtatious online as Harry found her to be in person at Fast Connections, she might have collected any number of disgruntled ex-boyfriends or stalkers along the way. When the page came up, I scrolled down through the previous entries, and clicked on the date we'd met for coffee just weeks ago. As with the others, it started out with a quote.

If you want to annoy your neighbors, tell the truth about them.
—Pietro Aretino

Dear Diary: Have I told you about my neighbors? While some of you may be living the life of the swinging singles scene, I've somehow bought into the Land of Nosy Old Biddies. The Realtor told me 70 percent of the residents were unmarried. She failed to mention that they take shifts as lookouts in this condo — some keep watch in the morning and others at night. And there's always a friendly comment to let you know your three a.m. arrival did not go unnoticed.

I giggled out loud. "She had 'em pegged," I said to the cat.

I think it was Cyril Connolly who said, "There are many who dare not kill themselves for fear of what the neighbors will say." I had coffee with a new one yesterday but they must have screened her to be sure she fit the mold — raise your hand if you'd pay a king's ransom for a sense of humor in your neighborhood!

My jaw locked. Much more amusing to imagine her making fun of Mrs. Dunbarton. Apparently I'd come across as quite dull.

A new e-mail chimed its arrival, then flashed on my desktop. *Harry.* In spite of my best attempt to squash the connection, he'd had a delightful evening. Most of all, he appreciated my honesty. Would I consider getting together this weekend? He'd made a reservation at his favorite bed-and-breakfast in Newport — two rooms. He'd taken to heart my comment that you couldn't "know" someone else in six minutes. He'd love to spend more time together. Could he pick me up Saturday at nine?

So much for being an expert on decoding the dating scene. I closed the e-mail — it would take some finesse to word the rejection carefully. I thought again about how badly Derek had wanted to see Madeline, then typed her e-mail address and password information into the Fast Connections website.

Derek had posted a second message.

I've been thinking about you since we met — can't get my mind off those velvet brown eyes. Desperate to talk to you again. You know the Stone House near the Guilford harbor? I'll be waiting there tonight at nine.

My heart started to pound. The Stone House was not even a half mile from our Soundside condos. I drew in a deep breath.

Here was a way to chat with him without pretending anything. And he wouldn't even have to know my name. It wasn't like me to be reckless, but I felt compelled to follow this last bit through. The plan:

1. *Interview Derek. Briefly. Safely. Anonymously.*
2. *Report to Meigs.*

I showered, toweled dry, and pulled on my tightest blue jeans — the ones that practically popped the zipper when I sat down — and a fuzzy white turtleneck. I brushed my hair vigorously and spritzed on perfume. How would I explain my appearance in the bar, to a man infatuated with Madeline? My mind felt blank. Something would come. I picked up the photograph I'd taken with me to Fast Connections — Madeline and her mother — and stuffed it into my purse. I would tell him the truth: Isabel had asked me to find out about her daughter's state of mind in the days before she died. The trail led to him.

Spencer followed me to the door and I bent down to kiss him. "I won't do anything crazy," I promised. "And I'll be home by ten."

CHAPTER 19

I walked the three blocks to the Stone House, partly to enjoy the crisp night — and partly to delay the charade with Derek as long as possible. Both the Big and Little Dippers hung low in the sky and choppy waves slapped against the breakwater across from the restaurant. A puff of wind brought the strong scent of beached mussels from the sound, and then a whiff of rotting food from the Dumpster. I circled through the back parking lot to the front door.

To the left of the vestibule just past the bar, a fire flickered in a freestanding wood stove surrounded by half a dozen tall tables. The air was thick with the tantalizing smell of charbroiled burgers and barbequed ribs. I'd nibbled on some wilted vegetables at home, for once my nerves too jumpy to cook and my gut too jumpy to eat.

"I'm meeting someone for a drink," I told the receptionist, a slim Asian woman in tight jeans — snugger even than mine.

I paused in the doorway, searching for Derek. He slouched on a stool at the far end of the small bar, tracing lines in the condensation on his beer glass, eyes focused on the TV hanging from the wall. New York Yankees versus Boston Red Sox — fans at the bar would be evenly split, knowing this town.

I took a deep breath, squared my shoulders, and glided across the room.

I tapped his shoulder. "Excuse me? Derek?"

He glanced over, drew his eyebrows together, then looked to the door. "Yeah? Do I know you?"

"I'm Rebecca Aster." I offered my hand, then dropped it when he didn't respond. "A friend of Madeline Stanton's? She was going to meet you here at nine?"

He pushed back a hank of almost-chocolate-colored hair and frowned. "What the fuck? She sent you to blow me off?"

"Not exactly. I'd like to explain." I gestured to the stool beside him. It did not sound as though he'd heard the news about Madeline's death. "May I sit?"

He nodded roughly and turned his attention back to the ballgame. "You'd think if they paid a pitcher a couple of million bucks he could throw a fucking strike."

My heart beat faster. I shifted to relieve the pressure of the denim waistband constricting my stomach.

"Something terrible has happened," I blurted out. "Madeline died."

His head jerked back from the TV. "What?"

My hand hovered above his arm but he pulled it away.

The bartender arrived and ran a damp rag across the wood in front of me. "What can I get ya?"

I plucked up the table talker listing the Stone House drink specialties. I couldn't think. My heart was hammering — I needed something to focus my eyes and hands on, other than Derek. A shot of Stoli came to mind. "A cranberry sparkle," I said. "That sounds fine."

"What do you mean, 'Madeline died'?" He looked truly stunned.

"It happened last week but they kept it out of the papers. And no one knew to tell you. I'm so sorry to have to break the news this way. Let me be honest with you, there's some question about whether it was a suicide — that's why I wanted to talk to you. You guys met just before she died and she seemed so fond of you" — babbling now

— "I wondered if I could ask a few questions?"

"And who are you?" He drained the last of his beer, watching me over the rim of his glass. Then he crumpled his damp napkin into a tight ball and flung it over the bar. "How the hell did you know I was going to wait for her here if she's dead?"

The bartender delivered a tall pink drink and I gulped an inch down. "Fast Connections. I guessed her password and then when I saw your message . . ."

Those green, green eyes narrowed to angry slits.

"You can understand that Madeline's family is devastated," I hurried on. "I promised them I'd try to help figure out what went wrong."

The skin across his face tightened, two white spots framing the nostrils.

"I know this is awkward —" I picked up my glass and drank. Already, my cranberry sparkle was half-gone.

"Awkward? It's more than fucking awkward." His voice trailed away. He slumped back into his seat and signaled for another beer.

"Did she seem depressed to you? Unhappy about her life?" I probed.

"Depressed?" he asked. "You've got to be

joking. That girl was alive." He licked his lips. "Have you even read her blog?"

I nodded. Hard to imagine he'd found this appealing. "It seemed a little gloomy to me. Stories about Princess Diana and her own crazy neighbors —"

"Not that one," Derek cut in. "The other website. She was hot. She was so cool." His eyes glittered. "She has — had — a huge following."

"Another website?'

"Click on the lips on the bottom of the blog." He swallowed a gulp of beer. "I couldn't believe my luck when she showed up at Fast Connections and then we hit it off. I recognized her right away. You have no idea: I must have sent her a million e-mails through the website — but she never answered those."

I patted his hand. "I know she liked you too. Did it seem like she was upset about anything? Her family, maybe? Work or friends?"

"Nah. She was, like, high on life. She got off on me being so into her blog."

"When you spent that time together at Rudy V's, did you talk about future plans?"

He leaned closer. A drop of sweat edged out from his hairline and trickled through his coarse sideburn stubble. "I told her about this erotic party network that's just getting started in New Haven. Like the ones in Manhattan, you know?"

I didn't — how would I unless a patient told me? Certainly this kind of event wouldn't make the Out and About section in the *Shore Line Times.* But I nodded to keep him talking.

"She was going to write about it after we went. I told her we didn't have to go as boyfriend and girlfriend. And once we got there she'd be free to do what she pleased. If it involved me, even better." His lips stretched into a repellent grin. "She said she had the idea we were gonna like each other — a lot." He looked angry again. "Then I never heard a damn thing. I figured she was just a Goddamn tease."

How to sound consoling but not heavy-handed? "You felt like Madeline led you on . . ."

He rolled his eyes.

"I'm sorry to disappoint you." Another question popped into my mind. "Did I see you at Rudy V's this week? After Fast Connections, in the bar? I didn't catch your name on the speed-dating rotation."

"What a joke. You think I'd spend any more money and time on those losers?"

"I was one of those losers," I said primly.

"Sorry." He laughed. "I thought if I hung out at the bar, I might see Madeline." He raised his eyebrows and flashed a rueful smile. Was he checking me out? "So. Rebecca. How about you and me give it a go? There's a party tomorrow night."

Talk about a quick recovery. But I wasn't offering that kind of consolation.

"Thanks for asking," I said with a regretful shrug. "I'm married." What was one more lie?

"Don't tell him." He glanced at my empty ring finger and skimmed his hand along my thigh, leaving my skin jangling unpleasantly.

"Thanks for asking," I repeated firmly. "I'm pretty well tied up."

"Oh, you're into another scene." He grinned and turned back to the television where a Red Sox base runner was caught in a rundown between first and second.

"Jesus fucking Christ!" Derek screamed, startling me. "Can't these idiots read a signal?"

I didn't like this guy. I drew a twenty-dollar bill out of my wallet and signaled to the bartender. "I'm awfully sorry to be the bearer of bad news."

He shrugged. "Sure you won't stay a little longer?"

"I'm sure. Take care." I grabbed my

change, flashed a phony smile, slid off the barstool, and hurried across the room into the ladies' lounge. When I came back out, Derek's seat was empty.

"I think he's waiting for you outside," said the receptionist.

"Who? Who's waiting for me?"

She waved at the stool where Derek had been sitting. "Your boyfriend. He stood around here a minute and then went out to smoke a cigarette."

I pulled back into the ladies' room entrance, squinting to place Derek in the shadows outdoors. The quick flash of a lighter exposed his face as he leaned against the flagpole in the middle of the courtyard. Why was he waiting? What did he want? What a dope. If I only had a car — if he followed — I could drive somewhere besides home to throw him off. Or lead him right to the cops. But the car was in my garage.

Across the room at one of the tall tables circling the woodstove, I spotted Craig Sebastian, one of Mark's hospital colleagues. He was mopping up after a plate of ribs, all while haranguing a narrow-faced woman I assumed was his wife. I'd used Craig as medical back-up for a couple of my patients in the early days of my practice. He turned out to be everything I didn't want in a psychiatric consultant — cold, officious, and quick to prescribe. Worst of all, my patients seemed to return to therapy with bony fingers of doubt fondling their confidence in our work. But tonight he would be my new best friend. I marched across the room to Craig's table. No way around it: I had to crash their evening and settle in like a shuttle on the moon.

"Craig, it's so good to see you." I kissed the air and stretched out my hand to his wife. "I'm Rebecca Butterman. I think we may have met at one of the department parties, but the old memory just ain't what she used to be." I tapped my forehead and grinned. What an idiot. The Sebastians looked confused and not altogether pleased.

"Mark's wife," Craig grunted to his spouse. "You met her at the Christmas party last year. This is Kristin."

"Ex-wife," I said and leaned close to whisper to Kristin. "I'm terribly sorry to interrupt your dinner. But I'm a little afraid the man outside intends to follow me home. I was hoping I could just stay with you a few minutes until he leaves." I tipped my head toward the window.

"Of course," said Kristin. She glared across the table at her husband. "You'll stay right here as long as you need."

"I'm going to call a friend and ask her to swing by and get me." I speed-dialed Angie's cell phone. *Pick up, pick up, pick up.* Her voicemail kicked in.

"It's me," I said, turning my face away from the Sebastians and whispering hoarsely into the phone. "I need you to stop by the Stone House and give me a ride home. Now. Call me as soon as humanly possible." I pressed *end.* "So how's business?" I asked Craig, smiling brightly and pushing back the tears.

Half an hour later, the Sebastians had finished coffee and cheesecake, and Derek was still outside. Kristin reported that he'd smoked three cigarettes and crossed the street to the harbor and back twice. Craig was mostly silent and obviously irritated. Whatever he and his wife had been discussing, it was not the decorator show house in Madison, the entertainment at last week's Guilford fair, or whether Breakwater Books would carry an ample supply of Oprah's next selection — all topics that Kristin and I covered thoroughly.

"Let's get out of here," said Craig. "We'll give you a lift." He ushered us outside, only Kristin sneaking a look at the flagpole. Now empty. I gave directions to my condo and collapsed in the backseat of Craig's Mercedes.

"I'm really so sorry for ruining your evening," I said.

"Don't be silly," said Kristin, craning around the headrest to wink at me. "This is a lot more important than anything we had on the agenda."

"Now how the hell did you meet this man and why was he following you?" Craig demanded.

"It's a long story." I met his eyes in the rearview mirror. "Let's just say this: The single life is not as glamorous as married people imagine. I'm newly divorced," I told Kristin. "The adjustment is a little hard." Better to leave them thinking it was a date gone bad than try to explain the truth.

The Mercedes pulled around the large stand of marsh grasses that hid my complex from passersby. A police cruiser was nosed into the bushes along my driveway, its lights flashing. I got out of the car.

A small crowd of neighbors was huddled around two policemen on my front lawn. I recognized Mrs. Dunbarton's ratty tartan terry robe and Babette Finster's pink polyester peignoir peeping out of her raincoat. Peter Morgan was still dressed in street clothes. Sooner or later in a condominium complex, you see everyone in pajamas. Bernd Becker stepped out of his Volvo and headed toward the neighbors as Angie's red Miata screeched to a stop behind us. She flung open the door and raced over to me.

"Rebecca? What the hell is going on?"

My knees buckled and I sagged against the Mercedes. "I have no idea."

CHAPTER 20

I approached the older cop, a stocky fellow with a pair of aviator sunglasses resting on his thinning gray hair. Sunglasses at night? It must be a look.

"Is there a problem, Officer?" I licked my lips and waved at the condo. "This is my home."

"There was a man in your bushes!" Mrs. Dunbarton crowed. She brandished a leaf rake. "I think we've found our murderer."

"I thought I saw a shadow when I was walking Wilson," Babette added. She trembled and pulled her raincoat tight around her thin frame.

"Babette called me and I called the police," said Bernd, holding up his cell phone. "Sorry I couldn't get here faster."

Peter edged around the women, moving close enough to squeeze my shoulders. "Are you okay?"

"I'd already notified the police." Mrs.

Dunbarton sniffed. "They were already on the way."

"Better than a burglar alarm," muttered the younger cop whom I now recognized as the man stationed outside Madeline's apartment after her shooting. The full lips and brush cut were unmistakable.

"Where's the prowler?" I pulled away from Peter. I didn't feel strong, but I felt like I should try to look that way.

"The perp was gone by the time we got here," said the young cop. "We were just obtaining a description from these ladies."

"He was short to medium," said Mrs. Dunbarton.

"Almost bald," added Babette. "I spotted him when I saw your floodlight reflecting off his head."

"Squat-shaped," said Mrs. Dunbarton, elbowing her way in front of Babette to point at Craig Sebastian. "Like him. He ducked around your place to the rear."

Craig pinched his lips. Probably a first — someone calling him "squat" — in public, anyway.

"Does this sound like someone you know?" the cop asked me.

I shook my head slowly. "Honestly, I don't have a clue."

Angie took a step forward. "It sounds a

little like that guy you met the other night."

I shot her a look to kill. Yes, it sounded like Harry, but who knew how many dozens if not hundreds of short, bald men there were just in our little local world. And what reason would any of them have to be in my yard?

"Who is this fellow and how did you meet?" asked the older cop, a gnawed pencil poised over his dog-eared notebook.

I cleared my throat. "His name is Harry. I met him at a speed-dating event. We had a drink last night. But it couldn't possibly be him. He doesn't know where I live."

The younger cop coughed. "You can get any information you want online — you don't need to be a genius. Did you have problems during your *date?*" He made it sound like a brothel visit. "Arguments? Odd behaviors? Indications that he might be stalking you?"

"Nothing like that," I whispered.

"You look like a ghost," said Angie, grasping my elbow. "Let's go sit down."

"Call us if you have any more trouble," said the gray-haired cop. "Right now we're going to take another look around." Bernd trailed them as they headed to the woods behind the condo.

"Fine." I retreated to the front steps and

melted down. The Sebastians, who'd hovered just within earshot, came closer. The departmental pipeline would be pulsing tomorrow.

"How can we help?" Kristin asked.

"Everything's under control, thanks." I only wanted to hole up in my condo, alone. "Thanks so much for bringing me home."

"Are you sure?" asked Kristin. She bent down to touch my knee. "We can stay." Craig frowned and gave his head a tiny shake.

"We'd be happy to have you spend the night at our place," Kristin said, holding both hands out.

I took one and squeezed it. "You've already done too much. You've been very kind. Thanks for everything." I mustered a shaky smile. "See you at grand rounds next week, Craig." He hustled her into their Mercedes, sitting up tall to get a good view over the wheel.

The two cops and Bernd emerged from the backyard. "Definitely no one there now," said the older cop. "And we saw no signs of attempt to break and enter. With your permission, we'll secure the apartment."

After a short search, they returned with another negative report. The cruiser peeled out of my driveway, and Peter and Bernd escorted the twittering neighbor ladies home.

"I'll be back in a couple of minutes," Peter called over his shoulder, "to make sure you two are safe and sound."

"Not necessary," I said, but he waved me away.

"Phone if you need me," said Bernd. "Any time."

Angie followed me into the condo. I changed into sweats and washed my face while she put the teakettle on. I heard her let Peter in the front door and settle them both in the living room, then the low hum of their conversation.

Angie pushed a mug of chamomile tea across the coffee table when I came back into the room. She'd uncovered a stash of homemade peanut-butter cookies in my freezer, tucked away for emergencies. This definitely qualified. She glanced at Peter — they'd obviously been discussing me.

"Start from the beginning," Angie said. "What the hell is going on?"

I sank back into the couch and closed my eyes. "I'm so tired."

Peter patted my knee. "But we're worried. How about the short version?"

I sighed. "Harry wouldn't have come here.

I told you" — I lifted my chin at Angie — "I had a perfectly uneventful drink with him last night."

"He was the guy you were going to meet after the cocktail party?" Peter asked.

I nodded. "I talked with him a little about Madeline. I know I made it quite clear I wasn't interested in him. Not interested at all," I added firmly, deciding not to mention his invitation to Newport. Harry might be clueless, but he wasn't a stalker.

"Guys can be dense sometimes," said Peter, grinning. "Was he upset about how you left things?"

"Not at all." I crossed my arms over my chest.

"What was going on at the Stone House?" Angie asked. "Your message scared the crap out of me. I rushed over there — the receptionist said someone resembling you had just left . . ."

"Sorry." I pressed myself back into the couch again, tucking my knees to my chest. "Derek is the man who met Madeline at Fast Connections right before she died. He'd written several e-mails to her suggesting drinks. I figured I'd stop by the Stone House to see if he was there — maybe he could describe Madeline's state of mind before her death."

"Does she always bolt off half-cocked like this?" Peter asked Angie.

"Not at all," Angie answered. "She's conservative at heart. She tends to hash out every possibility before she makes the smallest move."

"Thanks a lot," I snapped. Then I rubbed my neck and yawned. Hard to take too much offense when Angie was basically right. "Derek had invited her to some kind of a naked erotic party. Obviously, he was disappointed when she didn't respond. So he asked me instead."

Angie's eyes popped wide. "He wanted you to go to a sex party?"

I felt my cheeks flush, not wanting to meet Peter's eyes. "Is it that farfetched?" I giggled. "I guess it is. Can you imagine? All those gorgeous twenty-somethings and then middle-aged me: bags, sags, and wrinkles on parade."

"Don't be ridiculous." Peter smiled. "I'm sure you'd be very popular."

"Thanks. I think."

"Do they pay to have sex at the party?" Angie asked. "That sounds illegal."

"Not if it's private, and consenting adults. As far as I know, no one gets paid — except for the person clever enough to organize the party. Derek said Madeline had an alternative blog where she posted about her erotic adventures. I think he was looking forward to a starring role."

"So she goes out with a guy and then tells all to her readers. Doesn't that embarrass the people involved?" asked Angie.

Peter shook his head, reaching for another cookie. "I must be hopelessly old-fashioned. The whole scene leaves me cold. And how do you face your coworkers and family after that?" He glanced at his watch and back to Angie. "Speaking of work, I have to get to bed — big deposition tomorrow. But how do we talk this one" — he patted my head — "into staying out of any further trouble?"

"I should never have agreed to do the syntactical analysis," said Angie. "I'm afraid I egged her on."

"You're starting to piss me off," I said. "Don't talk as though I'm not here — please. I have no intention of getting more involved. First thing on my list tomorrow is talk with Meigs." I made a face.

"He's the detective who came around the night they found Madeline's body?" asked Peter. "An interesting character." The lift in his voice suggested he would have said more if he wasn't so polite.

A grin split my face. They weren't much alike, Meigs a sloppy, gruff bear of a man who couldn't step lightly if he tried.

Angie yawned. "Call me after you speak to him, okay?"

After Peter saw Angie to her car, I circled through the rooms, checking locks on the windows for a third time and, finally, the deadbolts on the doors. Then I slid between the covers, Spencer draped across one thigh and the computer on the other. Finding the cops outside the condo had shaken me up, more than I'd wanted to show. I was beginning to feel like my patient Wendy, rattled by tiny noises, afraid of bogeymen in the shrubbery. The Stone House caper was even worse. What if the Sebastians hadn't been there?

I typed in the address for Madeline's website and scanned the graphics for the portal that Derek had described. A small pair of coral lips had been tucked into the bottom left corner of the homepage. Not lips exactly, but the kind of grainy imprint a pair of heavily colored lips might make if pressed onto a blank page. I clicked. The title of the new page was "Kiss and Tell."

In the lead entry, just days before her death, Madeline reported that she'd interviewed the young woman who was running erotic parties in the New Haven area. She was terribly excited about her own invitation to join. In fact, she'd already made her first visit. She had not waited for Derek at all.

Don't be shocked, Dear Readers! I was invited to the most amazingly erotic networking scene. Shhh — I whispered the password: "Roll down my garter." Then the door opened as though I were Alice in Wonderland — a wonderland of gorgeous undulating bodies and a sexual charge like I've never felt in my life. And did I meet Alice and Ted and Carol and Bob? No, but I met Dustin and Brittany and Sam. Sam of the wide shoulders and washboard abs and oh — must I tell you everything? Let me leave it this way: When Sam was bad, he was very, very bad.

Are you troubled, Dear Readers? Please don't be concerned! Women have spent so many years waiting on the sidelines to be clipped like rosebuds. Should we be the wrong color or just past prime, we're passed over and left to fade among the thorns. These parties give us women the chance to choose for ourselves and then blossom.

They empower our sexuality — and entre nous, *Dear Readers, mine needed a little boost.*

And then she'd posted photos. Slightly out of focus and no recognizable faces, but clear enough to bear true witness. Eighty-seven comments followed, posted from Madeline's Dear Readers — a hell of a lot more activity than I got after one of my advice columns. The thought of skimming them filled me with exhausted dread.

Had Madeline really attended this event? You can do a lot by manipulating digital photography these days. Maybe I was naive, but it seemed possible that this was all an elaborate fantasy. Why would a young woman go to a party like this? There were certainly some answers in the readers' comments. I was horrified to admit that Madeline's description had left me aroused. Her intention, I was sure.

But probe a little further into the possibilities: The possible humiliation, competition, mistrust, and even something as unsexy as a life-threatening disease. I shut the computer down and inhaled deep and slow, transferring my attention to Spencer's ears. He responded with a long stretch and a contented purr.

"I need sleep," I whispered to Spencer. "You, my royal friend, have the right idea."

CHAPTER 21

Before sunrise, I pulled on the same sweats I'd worn the day before and carried a travel mug of coffee down to the town dock. If Wednesdays are supposed to be a haven of rest and relaxation, yesterday was a bust. I collapsed at the picnic table by the jetty and rested my chin on my hands. A few fishermen had already settled in, waiting for bluefish to crash the glassy surface of the sound. A flock of gulls circled the abandoned red shack across the inlet, flapping to alight on the ridgeline.

I felt exhausted and depressed. After hours of ruminating in the dark last night, I'd switched on the light and revisited Madeline's alternative blog. She'd had individual sexual encounters with dozens of men over the last year — if you believed her reports — and unconsummated dates with even more. All of this had been recorded in elaborate and sometimes unflattering detail, though none came through quite so titillating as that final erotic party. And there were dozens of photos. The night before she died, she had posted an entry about being authentic.

Readers: Authenticity means refusing to carry on a charade. Princess Di was working on this and she was up against the Goddamn royal family of England! Come friends, sally forth and be real. Tell the truth in your heart and to your neighbors and family and friends. Even if one or two don't like it . . . or maybe especially . . .

In the accompanying photograph, she had posed like the famous painting of a woman nearing orgasm: naked from the waist up, her eyes half-lidded in pleasure, a pair of large square hands wearing a gold signet ring spread across her breasts. No end to this woman's narcissism. No wonder people were drawn to peep.

Reading this stuff made me squirm, even in the privacy of my own bedroom. I had never considered myself to be a prude, but maybe that image needed revision. When lovemaking functions as a competitive sport, what happens to intimacy between two people when the right time comes? Madeline would never find out.

I found myself getting hot — angry first about my description in her blog, then pissed about the way Madeline had pushed me into giving her phony advice. Subtle maybe, but she'd led me by the nose just the way she'd led those men. And her readers.

I hated to think about the young women who read her stories and got inspired. A steamy fantasy doesn't necessarily translate into a grand reality. In real life, you don't have the same control: Your partners may have a different idea of where the encounter is headed. Something rough or demeaning, for example. And what appears exciting at the time can evolve into feelings of emptiness and exploitation back home. Madeline didn't suggest that she'd felt anything but pleasure at the party. On the other hand, if you believe the official story, days later she'd committed suicide.

The more I thought about it, the more puzzled I grew. No way in hell I would attend a nude gathering. Who *would* go to a party like that? I'd caught just the tail end of the women's movement in college — I'd seen smart women fight long and hard to be able to say their bodies belonged to them; they weren't objects for the pleasure of strange men. No matter how the organizers spun it, the sex parties stunk of regression. Like prostitution or geishas or the resurgence of Barbie dolls with huge plastic boobs and feet permanently bent into the shape of spike heels — okay, maybe I was getting carried away. But the Barbies reminded me that I had to call Janice.

I got up and ambled home, wondering again how the men Madeline had featured in her blog felt about their exposure online. Given that hogwash about authenticity, chances were she boasted about her online chronicles in advance or even during sex. Some of her partners, like Derek, might have gravitated to her specifically for the chance to appear as stud of the day in her blog. Others, I was certain, would not be so thrilled.

After showering, I poured another cup of coffee and began to make notes: Lists of all the people I'd talked with, web addresses, theories, *Shore Line Times* articles, and random thoughts. Detective Meigs was going to get it all. I hated to leave Madeline's case in the hands of professionals who probably didn't give a rat's butt crack. But after a possible break-in, a man in the bushes, and more unsavory invitations than I'd ever had in my life, it was time to move on.

I stopped by Royal Printing on the way to

the police station and made copies of my notes and my faux psychiatric interview. Meigs would probably deliver all of this directly to his trashcan, but I'd feel better not holding anything back. I'd had enough scolding for a lifetime. Or at least for a week.

The dispatcher informed me that Detective Meigs had stepped out but was expected back shortly. He would see me then. I should park it. Not those words exactly, but I knew what she meant. Probably his day for the Dunkin' Donuts run. I glanced at my watch. Just nine — I had an hour until my first patient arrived. I'd wait fifteen minutes. Tops. I nodded curtly and began to pace the length of the waiting area.

The upper half of the door to the records office swung open. Would they allow me to see the official police record of Madeline's case? Maybe then I'd know exactly what convinced Meigs to close it. Maybe then when we talked, I could relate my doubts directly to his boneheaded reasoning.

I approached the clerk with a friendly smile. "How does a citizen go about obtaining the records on a case?"

"You can have anything you want if you're willing to pay," she said, rubbing the fingers on her right hand together. She had a toothy smile and a voice like the bark of a seal.

"One dollar a page."

"Would you mind locating the Madeline Stanton records?" I asked. "That's S-T-A-N-T-O-N." I drummed my fingers on the counter and watched her type the name into her computer.

"Sorry," she said, stepping back to the Dutch door. "I should have been more clear. You can only obtain a police report if the case is closed."

"This case is closed," I insisted.

She looked at me, then went back and glanced at the screen, shaking her head. "The Stanton case is still open." The words reverberated around the reception area.

How bizarre was that? The next name popped into my head. "Could you get me the records on Alice Meigs?"

"You want Alice Meigs?" the clerk bellowed, her head goosed back in surprise. I nodded.

"Can I help you?" Detective Meigs was suddenly standing next to me, so close I could smell the coffee on his breath and his minty aftershave.

"I was just asking when you'd be back," I lied desperately.

"You want the whole Meigs record printed? That'll come to twenty-nine dollars. It'll just take a minute," said the clerk.

"Never mind," I croaked, a great wave of embarrassment sweeping from face to chest and then weakening my knees. "I was just curious."

I stepped away from the counter without looking at Meigs. No reasonable cover story came to mind. Excellent. Now he'd believe I was looking up his wife's police report out of prurient curiosity.

Once Meigs had ushered me into his office, I attacked. "You told me the case was closed on Madeline Stanton."

"I told you to keep your nosy face out of police work," he snapped back.

"I guess I don't listen very well."

"That's an understatement."

I slapped my notes and the copy of the psychiatric report on his desk, along with a couple of pages I'd printed out from Madeline's blog.

"She wasn't what she seemed," I said. "She wasn't a depressed, closing-in-on-middle-age woman who sat home in the dark and waited for her prince to call." I had a sudden, uncomfortable awareness that this sounded like me. I pushed the blog entries toward him. "Why did you tell me the case was closed?"

"I don't suppose it occurred to you that we might know what we're doing? Maybe we'd like the perpetrator to think we bought the suicide theory while we're pursuing a lead?" He rocked back in the chair and crossed his arms over his chest.

I swallowed. "What perpetrator?"

He scowled and pulled a form off a messy stack of papers.

"About last night, let's take it from the top."

"Not much to tell. The neighbors spotted a guy in the shrubbery and called the cops. Your guys didn't find anyone there."

"My guys said it might have been someone you dated? Someone you met at Fast Connections?"

"That's a big leap," I said. "The ladies said he was short and balding. That describes half the shoreline's male population."

"Tell me about the man," Meigs said, not smiling at all.

I reviewed the few facts I knew about Harry: He frequented the speed-dating scene, he'd been interested in Madeline, but not she in him, and I'd had a drink with him on Tuesday.

"So why was he in your bushes?" Meigs asked sternly.

I was about ready to cry. "I doubt it was him."

"You reported a possible break-in on Saturday night. Same guy?"

"I can't see how that would work. I only met Harry on Friday and we didn't exchange any identifying information. Those were the speed-dating rules." I rustled through my purse, found a scrap of Kleenex, and blew my nose.

"You met him on Friday, someone breaks in on Saturday, you have a drink with him Tuesday, he's in your bushes on Wednesday. Do you see a pattern here?"

I was suddenly scared. Had I misjudged Harry that badly? I met Meigs's eyes and shrugged.

"You meet people in settings like that, you know nothing about them. And then you're surprised when something ugly happens," he said coldly. "What did you tell him about who you are?"

"I told him my name was Rebecca Aster and that I write an advice column."

I pictured the title for my next column: "Don't Believe the Policeman Is Your Friend." Peter was right even if he hadn't come right out and said it — Meigs was a horse's ass.

"And your address?"

"Of course not! Do you think I'm a fool?"

He leaned back and frowned. "Did he

know Ms. Stanton was a neighbor?"

I tried to remember exactly what I'd said. If I'd told him we were neighbors and he had her address, he could have easily tracked me down. But how would he have her address? According to Harry, they never went out. I was shaking now, furious with myself — and Meigs.

I tapped the papers I'd put on his desk. "Look, I wouldn't have expected trouble from Harry. The guy I met last night was a lot scarier. It's all in here — Madeline had quite an active imagination and an active sex life to match. Then she wrote about these adventures in her blog."

"And was your Harry in the blog?"

"He's not *my* Harry." I gulped in some air and let it slowly hiss out. "I don't think she ever had a date with him."

Meigs sighed. "Run it by me again. Why were you meeting one of Ms. Stanton's former boyfriends last night?"

"A hunch," I said. "Harry told me they seemed to really hit it off at Rudy V's at Fast Connections a couple of weeks ago. I just wanted to understand her. And to tell her mother I'd done everything I could." I patted the crumpled tissue to my eyes. "What will I tell her now?" A torrent of tears cut loose. Meigs reached behind him for a box of generic-brand tissues and pushed it over to me.

"You'll tell her you didn't find anything the police hadn't already covered." He glowered. "Do you understand, Dr. Butterman, that if you continue to bumble around, you could cost us any progress we've made on the case? Besides stirring up unsavory characters who end up in your landscaping?"

"Why were you lurking outside Fast Connections?" I asked him suddenly. "Can't find a date and too damn cheap to pay for the program?"

He laughed loudly. "You do have spunk, lady. I was following leads."

"Do you think Madeline Stanton was murdered?" I asked.

"When we arrest someone, we'll certainly let you know."

I doubted I'd be getting a personal call. I'd read about it in the Wednesday edition of the *Shore Line Times* along with everyone else in town.

Meigs lumbered to his feet. "Feel free to call us if you have any more trouble. We'll send a patrol around whenever we can."

He looked at me, eyes almost kind. He seemed about to say something — Take care of yourself? Be careful? But he didn't, and after a moment, I nodded and left.

CHAPTER 22

When I'd finished with my morning patients, I walked downtown for lunch with Annabelle Hart. She'd rented space in an old brownstone behind the fancy high-rise buildings on Ninth Square and filled her office with miniature water fountains bubbling over smooth rocks, bead curtains on the windows, and a wall of diminutive figurines, which her patients arrange on trays of sand.

We have a standing monthly lunch date. Sometimes we talk about my patients, sometimes hers, sometimes just the world gone mad. Annabelle opened her office door and waved me in. I settled into a comfy upholstered rocker, unwrapped my tuna on wheat toast with roasted peppers, and opened a small bag of Cape Cod potato chips.

"Do you mind listening to me ramble about my neighbor today?" I asked.

"You know I love a good mystery," said

Annabelle, her black eyes gleaming. "Is there something new with her case?"

I summarized what I'd learned. "My question still stands, did she kill herself or was she murdered?"

Annabelle bit into a carrot stick, her brows drawn together. "You were a neighbor of hers, though hardly intimate friends. And her mother sent you on this quest, right?"

I nodded.

She tucked her legs up under her flowing paisley skirt and began to braid her hair, her eyes fluttering closed. From our year of supervision, I knew enough to wait while she organized her questions. She blinked and tossed the braid over her shoulder.

"You tell me she shot herself in the bathtub. Statistically speaking, that's an unusual suicide method for a woman. Not impossible, just unusual."

"Right."

Women are quieter than men as they live their lives, and quieter when they take them too. A handful of pills, the silent seeping of blood from slit wrists, gas from the oven where they've cooked so many meals: These are the methods most women choose. I set my sandwich down and waited.

"Don't you have to wonder why this mother's pushing you into detective work?"

Annabelle asked. "I presume she knows you're a psychologist. What does she really want you to rule out? Suicide or murder?"

"She says suicide. She says she can't believe her daughter was that depressed. Possibly she's just feeling guilty that she didn't recognize the signs. But as Angie pointed out, would a mother want to know the intimate details of her daughter's life? Probably not, if it was the kind of creepy stuff I've discovered."

I pulled a copy of the mock psychiatric interview out of my bag and handed it over. Annabelle skimmed the pages.

"You don't have much family psychiatric history. Which could be key couldn't it, class?" She grinned. "You know the drill: Has anyone in her immediate family suffered from major depression, alcoholism, or bipolar illness?"

"I have no idea. Her parents were divorced a while back — not a friendly split. Trouble is, none of the relatives are willing to talk to me. At least not honestly."

"What about friends?"

I thought of all the faceless people who posted responses to both of her weblogs. "I haven't met any," I said. "None of the neighbors seemed close to her either."

"How long has she lived in your neck of

the woods?"

"Longer than me." Not that I was a reasonable marker for neighborly relations. If it hadn't been for the condo association meetings and Mrs. Dunbarton's intrusiveness, I wouldn't have had anything to do with the neighborhood. "Attendance at the memorial service was sparse too."

"An empty room?"

I pictured the soaring ceiling of the meeting room at Evergreen Woods and the chairs filled with elderly residents. I remembered being slightly surprised about all of it — that the service wasn't held in a church, or even the chapel. And that the Guilford minister had been imported to preside. And that a pack of shocked young people hadn't come to mourn. The death of someone under fifty usually draws a crowd.

"Immediate family and some folks from the assisted-living facility. That's pretty much it. Oh, and a man who worked with her," I remembered. "I could try contacting him."

"How long did you say the family had lived in town?" Annabelle asked.

"Forever," I said slowly. "Generations. I see what you're getting at. The service should have been mobbed. Though Isabel did tell me she hadn't filed an obituary.

Still, word of mouth . . ."

Annabelle turned her attention back to my typed interview, flipped to the second page, then suddenly looked up. "You gave this to the cops?"

"Yeah."

She read aloud. "Annoying local detective informed Isabel that the death was a suicide, confirmed by regretful note conveniently left on the victim's laptop."

I clapped my hand to my mouth. "I totally forgot that."

She raised her eyebrows. Neither one of us much believes in psychological accidents. The unconscious is *always* at work behind the scenes, setting up echoes from the past to the present.

I snickered. "Actually, it could have been a hell of a lot more unflattering than that. He's a pain in the ass. And his wife's in some kind of legal trouble."

"And you? Are you all right?" She was staring at me now.

"I'm fine," I said.

"Your outing with the Sebastians ran through the department this morning like a flu virus."

I blushed. "Those prying buggers should mind their own business."

"What does Goldman say?" Annabelle asked.

It had been over a week since I'd thought about my therapist. "He's on vacation for a month."

She tapped her pursed lips. A nonaccident again.

"Could it be that you're acting out, darling? Punishing the good Dr. Goldman for going away?"

"Maybe," I said. "But what was I supposed to do, ignore this woman? I'd already done that to her daughter."

"I think you did just the right thing — turning everything over to the police, I mean," said Annabelle firmly. She wrapped up the remnants of her lunch, stuffed them into a paper bag, and carried them to a trashcan outside the office door. Nothing worse than smelling tuna fish and old onions while spilling your guts onto a sand tray.

"But that's not the expert opinion you wanted, is it?" she said, coming back in and pulling the door closed behind her. She smiled. "The girl's sexual acting out was very pronounced. The trouble with our voyeuristic culture is that no one's shocked by this sort of thing anymore. Reality shows, plastic surgery makeovers, confessions in front of Dr. Phil — anything's fair game." She curled back into her chair. "But it's not normal, Rebecca, having sex with so many different people and then reporting it to the world. If she was telling the truth, it makes one wonder about trauma and repetition, doesn't it?"

"Exactly," I said, leaning forward to rake a ridge smooth in the sand tray next to my chair. "I keep thinking about her Princess Diana fixation too."

"Check out the literature on narcissistic exhibitionism." Annabelle sat back and gazed at the ceiling. "If you had her in therapy," she said dreamily, "I'd advise you to learn what she's repeating. What's buried in her past that set her up for this kind of acting out? What did she see? What did she experience? Follow the trauma." She shook her head and smiled. "I don't mean that literally, of course. You've very wisely turned the job back over to the annoying cop. Where it belongs." We both rose and she folded me into a lavender-scented hug. "Be cautious and sensible, my friend."

I hurried back across the New Haven green, kicking brightly colored leaves off the sidewalk as I went. If I hadn't just eaten, I would have stopped for a grilled hot dog smothered in onions and sauerkraut from the stand on the corner, it smelled that good. My cell phone rang, saving me from the small temptation.

Meigs.

"It's okay if you keep thinking," he said.

"Excuse me?" I said coldly, certain this was an insult.

"I read through your notes. Your ideas aren't bad. They're not right, but not bad. So feel free to call me if you think of anything else." And he hung up.

I mulled that one over, pleased by the faint compliment but still blistered by our earlier conversation. Was this different than what Meigs would tell any random witness? *Call me if anything comes to mind.* Probably not.

Which reminded me of the humiliating scene in which he materialized in the hallway while I was trying to weasel Alice Meigs's records from the clerk. I was terribly curious about his wife's problem but could see no way to pursue it. Phone the *Shore Line Times* to find out who had been the officer on the scene? Then what? Call the guy and ask about Alice? With my luck, his office would be situated directly across the hall from Meigs.

"Hey Meigsy, there's a shrink on the phone who has a jones for your wife."

The phone rang again as I climbed the

stairs to my office. I checked the screen — not a number I recognized. Possibly a new referral, though I prefer to get those calls on my office line. Anyway, I felt tired and tapped out, not in the inquisitive, empathic mood needed to take on an unknown patient. A therapy prospect is usually in some serious psychic discomfort — it takes that to overcome the shame and fear of paying a stranger to listen.

"Hello?" I said, my voice not altogether welcoming.

"Dr. Butterman?"

"Yes." I sighed.

"This is Lorena Stanton, William's wife? Madeline's stepmother?"

That woke me right up.

"I heard your message on the answering machine. Then William told me you'd called again, and — well, it sounds to me like he was very rude. I apologize for that. I'm afraid all this has been a terrible shock."

"No problem," I said. "I certainly understand. So very sorry for your loss."

"Yes, well. As you might imagine, Madeline and I were not close." She sniffled. "I wanted to call you because I very much doubt anyone else in that family has bothered to tell you the truth."

I made sympathetic "please continue"

noises. Odd to hear from her, but after that start, I certainly wasn't going to cut her off.

"William and I met when Madeline was a young teenager," she said. "I was waitressing at the Guilford Tavern, and he came in for drinks from time to time. I'm a good listener," she added in a breathy voice. "He loved talking to me. Isabel didn't have the time. His sons were wild by then — we're both surprised they turned out as well as they did. And Madeline was a handful too."

"Not quiet and shy?" I asked, thinking about her mother's description.

"Quiet, yes, but in a sullen kind of way. He worried about her a lot." She sighed. "Then we fell in love. He told Isabel he wanted a divorce, but she was insanely jealous. She pressured him financially. The business had been in her family for generations, but it had performed poorly for years. William turned that around. She threatened to leave him penniless."

"Sounds awful," I said, thinking she wasn't so much a good listener as a good talker. Why tell me all this?

"Their marriage was over — she knew that. He moved into the apartment over her garage instead of coming to be with me because he didn't want to lose everything — including his kids."

"Things can really turn ugly in that kind of situation," I suggested.

"It took years for him to get up the nerve to move on with his life and propose," Lorena informed me. "Then everything went downhill fast. Isabel threatened to cut Madeline out of her inheritance if she attended the wedding. God knows what else she told her about me, but Madeline never wanted anything much to do with either one of us after that."

"She was that unhappy about the wedding?"

"Her mother was unhappy. Madeline was practically an adult by then — she understood that divorce is common and sometimes necessary. But everyone does what Isabel wants." She cleared her throat. "Isabel insisted that I'd broken them up."

"What about the boys?"

"The boys?"

"Did they come to the wedding?"

"Isabel spoiled it for us," she said after a minute. "We ended up eloping." Heavy breathing. "Did you tell my husband you're a psychologist?"

"Yes. I —"

"You probably don't need me to tell you what went wrong. It was hell for William moving into Isabel's little hometown, Isabel's family business . . . with me, he felt like a man." Her voice trembled, insistent and yet unsure.

"I hope things have gone well for you since," I said. "Nothing harder than lugging the baggage of the first marriage into your own."

The long pause told me what I needed to know.

"You shouldn't bother contacting William again," Lorena finally said. "Once he's clammed up on a subject, there's nothing else to learn." Her voice broke. "First that woman blames him for Steven's problem. Now the poor guy's torn up by Madeline's death. And not having the chance to attend her funeral . . . Hard to know how he'll pick up the pieces and move on."

She said good-bye and hung up before I could suggest that a reputable therapist might be a good place to start. When a therapy patient tells me there's no point in going down one alley, I highlight that alley on the map. We'll be visiting again to find out why. If Isabel had taken a harsh stance declaring William persona non grata at the memorial service, there had to be a better reason than an old divorce-related grudge. And what was Steven's problem?

I powered up my computer and typed *Wil-*

cox Metal Works into the Google search bar. Among others, an article surfaced from a New Haven industry news magazine. Ten years ago, William Stanton had filed suit for ownership of 50 percent of the business. Six months later, a short article reported that the lawsuit had been settled. Then I typed Steven Stanton into the search bar. Nothing interesting at all.

I dug the card out of my wallet that the skinny young man had given me at Madeline's funeral. Webflight Enterprises was a local number.

"Paul Petrie," a man's voice answered.

Once we'd established that we'd met at the service, I kept my explanation for calling brief and poignant: Madeline's mother was frantic to know why her daughter might have killed herself.

"I really can't say," he answered. "Honestly, she hadn't worked here that long and we weren't close friends."

"So no problems that you were aware of?" I waited.

"Okay, I think she was mad at her brother." He cleared his throat. "You won't tell them where this came from?"

"Absolutely not. Which brother?"

"The younger. He came by the week before she died and they had a pretty good fight. He wanted her to sell her shares of the family business at a deep discount. 'Why should we do all the work and take the risks and you reap the profits?' he asked her."

"What did she say?"

"She closed the door to her office and that's all I heard."

I thanked him for his time and wished him luck. The phone rang as soon as I hung up. I groaned — so much for my plan to get a jumpstart on the column and finish the dating article.

Mark didn't bother with a greeting. "I saw Craig Sebastian at rounds this morning. He said you intruded on their dinner and then he had to drive you home. For God's sake, Rebecca, are you out of your mind? How much are you drinking?"

"Just a damn minute, Mr. High-and-Mighty. First of all, this is not your business. Second, did it ever occur to you that Craig Sebastian hates my guts and might twist his story around?"

"Explain," he said coldly.

Which pissed me off all over, but I forced myself to calm down. I gave him a white-washed version of running into a guy in the bar whose intentions I didn't trust and an unrelated neighborhood incident at home.

"I've told you about those neighbor ladies.

They call the cops when they don't recognize the substitute mailman."

"That's not what Craig said. He said there was a man in your yard stalking you from an Internet dating service. For God's sake, Rebecca, can't you discuss these things with Goldman before you go off half-cocked? Isn't that why I'm paying him?"

For an instant I was speechless. "Why *you're* paying him?"

"That's what the divorce papers specified," he spat back. "You needed funds for rehabilitative alimony to cover your therapist's expenses."

My lawyer had insisted on that language. I hated it, but I'd been too upset to argue. And I did need the dough.

"He's on vacation," I said with as much dignity as I could muster and clicked the phone off. Which was not nearly as satisfying as the old-fashioned method of slamming down the receiver.

I burst into tears and called Angie.

"This is exactly why you divorced him," she said once I wound up my tirade. "He's a typical psychiatrist. Irritating, overbearing, insufferable, and certain he's always right."

"I divorced him because his answer to a rough patch in our marriage was to screw another woman."

"Same thing," said Angie, laughing. "I'm sure he's worried about you. I am too. But tell him to keep his fat head out of your business next time."

"Already did," I said, starting to feel a little better.

CHAPTER 23

Annoying as it was to have both Annabelle and Mark pointing out my reliance on Dr. Goldman, those sessions help me keep the strands of my own history separate from my patients' issues. Every therapist has the obligation to understand herself as completely as possible. With Goldman on vacation for just over a week, was I wandering into dangerous territory without even realizing that I'd left the road?

There was certainly more to learn about William Stanton. Maybe Steven too. And I was intrigued by Meigs's call. But for my own good, it was time to tell Isabel I was finished snooping. I'd volunteer the names of some therapists experienced in grief counseling. And the dates and times of parent support groups in the area. I would not offer to attend — one of her sons should step up. Better still, I'd tell her that Yale New Haven Hospital could provide information about the groups, as well as her own doctor. Someone else would have to hold her hand while she dialed the phone. That sounded harsh, but better for both of us in the end.

I packed up my computer and papers and headed for my car, wondering what to cook for dinner. The paper this morning had predicted an unusually early frost, which brought to mind vegetable soup and cheddar scones.

Should I warn Isabel I was coming? I decided not. If she wasn't there, I'd leave a message asking her to call. If she was, I'd catch her off guard for our final conversation. I took exit 55 off the highway and turned onto Route 1 toward Evergreen Woods, relieved at the prospect of getting this business over and done with.

Inside the facility's fancy reception area, a spidery-thin, trembling woman in a forest green pantsuit greeted me and phoned Isabel from the front desk. She clattered the handset into the receiver and offered a shaky smile. "She'll be right down." Ten minutes later, Isabel fluttered into the room.

"Dr. Rebecca Butterman, what a nice surprise!" She leaned forward for an air kiss and beckoned me back the way she'd come. As we passed through the carpeted corridors to the far end of the complex, she chatted about the latest scandals — whose wheelchair blocked egress to the fire escape, who brought their own flasks to dinner on no-alcohol Sundays, and most fascinating of all, who was caught coming out of whose apartment before dawn.

"Probably just borrowing their newspaper." She chuckled.

We climbed three flights of stairs — no elevators for Isabel until her legs gave out completely, she told me — and she unlocked the door to apartment 310.

"Welcome to what now passes for home." She flashed a chagrined smile.

It wasn't at all institutional, as I'd expected. The walls of the hall and the living room were hung with original watercolors and a stunning Oriental carpet covered the floor. Antiques and stone sculptures crowded the living room, which was lined with floor-to-ceiling bookshelves.

Isabel smiled again, seeming to recognize my astonishment. "They bring the most amazing small art exhibits to this place. Besides, it wasn't easy downsizing from thirty years in an old Colonial to this place. The sculptures were my hobby." She looked sad.

"The rug is remarkable," I said. "You

don't often see colors that intense."

"Handwoven by a co-op of Persian women," Isabel said. "Madeline loved them too. I gave her the two small ones that matched this one exactly." She frowned. "I noticed that the smallest has gone missing. I hope she didn't give it to one of her flaky friends. That would be just like her."

"It's a lovely home," I said, meaning it. "I came to tell you I've done everything I could to find out what happened to Madeline. It's probably not what you'd hoped for, but I did try."

"I'll make some tea," she said.

"I can't stay —"

"Sit, sit," said Isabel, touching my shoulder and pointing to the couch. "I'll put the kettle on. Perhaps you'll change your mind."

I sank down onto the couch. While she puttered in the kitchen, I tried to organize my thoughts. It was much easier to list what I wouldn't say: that her son had warned me off the investigation; that her daughter had been involved in a secret life, promiscuous and wild; that her ex-husband's wife blamed the family's troubles on Isabel's insistence on control. And that Meigs might have been setting a trap for a killer by publicly accepting the suicide — though, whether the local cops had the skill to pull this off was another question. I'd stick with the psychological material that was rightfully my department.

Isabel returned bearing a teapot, two cups, and a plate of chocolate-chip cookies on a painted tray. She slid the tray onto a wrought-iron end table and perched on the fringed hassock nearby to pour.

"I got the sense that Madeline was not so much depressed as a little melancholy," I said. "As with all of us, history takes its toll. I believe she was sad about her father and somewhat lonely. But without Madeline here to speak for herself, there's simply no answer to the most painful question — 'Why did this happen?' "

Isabel's eyes filled with tears. She poured tea, spilling as much liquid in the saucers as into the cups.

"This must be so hard for you," I continued. "But I've concluded that I can't help. I wish I could." I transferred to the footstool closer to her and patted her knee. "I'm terribly sorry." I extracted a square of paper from my pocket. "Here are the names of two therapists I trust. I think you'd like working with either one of them."

Isabel pushed her chin out, looking as though she wanted to argue.

"If you're not ready for individual therapy,

there are support groups available for parents who've lost a child. You'll have the opportunity to talk with folks who have suffered similar losses. Online if you'd rather, or here in the area." I stood up. This was going horribly. "Your doctor will have referrals."

"You won't help me," she said slowly.

"I can't," I repeated. "I'm not a detective. And you can't be my patient. Even if you wanted," I added quickly. "Too many complications. I'm sorry. Time will help. Grieving a loss like this takes time."

She gave her head a little shake and gestured at the steaming cups. "You'll have some tea before you go."

I couldn't just leave. With a sigh, I sat back down on the couch. We sipped the tea in silence, my mind whirring with all I knew and all I didn't. "May I ask one question?"

Isabel cocked her head hopefully.

"Where was Spencer when the police came into the apartment? Just out of curiosity."

"The cat?" Isabel looked perplexed.

"He seems a little nervous," I explained. "I just wondered how much he saw. How long he was with her after she died."

Tears washed Isabel's eyes. Feeling stupid and cruel, I flashed on an image of Spencer picking his way around Madeline's dead body. Why had I brought up the traumatized cat?

"He was under the bed when I arrived." She sniffled. "It took a bowl of milk to lure him out."

The next question also burst out unplanned. "Are you quite sure that the gun in question did not belong to Madeline?"

"That would surprise me." Isabel set her cup on the tray and dabbed at her mouth with a napkin. "But obviously, there was a great deal I didn't know about my daughter."

"Just out of curiosity" — I winced inwardly, hearing myself use that stupid phrase again — "do your boys own guns?"

Isabel shrugged. "The boys are not sportsmen." She looked up and frowned. "It certainly didn't belong to me."

Which hadn't crossed my mind. "I didn't get to meet any of Madeline's friends at the memorial service," I said, pausing to see how she would explain the fact that so few turned up to mourn a death in such a well-known family, with generations of local roots.

"We decided to keep it quiet. Her passing was such a shock, you understand. It seemed so important to have private family time." She grimaced and spread out her hands. "Private is all relative in a place like this. You can't really keep the old codgers out — they gather because they're lonely. And I think somehow it helps get them ready for what's to come, you know?"

A loud bang on the door startled both of us. I heard a key scraping in the lock and Isabel's younger son, Tom, burst in, stopping short when he saw me.

"I'm sorry, Mother. I didn't know you were . . . expecting company." He looked harried and annoyed.

"I'm just leaving," I said. "Stopped in to check on your mother. Hope you don't mind, but I brought the names of a couple of therapists I trust." Isabel might be more likely to follow through with pressure from her family.

She smiled weakly at her son. "Stantons aren't very good at that sort of thing, are we, dear?"

"Can I have a word?" Tom asked his mother.

I stood, picking up my purse. "I'll show myself out," I said, and started toward the door.

"This will take just a minute," Tom said to me. "Wait here and I'll walk you down." He grasped Isabel's arm and propelled her toward the back bedroom.

What did he want from me? I paced the foyer, feeling irritated with the Stantons in general, Tom in particular. And Isabel too. Why did I feel like I'd just emerged from a sappy movie — manipulated and wrung out?

I'd come to inform her I was "off the case." So why was I behaving as though I was a member of the investigation team, observing her like a prosecuting attorney choosing a jury: tics, twitches, involuntary winks, anything that might suggest a lie?

I stepped over to the bookshelf to admire a highly polished green marble oval, trying to block out the raised voices echoing down the hall. Family pictures were arranged on the shelf at eye level, including another shot of Madeline with a girlfriend. This time the girl's face was clear — recognizable even with fifteen or twenty years gone by. I knocked my fist lightly against my forehead. It was Pammy — Steven's wife — who had been her best friend.

Tom emerged from the bedroom, still frowning. Isabel stayed behind.

"She's exhausted. She sends her apologies. Shall we?" He opened the door and motioned me through. Downstairs, the heavy outer door whooshed closed behind us. He turned to face me on the sidewalk, pale and tense, arms crossed and legs spread wide.

"This family needs to move on."

"I came here to tell your mother the same thing."

He looked at me warily.

"A suicide is such a harsh blow," I continued. I was pretty sure Madeline hadn't killed herself, but what did Tom think? "You're always wondering what you missed, what you could have done, whether part of the fault was yours."

"Madeline made her own bed," Tom said, then added quickly, "Not that she deserved to die. But I'm not in favor of falling on our collective swords by spreading blame. We have enough trouble managing the business together without pointing fingers."

"Working together as a family is very challenging," I agreed. "Especially when you move past the founding generation. A tragedy like this one could tear even the strongest family apart."

He cleared his throat, his Adam's apple bobbing. "You've heard the saying about how you can't choose your relatives?"

I nodded. "Of course."

"You have to stick with your family. Even in the low times. Mother believes that and I do too." He squared his shoulders and ran both hands through his thick, bushy hair. "Once you start down a path, you need to keep on." His shoulders sagged.

Who was Tom was protecting? "You and Steven both work in the business. Why not Madeline?"

"Her choice," Tom said. "She found her brothers stuffy and the work itself dull."

"Hard to always play the little sister," I said with a smile.

But Tom bristled. "There were money issues too. How are two family members supposed to feel good about working their asses off and turning the profits over to the third?" He stopped speaking and stepped back.

"Anyway, thanks for your concern," Tom said. "We'll be over on the weekend to clear out the rest of Madeline's stuff. And the cat. One of Steven's neighbors has agreed to take him on. Hopefully I've talked mother into staying home."

I nodded, my throat suddenly too constricted to speak, and walked quickly to the car. I wasn't crazy about this man, even before he mentioned taking Spencer. I slammed the gearshift into reverse, nearly sideswiping a mint late-eighties Cadillac in my rush to leave.

I never should have taken the damn cat.
You don't miss what you never had.

CHAPTER 24

Babette Finster tottered out of the clubhouse shadows towing Wilson, her plaid-coated white rat-dog, as I navigated down Soundside toward home. I put the car in *park* and got out to join her by the mailboxes. She snatched up the quivering Wilson, who was shaved almost bald except for a mushroom of ringlets on his head, and squeezed him until he yelped.

"Good evening," I said. "It sure got chilly fast. At least your dog looks warm." I reached out to pat his tartan sweater. He snarled and tried to lunge at my fingers. I jerked them back.

"Wilson!" Babette scolded. "Don't bite the doctor." She hugged the dog to her neck. "We're both a little on edge."

I smiled reassuringly. "Everything okay around here?"

"I think so," she stammered. "The police have driven through twice today." Her eyes glistened. "I've been trying and trying to remember who else I might have seen going into Madeline's apartment. That detective left me feeling like I was letting everyone down because I couldn't come up with the right answers. Do you really think she was murdered, like Mrs. Dunbarton said? I'm so nervous, it makes it hard to remember anything at all. I feel like my memory is leaking away."

Now she was shaking as hard as her dog. Bernd Becker rounded the corner of the clubhouse carrying a ladder, causing Babette to startle and squawk.

"Oh Lord, I'm a wreck!" she said.

"It's only me," said Bernd. "Weatherman's predicting rain and a hard frost, so I got those gutters cleared out today. Can't risk the pipes clogging up and ruining the paint."

I nodded and smiled. Hiring Bernd had been an association high point: If the maintenance was left to the condo's inhabitants, the place would fall down around our ears. Cliché, but he had our condo complex ticking like a damn Swiss clock.

"I'll need to get into your apartments tomorrow to caulk around the sliders. Any time not convenient?"

"I'll shut Wilson in the bathroom when I leave," said Babette, planting a loud smooch on the dog's head. "Don't wet the wittle wascal out."

I grimaced. Rat-dog baby talk. "Any time is fine. I'll be at work until late afternoon."

Bernd swung the ladder over his shoulder and onto his Volvo station wagon's roof rack. I squinted at Babette, wondering if she really could fill in important details about Madeline's visitors. Easy to overlook such a major basket case. What else might she have registered last night about the man in the bushes? Would she talk more freely out from under Mrs. Dunbarton's critical eye? Assuming I could calm her down . . .

"Would you like to come in for a cup of tea and a cookie? It's not such a nice night to be alone."

Babette smiled tremulously, gold crowns sparkling in the reflected light of the club-house spotlight. "Thank you anyway. I have dinner in the oven. And now that Wilson's done his business," she cooed at him in a high voice, "we're on our way home." Wilson licked her neck.

"Well, don't worry about your memory," I said. "Most people retain more details about traumatic events than they remember right away. Information gets lost in the confusion, especially if you're upset and anxious, but it comes back over time. If something new pops up, you should definitely call Detective Meigs."

"That man scares me," she said. "I'd call Bernd or Peter Morgan. He's been so very kind. I told him this morning, I just don't think the man in Dr. Butterman's bushes was as short as Edith thinks he was. And I'm not so sure about his hair now either."

"That's fine," I said, "but call the detective too. He's not so bad once you get to know him." Ha. I nodded reassuringly. "One more tip: If you're having trouble remembering something, it can help to visualize what happened earlier in the day — what you had for lunch, when you walked Wilson, maybe a TV show you watched. As you imagine those details, the rest might get clear too."

I doubted very much that she'd recall anything new, but maybe a concrete suggestion would help her feel a little more in control. Bernd finished tying off the ladder and climbed into his car.

"Good night, ladies. I'll see you again tomorrow." He tipped an imaginary hat and drove away.

Babette took two steps back and shook her head. "This has gotten me so upset," she whispered hoarsely. "Madeline was deceased right in the next apartment and I didn't know a thing."

"I understand." Boy, did I understand. I started to lay a comforting hand on her shoulder, but pulled it back when Wilson bared his teeth.

"Good night." Babette waved one of her dog's skinny white paws at me and scuttled off.

I pulled my mail out of the mailbox, got into the car, and drove back to my driveway and into the garage. Babette's nervousness was infectious. I decided to tour the outside of my apartment while the shimmering pink sunset provided some light. Why in the name of God would Harry have been in my bushes? I simply couldn't believe it was him. Made no sense whatsoever — he seemed harmless. Even if he wasn't, I hadn't shown enough of myself to become the focal point of his obsession.

I circled around to the back deck, kicking through fallen leaves and into the shrubbery. Looking for what? Cigarette butts stained with the killer's DNA? Give it up, Rebecca. Through the adjoining glass of Madeline's bedroom slider, I noticed more boxes packed with my neighbor's stuff. Videotapes, mostly, from what I could see, Diana's wedding on top.

Inside, I scooped up Spencer, gave him a

gentle squeeze, and let him go, surprised to feel near tears. He followed me as I checked the locks on all doors and windows, alternately meowing and purring to drooling. I filled his bowl with kibble and shredded chicken, and let his tail drift through my fingers while he began to eat.

Turning away quickly, I pulled up the cornmeal-cheddar scone recipe on my computer and turned on NPR's *All Things Considered.* I whisked together cornmeal, flour, and baking powder with cayenne pepper, then cut in butter and cheese. I kneaded the dough gently and patted it into a round. The phone rang while the scones were in the oven and a quart of vegetable soup from the freezer bubbled on low.

It was Jillian, pressing for progress on the dating article.

"I can't write —" I started.

"No, no, darling, don't even start that. We've been whetting the readers' appetites for this installment all week long. It doesn't have to be a masterpiece. Just dash it off and send it on. We can tweak later."

Without the truth or a more exaggerated version, she wouldn't let up.

"Listen," I pleaded. "The cops wrestled the guy I dated out of my hydrangeas last night."

"Gawd, you're joking!" Jillian squealed.

"And the man my neighbor fell for from Fast Connections turns out to be a voyeur involved in the sex-party scene. Is this what our readers want to hear about? If they decide to attend one of these things and it goes bad, you could get lawsuits and God know what else."

"Hmm," Jillian mused. "Maybe it would bump our sales figures." A peal of laughter. "I'm kidding, of course. But what about all the couples that are getting engaged after meeting online?"

We agreed to compromise: I would draft the article and take the night to think it over. She'd call me back tomorrow to check in (read: nag). I sat down to supper with the *Shore Line Times* open on the table. Today's front-page controversy involved opposition to a proposed bed-and-breakfast in a residential neighborhood; concerned residents petitioned that it would attract Internet strangers and pedophiles. Small-minded, yes. But now I could relate to that kind of fear.

Janice called while I was washing the dishes.

"Where've you been?" she demanded. "I was about to get in my car and drive over. I was beginning to think you'd died."

"Sorry," I said.

Normal people don't jump to that kind of conclusion, but I was sympathetic and guilty. I felt jumpy too.

"I've been swamped. Can we get together for dinner on Sunday? Just us girls? You choose the place." We chatted for a few more minutes about my niece, the cancellation of Meals on Wheels ("Don't they think we have poor people in Madison?"), and my brother-in-law's overbooked travel schedule.

"Janice," I said, as she was about to hang up, "do you ever think about looking for Dad?"

Dad. We'd only seen him a handful of times since adolescence — I'd spent the remaining years pushing the thought of him away. Even saying the name aloud felt odd.

She didn't hesitate. "Why? Brittany has a grandfather she loves, who loves her back. How would I explain a strange man showing up at this point in her life? She'd have no use for him, Rebecca. Have a good night — I'll talk to you later." It was always about Brittany for Janice — she carries her daughter's needs with her like an impermeable shield.

I washed my face, pulled on flannel pajamas, and got into bed with Spencer and the laptop. I typed "narcissistic exhibitionism" into the Google toolbar and ran my hand over Spencer's belly while the results loaded. He sighed and stretched, extending and retracting his claws.

I switched my attention back to the screen. Why do people in my field feel the need to couch their theories in unintelligible jargon? My head was spinning with phrases like "shoring up breaches in self-cohesiveness" and "sex as an instrument to increase the sources of narcissistic supply." I'd never submit a column on this crazy subject, but sometimes just drafting answers to my own questions helps me sort things out. I started with Madeline's pretend concern.

Dear Dr. Aster:
I love my boyfriend deeply. In fact, I hope we'll spend the rest of our lives together. But just lately, he's gotten interested in the erotic party scene. He says he wants to include me in this — the idea of us attending together really turns him on. He says I should loosen up and let my inhibitions go.
First of all, I'm not so sure this is for me. And second, I'm not sure I want to see all this reported in his blog. Can you help?
Sincerely,
Prudish in Providence

Dear Prudish:

You'll need to trust your gut on this one. It could be that your boyfriend is encouraging you to expand your horizons in a positive way. As long as you're consenting adults, it's okay to let go and be playful — in the context of a safe and loving relationship.

That's what I remembered telling Madeline.

But on the famous other hand, if your boyfriend's requests feel wrong, you owe it to yourself to decline. You two may need to address some important issues before a healthy relationship is possible. For example, professionals sometimes refer to sex in the kind of group situations you're describing as "emotionally neutral." In other words, it's very difficult to maintain a deep emotional connection to one person at a sex party. If your boyfriend tends to prefer this kind of sexual experience, he may have a problem with his own self-esteem. Not to mention his ability to maintain the quiet and steady attention that a one-on-one relationship requires. And that's going to cost you in the long run.

As for blogging about private matters, may I show my old-fashioned streak by saying I just don't get it? I concede that we live in a voyeuristic culture that encourages us to "bare it all" in public. But do ask yourself what it means that your boyfriend needs to see this most private of human activities reflected in the public eye. Good luck and be careful!

Bottom line? Someone who blogged about her sexual adventures and got a kick out of group sex scenes had a serious screw loose, in my mind. Somewhere in her childhood, Madeline didn't receive the attention she needed to develop a healthy sense of herself. But why? Was Isabel too focused on the business? Too controlling? What about William? I clicked on another link — a study that concluded women who developed narcissistic traits as children were more vulnerable to sexual exploitation as adults. And I remembered Annabelle's advice: If she were your patient, you would follow her trauma.

But she's not.

I shut down the computer and flicked on the TV, shuttling from channel to channel but finding nothing worth watching. Spencer was cleaning himself, inch by inch, licking his paw and stroking it over the areas of fur he couldn't reach with his tongue. Then he settled into a fold in the down comforter, resting his head on my leg and stacking one paw on top of the other.

I pictured him sniffing around Madeline's body. He was fastidious, affectionate, loyal, and curious. How would he have reacted to being shut in the house with his dead mother? He would surely have been worried in his own feline way. And hungry. I tried to remember if I'd seen him in the window over the two days that Madeline had been dead. Why hadn't I noticed? I turned out the light and snuggled under the covers, reaching down to stroke him.

Meigs had mentioned the cops laying a trap for the killer. He hadn't spelled it out that way exactly, but what other interpretation could there be? If the suicide theory was the bait, who was the mouse? Isabel? Or . . . Tom? Or Steven? Ridiculous — as odd as I found it that both her brothers had instructed me to quit nosing around, I had no good reason to suspect Madeline's own family. More likely one of the loonies she met at a sex party.

Outside, the wind picked up into a low moaning whistle that rattled the slider doors. And then I heard a faint yapping. Had Babette Finster's little rat-dog cornered a possum? I chuckled, picturing Wilson in his jacket, bouncing around a hissing rodent — or something much smaller, more likely. After lying there listening to it for half an hour, I concluded that the barking was not going to stop. If anything, the cries were growing more urgent. I rolled over, switched the light back on, and called Babette. No answer. Very odd; Babette was never out this late. Had Wilson run away? Was my neighbor frantically searching the dark woods for her precious baby?

You're not going out there alone, Rebecca.

So what? Call the cops about a barking dog? I pulled on Mark's old bathrobe, a faded navy terrycloth that I loved but he'd hardly worn. Which made it okay to hide in the bottom of my suitcase the day I was packing to leave home. I padded to the living room and looked out at the other condo units. Peter Morgan's lights were still blazing. I dialed his number and explained.

"I'll come right over," he said. "Bring your flashlight and your cell phone. We'll call for reinforcements if needed." He laughed. "And I don't mean Mrs. Dunbarton."

CHAPTER 25

After snapping on every light in the house, I pulled my raincoat over the bathrobe and went out through the garage. Peter's flashlight bobbed down my driveway and his smile gleamed in the reflected floodlight. He wore freshly pressed jeans and a navy wool blazer. I smelled whiskey on his breath as he circled his arm around my shoulders and squeezed.

"I'm glad you called —"

"Listen." I stiffened, my hand on his arm. The faint yapping started up again, echoing from the woods behind the clubhouse. "Should we call the cops now?"

"If we need to. Let's find out what we're dealing with first." He strode around the back of the condo and into the brush, holding branches back and pointing out areas of uneven turf. The chop of the surf pounded in the distance. It was cold, pitch dark, and starting to mist — Bernd Becker's weather forecast to a tee. In my current state of dread, Mrs. Dunbarton's project, the prison spotlights, was beginning to seem like a damn good idea. Next association meeting, I'd propose we install enough lights to cover the woods as well as the lawn. The slick rubber soles of my slippers lost traction on a patch of wet leaves. My knee twisted and I went down, cursing.

Peter hurried back and reached out a hand to haul me up. "Are you hurt?"

I brushed dirt and rotting leaves off my knees and shins and shook my head. "Just clumsy."

We crept forward, listening for the dog. "Wilson?" I called. "Babette? Are you here?"

A faint white shape burst out of the bushes, startling me with a sharp spurt of adrenaline and fear. Wilson raced around us, snapping at our heels, and then disappeared deeper into the woods. We picked through the brambles after him.

Peter stopped abruptly. "Oh, Christ."

The dog was hysterical now — frantically yelping as he circled a prone figure half-buried in leaves. Babette? I grabbed Wilson's trailing leash, reeled him in, and snatched him up, thinking of the damage he could do to his injured owner with those sharp little claws. He bucked and struggled, just barely missing my nose with a nasty nip. Peter squatted next to Babette and shone his flashlight down the length of her body.

"Oh God," I said, "is she okay? What the hell happened?"

He ran the light over her head. Babette's blond pageboy was off-kilter, exposing a ragged gash in her thin gray hair. Globs of blackened blood had stained the wig and spackled the folds of her neck.

"She wears a wig!" I snorted, hybrid of a laugh and sob. "Oh God, that sounds awful — you know what I mean. God, I'm babbling." I started to cry. *Pull yourself together, Rebecca.* "Is she . . . alive?"

Peter shrugged, reached up to grip my hand briefly, and then started to roll her over.

"Don't touch her!" I said. "Wait for the paramedics." I shifted the dog to my left arm, pulled out my cell phone, and dialed 911. The dispatcher took a full report.

"We should have brought a blanket," said Peter.

I passed him the squirming animal, peeled off my raincoat, and tucked it around Babette's body. She had not moved or made a sound since we arrived. I began to shiver in spite of Mark's bathrobe and my flannel pajamas.

"Do you think she'll live?" I asked again.

"I'm not trained in this sort of thing." A chagrined smile. "I'd be more use if we were dealing with bankruptcy or torts. Look, one of us should go back to the complex and show them where we are."

I considered the cold, dark vigil next to Babette, unsure if she were dead or alive. Next I thought about a possible ambush by the would-be killer on the path through the woods, me with a sore knee and floppy slippers.

"We've got to stick together. We'll both go — we don't know where her attacker might be."

The cops and an ambulance arrived within minutes. After a quick argument about civilians mucking up a crime scene versus time wasted searching, we tromped back through the woods to show the professionals the way. The paramedics braced her neck, pressed a bandage to her head, lifted her onto the stretcher, and slid an oxygen mask over her gray face. The young cop who'd answered the call for Madeline just two weeks ago, and chased would-be prowlers from my home last night, slid the bloody wig into a plastic bag.

"Will she be all right?" I stammered.

No answer. As we trailed out of the woods behind the EMTs with their loaded stretcher, Meigs's white minivan roared into the clubhouse parking lot. The shriek of the sirens had already brought out the most curious neighbors — the Nelsons and Mrs. Dunbarton. Only Babette was missing. I sank down on the clubhouse steps, away from the milling and curious onlookers, wet and cold, sick and scared. And my knee hurt like hell.

Wilson squirmed out of Peter's arms, raced across the parking lot, and sank his teeth into one of the rescue worker's calves. The young cop snatched him up and locked him in the back of his patrol car. Every couple of seconds, there was a volley of furious and now-hoarse barking, and his curly white head surfaced in the window. I had to admire the little guy. He had a Lassie complex, in a yapping sort of way.

Meigs waved me over after conferring with the ambulance driver and the cops who'd answered my call. Peter, Mrs. Dunbarton, and the Nelsons closed the circle.

"What happened here?"

Shivering, I pulled my bathrobe tighter. My bloodstained raincoat had been taken off in the ambulance with Babette.

"I went to bed around eleven. Then I

heard Wilson barking behind the complex."

"Ms. Finster is never out this late," said Peter. "Dr. Butterman got worried because she heard the dog and we decided to go out and take a look."

"This neighborhood is not safe anymore," announced Mrs. Dunbarton to the detective. "We insist on more frequent patrols."

"Do you need volunteers to canvas the woods?" asked Mr. Nelson. He reeked of alcohol — one lit match and we would all be blown to hell.

My teeth began to chatter loudly: My feet, hands, and ankles were freezing. The cold mist was edging toward rain.

"I have the key to the clubhouse," said Peter. "If it's all right with you" — he nodded at Meigs — "we could move inside."

Meigs stared at me and then Peter, his eyes flat and hard. He took a notepad from his pocket and addressed the other residents. "We'll be around to talk with you folks in the morning. There's nothing else to do here this evening. You can get back to bed. We'll send patrols through the night." He turned back and lifted his chin. "Let's go."

In the harsh fluorescent light of the clubhouse meeting room, Meigs looked even more rumpled than usual, the tired lines around his eyes and mouth pulling his features down. I collapsed into a white plastic chair, clutching the blue robe tight at my neck. For sure, I was no vision either. My right pajama leg had been ripped when I fell; my knee was muddy and scraped. I patted my head — the damp night had frizzed my hair into an unmanageable halo.

"What do you know about all this?" Meigs asked brusquely.

"Nothing, really." Why was he so focused on me? "I can't imagine why Babette was out there. I spoke with her earlier this evening — she was a nervous wreck. Last thing in the world she would do is go out in the dark alone."

"Unless that silly mutt got away," Peter said.

I nodded and stared at Meigs. "She's been feeling a lot of pressure since Madeline died." My lips trembled. I sat up and squared my shoulders. "It's spooky living so close to our neighbor's place and not knowing how it happened and why. This afternoon Babette told me she'd failed the police — that you think she knows more about Madeline's murder than what she's told."

"Madeline was murdered?" Peter's brow furrowed. "Last I heard, you told us it was suicide."

"Butt out." Meigs glared. "I'm talking to the lady."

Peter cleared his throat. He took a breath, let it out, and smiled. "I'll be outside, should you wish to interview me. I did find Ms. Finster too."

How could he be so polite when Meigs was so rude?

"I'll walk Dr. Butterman home and check the premises," said Meigs. "There's no need for you to wait."

Peter shrugged, the conciliatory smile evaporating. "I'll call you tomorrow and we'll set a date for the Cuban place." He tucked a strand of frizzy hair behind my ear, then turned and left.

"He's trying to be helpful," I snapped at Meigs. "He was with me when I found Babette."

"What did Ms. Finster say about remembering the murder?" Meigs asked.

I sighed and summarized my conversation with Babette. "Bernd Becker, the condo association manager, was standing with us," I told him, pointing out the window to the spot where his Volvo had been. "He might remember more."

"Anything else?" Meigs asked.

"I've been thinking." I flashed him a weak grin. "You said I could. I talked with a col-

323

league — confidentially, of course — who diagnosed Madeline with narcissistic exhibitionist traits. I have to agree. Chances are, someone in her family blazed the trail. That's how these things work. I'd bet money on the father, but no one in the family will talk openly. Not to me anyway."

"What do you mean, no one's talking to you?" Meigs demanded, his eyes suddenly stony.

"I saw Isabel Stanton today," I admitted.

Meigs's face flushed red.

"I went to tell her I was finished snooping, but then her son came by and they got into an argument. Tom." I swept my hair back from my face and wound it into a knot at the base of my neck. "He's very protective of his mother, just like his brother, Steven. He admitted having an argument with Madeline about the business — whether or not she deserved an equal share of the profits or something. Her former coworker confirmed the tension." Meigs frowned. "But I guess all that's in your department."

"Correct." He rubbed his jaw, which glinted with a reddish stubble. "What do you know about Bernd Becker?"

I swallowed. "Not much. He was hired early in the summer, before I moved in.

He's Swiss. Or maybe German." I shrugged and shivered. "He's very good at what he does."

Meigs glanced at his watch and lumbered to his feet. "Let's go."

I trudged behind him to my condo and stayed in the kitchen while he searched each room. For a moment, I wished I'd made the bed before I left, but I quickly brushed off the thought. This was a police emergency, not a *House Beautiful* tour. Besides, it was midnight and normal people were in bed.

"Do you think she'll be all right?" I asked as I trailed him to the door. "Babette?"

"I'm not a doctor," he said, and sprinted down my front walk through the rain.

Which I took as a no. Maybe it didn't mean that — he probably didn't know. The oxygen mask seemed like a good sign. Surely they wouldn't have bothered if she were dead. I flashed on Madeline's body, rolled out of her home in a black bag. And Wilson, carted off to the pound.

I pressed my face against the thick gray velvet of Spencer's back. "I guess we should have offered to take him in." Spencer blinked, stretched, and yawned. Also a no.

Would I ever sleep again?

CHAPTER 26

Friday morning, I sleepwalked through five patients in sequence, amazed that I was able to concentrate at all. Sometimes focusing on someone else's worries helps contain your own.

After a few bites of a veggie wrap from the corner deli, I called Yale New Haven Hospital to check on Babette's status. A snippy receptionist froze me out.

"The new government regulations about privacy don't permit us to disclose our patients' status," she said. "You'll appreciate the confidentiality when your turn comes."

My turn. Gee, thanks. At least they weren't denying that Babette existed. Which I chose to take as another sign that she was still alive. Feeling restless and helpless, I called the police station and asked for Detective Meigs. Out of the office and not expected back until Monday. Just great.

Was the attack on Babette related to Madeline's death? Next-door neighbors attacked within a few weeks — it seemed like one hell of a coincidence.

Among all the loose ends in the Stanton situation, I was most curious about Madeline's father. My own father had pulled out of my life, as had hers. I understood, intellectually anyway, that he wasn't strong enough to stay and face the responsibility of two small girls. Maybe William Stanton was the same sort of man. But what had he run from?

I dialed Nancy Griswold at the church office. It wouldn't hurt to ask if she knew anything more about the Stantons.

Nancy sounded regretful, but said she couldn't help. I suspected Reverend Wesley had lectured her about confidentiality and church business since we'd connected last.

"I understand," I assured her. "People have to feel like they can trust you or they won't come in. Just one more question — I don't think this is asking you to break a confidence. Would you say Pammy Stanton was Madeline's closest friend?"

"Oh yes," said Nancy, sounding relieved to have something she could tell. "Right up to Steven's wedding. Madeline was the maid of honor. It was so sweet. I gather they haven't been close lately, but that's only natural, don't you think? Once you get married, it's natural that your girlfriends drift away. Right now she's working as the receptionist for the family business."

I hung up sure about one thing: Pammy Stanton was next on my contact list. But an e-mail chimed its arrival before I could dial.

"It's Harry, remember me?" read the subject line.

My heart froze.

"Listen, I must have sounded a little overeager in my last message. I may be dense, but when a girl doesn't answer an e-mail within twenty-four hours, I suspect I've screwed something up. Sorry for assuming you'd be ready to do an overnight. I'm keeping my fingers crossed that you'll consider another margarita? You name the time and place and yours truly will be there, sombrero in hand."

Well, knock me over with tequila breath. Unlikely that a guy who'd lurked in my bushes two nights ago would have the gall to apologize, and ask me for another date. I phoned the police station and left a message on Meigs's voicemail suggesting he start scanning for other suspects in the prowler incident, and asking for news on Babette.

Then I punched in the number for Wilcox

Metal Works. Pammy Stanton answered the phone with just the kind of chipper receptionist welcome a company would want. The temperature of her voice dropped a good ten degrees once I identified myself.

"I have a few questions about Madeline. I understand you two were close friends."

"I have nothing to say."

I stayed quiet. This is one of the first techniques they teach in graduate school: If you can avoid rushing in to fill every awkward silence with your own anxious yakking, confidences emerge. But she held out longer than I expected.

"I was hoping to buy you a cup of coffee," I said finally. "I know this has been hard on the whole family, but you especially. You grew up with her, didn't you?"

"I have nothing to say," she repeated.

"Do you think Madeline's death was related to Steven's problem?" I was fishing.

I heard a catch in her breathing. "I can't discuss this on the phone," Pammy said. "And I can't be seen with you. Steven would kill me."

"I'll meet you anywhere; you choose it," I said. "My last patient finishes at three thirty. I can be in Guilford by four fifteen."

Nothing from Pammy.

"This must be awfully difficult," I tried

again. "You lost your best friend. But now you're inside the family. Different loyalties, I imagine."

"Meigs Point Nature Preserve, four thirty," she said. "Pass East Beach, the nature center, and park all the way at the end. Fifteen minutes, that's all I have. Steven would be furious if he knew. And you can't tell anyone."

"Promise."

"And if I talk with you, you'll leave us alone?"

"Promise," I said, crossing fingers on both hands. I hung up and leafed through the Guilford phone book until I found the listing for Mrs. Dunbarton.

"Edith?" I said when she answered. "This is Rebecca Butterman. How are you this morning?"

I held the phone away from my ear as she reported in minute detail the calls she'd made to the police and two security companies.

"Good work," I said. "I have another question. You collected the references for our condo manager candidates, correct? I wondered what you could tell me about Bernd — his history before this job. A dear friend lives in Branford and they're hoping to find someone with his skills. I told her

330

you'd chosen someone with an unusual background and it worked out very well."

"Hold on. I'll pull his application from my files," said Edith. Two minutes later she returned to the phone, rasping heavily. "He was in banking. In Europe."

Why move from a lucrative and prestigious job like that to a condominium complex full of annoying patrons? "Any idea why he made that kind of career change?"

"He was burnt out," Mrs. Dunbarton said stiffly. "And he's always loved tinkering." It sounded like she was reading from his application.

"References were good, I presume?" I asked.

"I myself called the one in Massachusetts and the line had been disconnected. As for the others, who was going to pay for the overseas phone bill? He had been offered another position and we certainly didn't want to lose him," she sniffed. "Are you having a problem with Mr. Becker's work?"

"No, no. He does a wonderful job."

Once I'd gotten off the line with Mrs. Dunbarton, I called Meigs again and left another message. "It occurs to me that our handyman makes an appearance every time something bad happens around here. I checked with Mrs. Dunbarton — they never reached his character references. He could have come from anywhere. He could be anyone." I paused. "That's all. Sorry to bother you. I'm just nervous, I guess."

I drove through the empty gates into Hammonasset State Park. Fire bushes had reddened to brilliant along the entrance to the campground. Circling through two roundabouts, I passed the long stretch of East Beach, where anyone, even those without expensive mansions and high-priced beach rights, can enjoy the salt water and the sun. Next came the Meigs Point nature center — empty of visitors — and a brown expanse of salt marsh. I wondered if this Meigs namesake was any relation to my pal the detective?

"Could she have chosen anything more remote?" I muttered, my heart rate beginning to rise.

The wind had also picked up, whipping the sound into rollers and white caps. A few cars were parked at the end of the lot: a couple making out in a red Saturn, a pair of fishermen in full rubber regalia loading fishing gear and empty beer cans into their pickup, and an empty silver Mercedes. But no sign of Pammy. My watch said four twenty-nine.

I got out of the car and killed a few minutes reading a historical marker, learning that *Hammonasset* translated to "where we dig holes in the ground" for the Eastern Woodland Indians. And that the Winchester rifle company had used the beach as a testing site for new products. I glanced at my watch again. My hands felt damp. Had Pammy meant she'd meet me at the lookout point?

I climbed the hard packed path and then a set of steep wooden stairs to the top of the hill. High tide — the jetty was almost covered and waves sloshed hard against the rocks. I stalked to the end of the weatherbeaten deck, where a bench and a telescope were bolted to the wooden planking. A few wind-buffeted cedars framed a stunning view of the salt marsh to the north; to the south stretched the thin gray line of Long Island. One sailboat skidded across the choppy water. I could appreciate the melancholy fall beauty, but I didn't appreciate being here alone.

"Dr. Butterman?"

I startled, clapping my hand to my chest, then summoned a smile. "Pammy. Hello. Thank you so much for coming." She looked more subdued than the young woman I remembered from the memorial

— the same heavy layer of makeup, hair teased high, and expensive clothing, but this time, no attitude.

She clutched a brown calfskin jacket closed over a cashmere turtleneck. "What can I tell you? I don't know what happened to Maddie. Whatever." She wiped her eyes with her sleeve, smudging mascara across her cheek. "She's dead."

"Can we sit?" I gestured to the bench. "I'm just trying to understand her — something I didn't do very well while she was alive." I smiled ruefully. "In my line of work, the family is always the key."

Pammy shrugged, her gaze drifting across the water.

"Something happened with her father," I continued, "around the time he moved out. There was a problem in their business with money, am I right?"

Pammy faced me, gray eyes flashing. "So wrong." More silence.

"It couldn't have been easy, marrying Steven," I said. "Your loyalties shifting and all. I get the idea that Madeline felt cut off from the others — but once you married a Stanton brother, you'd crossed over to the other side."

Tears filled her eyes and slid down cheeks. "I didn't realize I would lose her," she said.

"But the messes she was getting herself mixed up in — Steven said if I loved him, I'd have to choose."

She snuffled. I found a Kleenex in my pocket and handed it over.

"The messes?"

"Always the drinking. And too many guys. Her judgment seemed to get worse and worse. One asshole gave her a wicked shiner — even that didn't slow her down."

"She got beaten up? That's awful."

Pammy looked away. "I told her she should buy a gun but she said she wouldn't have a clue how to use it. So I said: Just stick it in your nightstand. You can scare someone off if you need to by just waving the damn thing around." Hands trembling, she blew her nose.

"What happened between her parents? Why did Isabel make him leave?"

Pammy pulled a compact out of her bag, dabbed at the mascara on her cheek, and sighed heavily.

"Her dad was caught in a sting off I-95 — a state park in Fairfield County where homosexual men gathered. The one and only time for him, if you believe his story. The cops had been staking the place out for months and they rounded up dozens of men — fathers and husbands like Mr. Stanton, some prostitutes, some gay men just looking for company." She tucked the compact back into her purse. "Isabel used every ounce of influence her family had to keep his name out of the paper. When it was over, she threw him out of the house. It took several years to force him out of the business. And out of their lives."

"Is Mr. Stanton homosexual?"

She shook her head. "I don't think so. Maybe. Some of the time? Who knows how these things work? Isabel was always in control and he struggled with that. You're the shrink, you figure it out."

"So the boys went along with their mother, but Madeline didn't want to let her father go."

She nodded and narrowed her eyes. "You promised you'd leave us alone if I spoke with you. Please. This has nothing to do with Madeline's death. We all need to move on with our lives."

The Stanton party line. Pammy sprang up and started toward the stairs. I hurried behind, not wanting to be left alone in the gathering dusk.

"What about Steven?" I called. "Lorena Stanton said he'd had some trouble too."

She stopped so abruptly that I almost mowed her down.

"Steven has nothing to do with this," she said through clenched teeth, crying again. "Just leave us alone."

She reached the Mercedes, flung the door open and herself in.

"Take care and thanks for coming," I said as the car wheeled away.

My cell phone rang as I drove out of the park. I inserted my ear bud. "Hello?"

"What're you up to?" Angie asked. "What's for dinner?" Hinting that she wouldn't mind mooching a meal.

"Not cooking tonight," I said.

"You're not cooking?"

"I'm beat. We had another incident at our complex last night. I found one of my neighbors in the woods. She'd been hammered by someone. I'm going to grab some sesame noodles at Perfect Parties and get in bed."

"Alone?" she laughed.

"Of course not," I said. "I'll be with Spencer."

"Are you safe? You're welcome to spend the night here. I'll pop a few Lean Cuisines in the microwave . . ."

Angie's idea of cooking — ick. "Thanks. Come over tomorrow and I'll fill you in. I'll make you a pesto pizza. With fresh mozzarella and tomatoes."

Angie moaned. "See you then. Holler if you need me."

After a quick stop for takeout, I drove down Soundside Drive and pulled into my garage. I'd call Annabelle Hart after supper. She'd be interested to know that I'd partially solved the mystery of which trauma Madeline was repeating. If I had to guess, I'd say Madeline's wild life was an unconscious attempt to connect with her father. Unlikely that Mr. Stanton had gotten caught the one and only time he made an appearance at that rest stop, I thought as I opened the door.

I dropped my stuff on the kitchen counter and walked to the living room, calling for Spencer. And froze. Books had been yanked from their shelves and tossed to the floor, along with couch cushions, file folders, and photographs. A wash of fear gripped me, swelling into a wracking sob, which I attempted to fight with a dose of reason. I handle things calmly. A cool customer. Ice in my veins, so I can absorb chaos from other psyches. I started to pant.

Calm down, inhale, Rebecca. Have to stay calm. Can't think, can't breathe. Outside. I have to get out. Where's Spencer? Get out, Rebecca. He'll be fine.

I fumbled the deadbolt open and stumbled

out the front door. A dark figure loomed in the yard. I was sucking air, crouched to the ground, crying. "Who are you? What do you want?"

"Rebecca? It's me. It's Peter. What's the matter?"

"Someone broke in," I sobbed.

He squatted down and tried to gather me in his arms.

I stiffened, wanting to lean into him but hating that he was seeing me this way.

"Come on. We're going to my place to call the cops. I'll make you a cup of tea while we wait." He strode up the walk to close my front door and led me toward his home.

CHAPTER 27

While Peter went off to make tea, I paced the length of his living room, too nervous to sit. I vaguely registered his expensive, masculine décor — suede couch, American Indian–design rugs, mahogany bookcases filled with leather-bound books, a video camera, a massive flat-screen TV.

Who the hell had broken into my place? And what the hell did they want? I was embarrassed by the way I'd collapsed — my reliable control overwhelmed by pure fear. Maybe if I constructed a timeline of events from the past few weeks, I'd have a better shot at sorting things out. A large calendar blotter protected Peter's burnished teak desk. I crossed the room to study the calendar: Three weeks since Madeline died. Seemed so much longer.

Peter came around the corner from the kitchen carrying two steaming mugs. As he held one out, the track light from the ceiling glinted off the gold signet ring settled on his square finger with its perfectly manicured nail. I stared at the ring and then at Peter's face, then back at the ring.

My upper lip broke out in sweat. My God, Peter was the man in the photo on Madeline's blog. I stumbled back, knocking a pile of legal documents and a letter opener from the desk to the floor. Flashing a weak smile, I crouched to pick them up.

"Don't worry about the mess," said Peter pleasantly. "Just stand up and fold your hands on your head."

He set our mugs of tea on a side table, slid open the top drawer of an antique highboy, and pulled out a gun. I moved my hands slowly to my head.

"You can't seem to mind your own business." He walked to the window and closed the blinds and the drapes, then rubbed his forehead with his free hand, grimacing.

"Have to think. What to do next?"

My heart drummed. I cleared my throat, willing back the panic. "Let's talk with Detective Meigs when he gets here. I know he'll understand." Understand what? It didn't matter, I had to keep both of us calm.

He barked a laugh. "There isn't a cop in the world who would believe the truth. No, the police won't be coming."

"But you called . . ." My voice trailed off as he shook his head slowly.

"Please, Peter. Things will go fine if you're honest." I took one step toward the door.

"Ah, authenticity." He motioned me back with the gun, his eyes gleaming. "We're in this already. What say we have some authentic fun?"

"Please let me go home and I swear I won't tell anyone." Which sounded completely inane. By all appearances, he'd killed my neighbor and now he was pointing a gun at me.

He shook his head, a sly smile flickering. "You might be interested in my projects, like Madeline." He flipped on bright lights in the corner of the room, where a video camera, a digital camera mounted on a tripod, and a small printer were arranged. And then he moved closer. "Would you like to audition?"

"No thanks," I said firmly. "I'm not into that stuff."

He grabbed my wrist and wrenched it behind my back. "I didn't mean to give you the impression you had a choice." He laughed and shoved me back toward the desk. "I'm looking forward to seeing you dance. The day you moved in, I wondered whether you'd make it as an actress. Peter, I asked myself, what's behind those prissy Talbot's clothes? Will she have the faintest idea how to get a man excited?"

Prissy Talbot's clothes? Keep the bastard talking. I tugged my blouse and sweater down over my hips and lifted my chin at the video equipment. "How did Madeline get involved?"

He raised his shoulders in an easy shrug. "She liked to check out the new neighbors — she introduced herself to you too, no? I saw you in her blog." He laughed. "I invited her over for a nightcap and she was curious about my equipment." He gestured at the cameras. "Somehow we got to talking about private lives." He lifted his eyebrows. "May I say without appearing indelicate that we shared similar tastes? I'm sure you read all about it — she loved the camera, loved the spotlight."

His posture stiffened and the gun wobbled.

"I want to see you dance, Miss Priss."

He flicked on the Bose radio perched on the bookshelf beside the desk. It piped out a sexy Latin dance tune. Merengue, maybe? I wondered idiotically. He walked over to the video camera, sighted through the viewfinder, then turned it on. A small red light flashed green and a faint whirring started.

"All set. Go ahead," he said, "dance."

I planted my hands on my waist. "You've got to be kidding."

He strode across the room, slapped the side of my face, and jabbed the butt of the gun into my ribs. "Do it."

Ear ringing and nearly paralyzed with fright, I cradled my stinging cheek and began to sway.

Peter burst out in loud laughter. "I knew you didn't have any rhythm. I knew you couldn't compete with Madeline."

"Did you slap her around and hold her at gunpoint too?" I snapped.

His eyes widened. Did I deserve to be shot or congratulated? I wasn't sure myself.

"So the atmosphere is not to your liking." He went to a panel of switches by the front door, dimmed the lights, then crossed the room to raise the volume on the radio. Turning back to face me, his smile faded into a scowl. "Now dance."

I tried. Even under the best of circumstances, I've never been a relaxed dancer. And this was an ice age away from the best of circumstances. Besides, the merengue is impossible without Latin blood.

Peter watched for a few moments, then snorted.

"We should have a drink. That might

loosen you up, eh?"

He laid the gun on the desk, slid open a glass door on the bookcase against the wall, and brought out a crystal flask and two highball glasses. Then he unscrewed the cap, poured a generous two fingers of liquid in each, and drank deeply. "Now you." He held out the second glass.

"No thanks." If I had any chance of finding a way out of this, I would need all my wits about me.

"Take it."

I sipped a tiny mouthful, then spat the harsh whiskey out on the carpet. Peter grabbed my hair, yanked my head back, and sloshed a stream of brown booze down my throat, neck, and chest. I swallowed frantically to keep from choking — three, four, five times. He shoved me away and picked up the gun as I stumbled back against the wall, coughing.

"Your clothes are wet, Doctor. You'll feel more comfortable if you take them off. And it might make you easier to watch." He stroked the butt of the pistol. "Do it slowly." He waved at the camera.

I wasn't big enough to bull my way by him. The Nelsons weren't home — their condo had been silent and dark when we came in. Besides, the loud music would cover any cries for help. I turned away and pulled the sweater over my head, trying to imagine I was somewhere else. Anywhere but here. And praying to God for a brainstorm. Acutely aware of both the green light on the video camera and the gun, I pulled out my shirttails and undid the top two buttons of my blouse.

His voice thickened. "Come, Doctor, this way." He was twirling his finger and smiling when I turned. "Take your time if you like, but it's all coming off." He grinned. "Now show me sexy."

Terrified, disgusted, I tried to comply. My legs felt weak and my mind achingly numb.

"Dance like you mean it," he said.

I thought I detected a slight relaxation in his posture, a slackening of his facial muscles. I shimmied and wiggled. Maybe he'd be satisfied just to watch me. Why had I not seen this coming? I would not cry. Yet.

"How did you talk Madeline into this?" I asked as I danced.

Peter snickered. "Surely a psychologist could tell from reading her blog how desperately she wanted attention from men. She was fascinated about the idea of starting a video weblog. Surveillant narcissism, isn't that the technical term? Besides, I can be a very charming host."

346

The song on the radio ended. "Was she a good dancer?" I asked, gripping my shirt collar tight.

Peter swung the gun up level with my head and snorted. "Not a stick like you. Her problem was she couldn't do anything without telling the whole Goddamn world."

"That's how the trouble between you started?"

He swigged another mouthful of whiskey. "She loved making our movie and posing for photographs. But they were not for public consumption, of course. It's my hobby, Doctor. My *private* life."

"She told you about the blog and said . . ."

"She wanted to write about us. And she wanted to post the photographs on the web. Can you imagine how my law firm would go for that?"

He cackled. Why hadn't I noticed the annoying laugh and the pointed incisors before tonight? Let's face it, when it came to men, my judgment sucked. I stifled a sob. If I made it out of here, I was never going on another date.

"Then she tried to talk me into posting the video on her website. That girl was sick," he said.

He should know.

"Once she'd gone home, I noticed several

of our photographs were missing. I called her and explained nicely that I couldn't afford to show up in her blog. Even incognito. I insisted that she return the photos. She told me to check her website. 'We're already there,' she said. 'No one will ever know it's you, Peter.' " He gulped. "I had to get the others back before she did more damage."

"After she died, you thought I had them."

He nodded. "I saw you over there all the time. I saw you carrying things out of her condo and talking with her mother."

"Supplies for the cat," I said. "Kitty litter. And Isabel just wanted someone to talk to about her daughter. Madeline never confided in me. We weren't even friends."

He shrugged. "You know now."

"So you killed her?"

"I didn't kill her, Goddammit, that's just it." He sloshed more whiskey into his glass and knocked it back. "Look, this could ruin my reputation, even get me disbarred. So I went over to her place the next night to request respectfully that she reconsider." He massaged his chest. I wrapped my arms more tightly around me. "She refused. She kept teasing me with the possibilities. When I got upset and followed her into the bedroom, she pulled a gun. I admit, I panicked and pushed her. She stumbled and banged her head on the nightstand." He held one hand against his cheek and shook his head. "I tried to revive her, but it was too late — she was dead."

"It's not too late," I said. "You can go to the cops, explain it all."

"My life would be finished."

Especially when I got done talking.

"She bled like a stuck pig but luckily for me, she'd fallen on a little rug. Then I thought of disguising her death as a suicide so I dragged her into the bathroom and rolled her into the tub. Then I wrapped her hand around the gun and pressed the barrel against the wound on her temple. And fired." He scowled, scanning my expression carefully. "You don't believe me. No one else would have either. So I had to make it look like she did herself in."

"You wrote the note on her computer?"

He nodded. "It wasn't hard. She was always whining about her father."

"And Babette Finster?"

"She condemned herself," he said dismissively. "The woman never shuts up. She had to babble on all about how you advised her to imagine the days before Madeline died and how she'd gotten a mental image of the last man she'd seen leaving Madeline's place. She described me exactly, but she was too dizzy to realize it. Another twenty-four hours and she'd have put my name to the memory. I couldn't risk it."

"You couldn't have been the man in the bushes — the squat, bald man?"

He laughed. "I had a stocking cap on that night. And a lot of layers of clothing. But you'd set your alarm so I couldn't get in. You should always be that careful, Dr. Butterman. You could end up like your foolish neighbor."

I shivered. Did he know Babette had survived the night? It almost sounded as if he didn't. "She was a harmless old woman," I protested.

"If she'd kept her mouth shut she'd be alive today." Sweat had broken out on his forehead and the hand holding the gun was shaking.

"So Madeline's death wasn't your fault at all," I said. "It was an accident."

"Oh come on," he snapped. "You don't believe that and neither will they. Now dance."

He wanted the upper hand — I would not have to fake my fear. Could I draw the evening out in hopes of help arriving by pretending to comply? I closed my eyes and rolled my hips, trying to appear dreamy, trying not to think about the video. And thanking God no one else was here to see.

"May I have another drink?" I asked in a little girl voice. "Do you by any chance have a cigarette?"

Looking amused, he splashed another inch of liquid into my glass and watched me swallow. He pulled a pack of Marlboros from the desk drawer, lit one, and handed it to me. I inhaled and coughed sharply, feeling a rush of light-headedness. I hadn't smoked a cigarette since graduate school.

"Now take off the shirt."

Hands trembling, I unbuttoned the remaining buttons, extracted my arms, and dropped the blouse on the floor.

He leaned back against the wall, a hint of spittle in the corner of his mouth. "Dance," he said.

Another Spanish song was playing; I visualized the sexy photograph of Madeline, imagining how she might have moved. I glided, I slunk, I ducked and swayed, stopping to puff on the cigarette and trying to push back the realization that I was pirouetting half-naked in front of a psychopath. How had I missed the signs? Peter let the hand holding the gun drop to his side while he drank again from the flask: a reprieve.

"Take your pants off," he said.

"Not a chance."

In two strides he was across the room — another deafening slap across the side of my head. "Now!"

I fumbled with the top button, unzipped the zipper, and stopped.

"Keep going, Doctor."

"Mrs. Dunbarton will have seen me come over here, Peter," I begged. "She's probably gone for the police."

He snorted. "The police aren't interested in you."

"But Mrs. Dunbarton is. You'll only cause more trouble if you harm me." I couldn't have sounded less convinced.

"We're going to make a movie," he said. "Starring you and me."

He gestured with the gun. I dropped my pants, stepped out of them, and kicked both my pants and clogs aside. If there was any chance of running, I wanted to be ready. Switching the gun from hand to hand, Peter removed his jacket, unbuttoned his own shirt, and shrugged out of it. He came closer and prodded me hard in the buttock with the gun.

"On your hands and knees," he said.

I dropped to my knees. Then I felt the weight of him and his coarse chest hair against my back. And cold metal pressing against the thin cotton of my underwear.

He looped the barrel of the gun into my underpants and inched them down.

CHAPTER 28

The gun clanked to the floor as he shifted into position. Where had he dropped it? Could I get to it before he did? I desperately scanned my memory for the literature on rape. Did victims who submitted peaceably survive more often than ones who fought? And was the psychological fallout of the survivors worth the fight? All moot anyway — I'm a smallish person, only as strong as my weekly downward facing dog — a yoga pose I'd never be able to hold again without thinking of this awful man.

"Smile for the camera, Doctor." He reached around and ran his hand across my chest, his breath rasping raggedly. Then he lifted away to struggle with my bra, panting and rubbing against me in a revolting way. "Madeline liked it like this."

The terror that had frozen my muscles shifted to outrage. Not just for the disgusting intrusion of his intimacy, but for Madeline too. And hapless Babette. I collapsed flat, twisted under him, and scrabbled for the gun.

Peter laughed, pinning me to the floor. "You're a feisty little butterball!" His left hand grasped both of mine, his right forearm crushing my windpipe. I choked for air.

"You're a lousy dancer, Doctor. But maybe there's a market for this." Eyes half-closed, he began to fondle me, nuzzling my neck, pinching and squeezing my skin. He arched away slightly, tugging at a catch in the zipper of his pinstripe trousers. Above him, the green light of the video camera beamed steadily. His weight shifted as his hand groped my stomach, then started lower, setting my right arm free.

My fingers closed on the letter opener I'd knocked to the floor earlier. I took a ragged breath, plunged it at his neck, and screamed: "No!"

He rolled away grasping his collarbone, howling like the miserable coward he was. I straightened my underwear and scrambled toward my clothes. I yanked the sweater over my head and jabbed my legs into the pants.

The front door banged open and Detective Meigs and two other policemen burst into the room, guns cocked. Bernd Becker followed carrying a ring of keys, and at the sight of me half-dressed, instantly turned away. I curled into a hyperventilating ball. The uniforms wrestled Peter onto his back, handcuffed him, and yanked him to his feet.

"Call for two ambulances and get that asshole the hell out of here," said Meigs.

Angie darted past him to me. "Sweet Jesus, did he hurt you?" She yanked off her hoodie sweatshirt and tucked it around me.

I pulled my pants zipper up. "I'm okay."

She hugged me, crying and laughing. My legs buckled as I tried to stand. Meigs nudged me onto the couch and crouched down, a gentle hand on my knee. "Take some deep breaths. The ambulance is on the way."

"I'm not hurt," I repeated, wiping tears from both cheeks. I was shaking, my teeth chattering. "Just a little . . ." I couldn't think of the word.

"Can you tell me what happened?" he asked.

I leaned over and threw up onto Peter's coffee table.

Angie wrinkled her nose slightly and snapped at Meigs. "Could you get the lady a glass of water and a damp towel?"

A sharp knock echoed, and then I heard a

distinctive, nasal voice.

"Detective, what's going on?" Mrs. Dunbarton asked.

Then Bernd Becker's clipped words: "You'll need to step back, Mrs. Dunbarton. Official business only in here." Her head bobbed around his body block, eyes widening at the sight of blood everywhere, and me crumpled on the couch. For once, she was speechless.

After the paramedics had checked me out and I'd refused to be photographed by the police photographer, Meigs escorted Angie and me back to my apartment.

"I'll call you tomorrow," he said. "Any problems at all, you have my cell."

"Thank you."

I took the hottest shower I could stand, trying to wash away the cloying smell of Peter's cologne. When I emerged in pajamas and Mark's robe, Angie was straightening up the mess that Peter had made.

"I can finish that," I said, patting the couch beside me. "Tell me everything. Tell me how you guys showed up when I needed you most of all." Hot tears leaked down my cheeks.

"I got worried after we talked." Angie sat, took my hands and stroked them. "You sounded down. And the sesame noodles were calling." She gave me a shaky smile. "When I got to your place, the door was open and your condo was a mess. So I phoned the police. Your handyman was finishing the caulking on the sliders in the clubhouse. He said he thought he'd seen you go into Peter's place.

"The cops met us over there — we heard the most awful loud music and your banshee screaming," Angie added. "Bernd unlocked the door."

"Thanks, Angie." It came out in a strangled whisper. What else was there to say?

CHAPTER 29

I hadn't been to the graveyard in many years, but who was counting. Not my mother, certainly. Janice, probably. She kept the plot weeded and made visits on all major holidays, providing Christmas grave blankets, Easter lilies, Memorial Day mini-flags, and gingham-checked foil balloons for Mother's Day. She wiped down the head-stone with Murphy's Oil Soap once a month and polished it with a chamois cloth. I knew all these details because she reported them at length.

"You should go and see how pretty it looks," she'd told me more than once.

I had no trouble locating the site, on a hilly spot fifty yards or so off the unpaved road that wound through Westside Cemetery. Our mother's grave was among the most carefully tended, though I'd stop short of calling it "pretty." Standing in front of the marker, I felt sad and angry, but in the muddled way that a child might. I kicked at the turf and scowled.

Evelyn Butterman,
whose short life on Earth was God's gift
of love and joy to all
whose lives she touched.

Not hardly.

I wandered past a group of gravestones that listed drunkenly, their inscriptions worn shallow with age. At the back of the graveyard, I perched on a granite bench shaded by a stand of gnarled cedars. A carpet of fuzzy moss grew up to the edge of the facing stone.

Felice Damion, M.D.,
Mother to Four,
Friend to All.

Dr. Damion had lived a good, long life: ninety-one years. Well, a long one anyway.

"Why the hell," I asked aloud, "couldn't you have talked to someone if you were that unhappy? Did you ever think about me and Janice?" I began to cry, deep shuddering sobs.

"Dr. Butterman? Rebecca? Are you okay?" I leaped up, brushing the tears away with the back of my hand. Isabel Stanton stood watching me.

"I'm sorry to intrude," she said. "I was just here visiting Madeline. Her stone came yesterday. And then I heard someone crying. I just wanted to say I'm here if you need me."

"I'm fine." It came out terse, almost rude. Meigs had told me earlier in the week that Isabel knew all along about Madeline's secret life. I dug a tissue out of my jeans pocket and sat down again.

"Is this your —" Isabel glanced at Felice Damion's stone and back at my face, "grandmother?"

"My mother's over there." I flipped my hand toward the hill.

"May I sit?"

I shrugged. Isabel perched on the edge of the bench.

"I'm sorry about your mother," she said.

"It's old news," I said coldly.

"I'm really very sorry." She stretched to pat my knee awkwardly, not seeming to notice that I was shrinking away.

"How did she die?" she finally asked, then added: "You don't have to tell me." When I said nothing, she sighed. "Would you like to see Madeline's stone?"

Not really. But I'd reached the limit of my

rudeness. I followed her to her daughter's gravestone, white marble inscribed with a poem and a boat in full sail.

"Oh, I have slipped the surly bonds of Earth and danced the skies on laughter-silvered wings," she read. "It's by John Gillespie McGee." The words caught in her throat. "It was written for a pilot but it works for sailors too. Don't you think?"

"Lovely," I said. And after a moment, "She was a sailor?"

"Her father was. He took her out every Saturday on the Sound when she was little."

"You should have told me the truth about William — and Madeline — before you sent me out looking for a story that nearly got me killed." Unfair to blame her, really. My own curiosity took me a lot further than her early questions.

Isabel straightened her shoulders. "William humiliated me — all of us — with his sick fun. Madeline was taking the same path with that disgusting website."

"How did you find out about it?"

"I came across some awful photographs in her apartment and I confronted her the day before she died. What are you doing with these? I asked. She had to tell me."

"You had Peter's missing photos all along," I said slowly, imagining her ransacking her daughter's home for some kind of evidence. Madeline must have been livid.

Isabel ignored me. "I insisted that she cancel the website. When she refused, I told her about her father. How he'd been caught with those disgusting men." She shivered. " 'Do you want to walk in those footsteps?' I asked her. She told me to leave."

"You wondered if that's why she killed herself. That's what you needed to know."

Isabel nodded, her face looking shrunken and pale. "Nothing else seemed important after that — not protecting the family name; nothing but finding the truth about Madeline."

"But you knew about the website when you called me over to read her diary," I said.

"Of course I knew. I printed out the notes so you'd have something to work from. I didn't want to shade your judgment, I just needed a professional opinion."

A surge of rage left me momentarily speechless.

"And Steven?" I asked, pushing back my fury. "What happened to Steven?"

Her gaze dropped. She plucked at a pearl button on her argyle sweater, the loose skin of her neck quivering. "He was helping an Eagle Scout with a project at our church, building shelves in the pews to hold the hymnals. The kid filed a complaint about him." She frowned and looked up. "Could have ruined Steven — it almost destroyed his marriage. But nothing was ever proven and the charges were dropped. There was something really wrong with that boy, to need attention that badly."

Could she not hear what she was saying?

She knelt on the fresh dirt in front of Madeline's stone, brushed her lips on the white marble, then got to her feet. Her eyes glistened. She'd lost everything that mattered.

"When a person dies before her time, she leaves questions her survivors can't ever really answer," I said, holding my hand up against the late-afternoon sun. "At least they got Peter."

"That bastard!" She began to cry, then gathered her coat closely around her. "I'm sorry for your trouble," she said.

I gave a tiny nod. "By the way, please tell Tom he needn't bother coming for Spencer. I'm keeping him," I said, my chin jutting out fiercely.

"Okay," she said. "Thank you."

I watched her pick her way over the uneven ground to the stone gate that marked the cemetery's exit, her trench coat flapping. When I followed her out some minutes later, I spotted Detective Meigs's white minivan idling alongside the road. Meigs was leaning against the van.

"Everything all right? I saw your cars parked here." He pointed to the receding taillights of Isabel's Oldsmobile.

"Fine." Why was he here? "She thought she was responsible for Madeline's suicide. That's why she got me involved. Were you aware that she actually printed out diary notes from Madeline's computer before she called me over to consult?"

He shook his head. "I'm not entirely surprised."

"She tried to apologize, but she doesn't quite have it in her."

"That family is a disaster," Meigs said. "Steven Stanton came into the station the morning Peter Morgan took you hostage. He confessed that he'd visited Madeline just before she died to confront her about her blog. He told her she'd kill her mother by continuing to behave that way."

"How did Madeline answer?"

Meigs shrugged. "She was sick of their meddling. She was doing her own thing now." He looked directly at me. "Why would a woman want all that? I know I tend to take a dark view of people, but I don't get it."

"You repeat a trauma until it's worked out," I said. "Who knows how many times her father did what he did and how many vicious arguments it caused between her parents? And then he was banished. So she connected with him by repeating a similar thing in her own life. Unconsciously, of course."

Meigs raised his eyebrows. "That's a little over my head, Doctor."

I smiled and swatted his arm. "So Steven thought he set off Madeline's suicide?"

Meigs nodded.

"I suspect Tom thought he was responsible too. But instead, it was a stranger." I shuddered, suddenly cold and frightened.

"Peter's request for reduced bond was denied," Meigs told me. "That scumbag will be locked up for a long time."

I shifted my gaze to the bright red canopy of the maple tree across the street.

"He was reported earlier this year for sexual harassment at work," Meigs said. "The partners kept it from going public, but he couldn't afford another scandal with Madeline's blog. He panicked. And then he was afraid Babette could finger him. His lawyer is making noises about mental incompetence, but I think we'll nail him." He cleared his throat. "How are you feeling?"

"Lots of nightmares," I started, but my voice caught.

"That sounds perfectly normal," he said. "You might want to consider talking with someone —" He stopped and smiled. "You know that."

"But still good to hear it," I said, smiling back.

Meigs waved at the sea of headstones. "What are you doing here?" he asked, but with no confrontational edge.

I cocked my head. "Have you always lived in Guilford?"

He nodded. "Except for the time I spent in the military. Homegrown boy."

"Then you might remember the woman who killed herself, leaving two young children alone in the house with her body for twenty-four hours. It made quite a splash in the papers."

The words felt hard and smooth, like the shell of a hazelnut, protecting the kernel inside. I could count on the fingers of one hand the times I'd told this story. This was why — the wave of bile that rolled in with the memories.

"I remember hearing about the case," he said. "My father was one of the uniforms who took the call."

"Your father?" All the questions that

couldn't — or wouldn't — get answered by my mother's short obituary and my taciturn grandparents rushed to mind. All these years, I'd pictured her putting us girls to bed and settling into my father's recliner with a full bottle of Valium and a half liter of scotch . . . What had she been feeling? What was bad enough that she chose to take her life and leave her girls?

I found her in the morning but had little memory of the details: how long I might have lain in bed calling for her, how long the vigil by her body, how we were discovered. I shuddered, rubbing both arms. Meigs's father might have some answers.

"He's dead now," Meigs said gently. "I'm sorry."

I slumped back against his car.

Meigs looked away.

"She left a note for my father, said she couldn't face the future. She thought we would be better off with him and his new wife than being saddled with a crazy mother. Can you imagine? I can't. As sad or upset as I've ever gotten, I can't picture leaving my children alone like that. And I don't even have children. I'm just guessing here."

The detective touched my hand. "What about your dad?"

"He couldn't handle it. His new wife was

hysterical, and he was drowning in guilt. My grandparents raised us. They both died last year. I haven't seen him in ages." I laughed. "I guess I'm starting with the easier parent — whatever I say, Mom's not likely to talk back."

He leaned against the hood, arms crossed over his chest. "My wife has ALS. Lou Gehrig's disease. In a wheelchair most the time. And black with the blues." His voice broke. "So it's not like I can't understand a little of what you've gone through."

Years of damn schooling and "Sorry to hear that" was all I could think to mumble. He nodded and looked away again, toward the sound of cars passing below us on Route 1.

"These days, there are medications that really help with depression —"

"You can't fix the base problem with all the medicine in the world — she's very sick, and she isn't going to get well."

"I'm sorry," I said again.

"You were curious about the entry in the police log." His gaze flickered back to my face. "That's when we nailed down the diagnosis. Alice had to brake to avoid a collision and she couldn't get her foot to work. People thought she'd been drinking. It was muscle weakness — almost always the first sign of ALS.

"Every day she talks about killing herself. I only have a year or two left, she says, and it's only going to get harder. For both of us. And she's absolutely right."

"I'm so sorry. That's awful."

"I was just starting to think about leaving her when she got sick," Meigs continued. "Not now. What would that do to her?"

"Have you tried counseling?" I asked. "Maybe things between you would improve if you were able to talk about them."

"We're just surviving, Rebecca." It was the first time I'd heard him use my name. "We're not trying to fix anything, just live through it," he finished flatly.

"I'm sorry." All the words in the world and I could only come up with two.

"It makes no difference whether I meet a woman who's beautiful, smart, and complicated. My wife is sick as a dog and wishes she were dead." He looked at me straight on. "I plan to see it through."

I reached over and touched his wedding ring. "You're a good man, Jack Meigs."

Setting a platter of pesto pizza on the coffee table in front of Janice and Angie, I crossed the room to switch on the gas fireplace. Hard to get warm the last few days. I told them about meeting Isabel Stanton and Detective Meigs in the graveyard.

"The grave looks nice," I told Janice.

She smiled broadly. "I'm so glad you went."

"I'm thinking of tracking Dad down."

The smile faded. "Can't you wait and discuss this with Dr. Goldman?" she asked irritably.

"You don't approve of therapy," I said to Janice with a wink at Angie.

"Maybe you need more help than I thought," Janice said. "Maybe we could work on your love life instead."

"I'm not going there," I said, holding my hands up and tucking my feet under my legs. "My husband's caught cheating —"

"Old news," said Angie, wiping pesto off her plate with a piece of crust. "Practically hieroglyphics."

"And the next guy I consider turns out to be a psycho sex addict." Not that I'd really considered Peter. I moved Spencer off the coffee table and onto my lap.

"How about that nice young man from Fast Connections?" Janice asked.

"The one the cops pulled out of my bushes?"

"That wasn't him at all. You said so yourself. You said Peter was the one who

371

searched your place."

"I'd never be able to look at Harry without thinking of this week."

"Speaking of old maids," Angie said, "how's Babette?"

I socked her in the arm and she giggled. "She's home. She's having awful headaches but at least she doesn't remember the attack. Of course, she's terribly nervous anyway. Very worried about choosing a new wig. And how badly Wilson's been traumatized. And who'll take care of him until she's able." I stroked Spencer's stomach and rolled my eyes. "I'm taking the morning walk shift this week."

"Odd," said Angie, "all the times you talked about this case, you never mentioned Peter. And we sat there having tea and cookies with a psychopath. Did you ever suspect him?"

"Never," I said, frowning. "He seemed so self-contained and proper. He's the last one I would have imagined with a secret life."

"I wish I'd warned you," she said. "Some of my colleagues have seen him in action in court. If only I had asked them."

"Jim knows him too," said Janice. "He can't stand the guy."

"I only wish I'd said something," Angie repeated.

"Like what? The guy's a jerk in court? Watch out, he might rape you?" My eyes filled but I patted her hand. "It's not your fault. Either of you. I actually liked him. Whereas Meigs" — I made a face and pressed the cat's paw until his claws extended — "I didn't care for him at all. Funny, isn't it, just how wrong your first impressions can be?"

ABOUT THE AUTHOR

Anthony and Agatha Award nominee **Roberta Isleib** is a clinical psychologist who lives with her family in Connecticut. Visit her website at www.robertaisleib.com or email her at Roberta@robertaisleib.com.

We hope you have enjoyed this Large Print book. Other Thorndike, Wheeler, and Chivers Press Large Print books are available at your library or directly from the publishers.

For information about current and upcoming titles, please call or write, without obligation, to:

Publisher
Thorndike Press
295 Kennedy Memorial Drive
Waterville, ME 04901
Tel. (800) 223-1244

or visit our Web site at:

www.gale.com/thorndike
www.gale.com/wheeler

OR

Chivers Large Print
published by BBC Audiobooks Ltd
St James House, The Square
Lower Bristol Road
Bath BA2 3SB
England
Tel. +44(0) 800 136919
email: bbcaudiobooks@bbc.co.uk
www.bbcaudiobooks.co.uk

All our Large Print titles are designed for easy reading, and all our books are made to last.